"So the o_____d,"
Cate said

Liam nodde_____go."

"Vishenko r_____ent.

"Maybe," he said. "There's no proof of that. Not yet."

"There may never be proof. But I know." She tapped a hand against her breastbone. "I know it here. Just as I know he's the one who tried to have me killed. He is ruthless. Amoral. An animal. He'll do anything to prevent me from testifying."

"But you're going to testify anyway. Why?" he asked, curious to understand what drove her to take the risk when so many men had refused to flip on Vishenko in the past.

"Because your brother Alec and my cousin Angelina are right. He is evil, and he must be stopped. No matter the cost." Her voice dropped to a whisper as if she were reciting an oft-repeated mantra, so that Liam had to strain to hear her next words. "'I am only one, but I am one. I cannot do everything, but I can do something.'"

He recognized the quotation with a sense of shock. There was more to Cate than he knew.

* * *

Be sure to check out the next books in Amelia Autin's exciting miniseries.

Man on a Mission: These heroes, working at home and overseas, will do anything for justice, honor...and love.

* * *

If you're on Twitter, tell us what you think of Harlequin Romantic Suspense! #harlequinromsuspense

Dear Reader,

When I wrote *McKinnon's Royal Mission*, part of my Man on a Mission miniseries, two characters who intrigued me were Princess Mara's other two bodyguards—Diplomatic Security Service agents and brothers, Alec and Liam Jones. Alike in many ways, and yet so different in others. They are emotionally close, as brothers should be, so I started writing their stories simultaneously, weaving the plots together into a cohesive whole, although each book stands on its own, as it should.

But it was the brothers' differences that caught my imagination. While both men are protectors, Liam, the younger of the two, is *more*—more concerned, more protective, more emotionally involved. Liam is also more idealistic than his pragmatic brother. As I saw him, he should have been born in the twelfth century, roaming the world as a knight-errant, saving damsels in distress.

So the only woman for Liam was either pure as the driven snow...or something else. And I settled on the something else for my heroine because she was more appealing to me. True or not, Caterina "Cate" Mateja has judged herself unworthy of a good man's love after everything she has survived. Can Liam convince his lady otherwise in *Liam's Witness Protection*?

I love hearing from my readers. Please email me at AmeliaAutin@aol.com and let me know what you think.

Amelia Autin

LIAM'S WITNESS PROTECTION

Amelia Autin

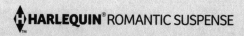

HARLEQUIN® ROMANTIC SUSPENSE

Recycling programs
for this product may
not exist in your area.

ISBN-13: 978-0-373-27940-1

Liam's Witness Protection

Copyright © 2015 by Amelia Autin Lam

Printed in U.S.A.

Amelia Autin is a voracious reader who can't bear to put a good book down...or part with it. Her bookshelves are crammed with books her husband periodically threatens to donate to a good cause, but he always relents...eventually.

Amelia returned to her first love, romance writing, after a long hiatus, during which she wrote numerous technical manuals and how-to guides, as well as designed and taught classes on a variety of subjects, including technical writing. She is a longtime member of Romance Writers of America (RWA), and served three years as its treasurer.

Amelia currently resides with her PhD engineer husband in quiet Vail, Arizona, where they can see the stars at night and have a "million-dollar view" of the Rincon Mountains from their backyard.

Books by Amelia Autin

Harlequin Romantic Suspense

Man on a Mission

Silhouette Intimate Moments

Visit the Author Profile page at Harlequin.com.

For Sharon Treister, Stephanie Hyacinth, Susan Kyser Frank, Debbie Oxier, Sharon Wade and a host of other readers whose emails, book reviews and posts kept me going in 2014 and helped me make my deadline for this book—this one's for you. For my sister, Diana MTK Autin, Esq., who helped me get the legal details correct (any errors are mine and mine alone).
And for Vincent...always.

Acknowledgments

Though itself part of the US Department of State, the Bureau of Diplomatic Security is the parent organization of the Diplomatic Security Service (DSS). The DSS is the primary tool by which the DS carries out its security and law enforcement mandate. For more information, please visit www.state.gov/m/ds.

I have the highest regard for the work these federal agencies perform. Nothing in this story is intended as a negative representation of the Bureau of Diplomatic Security or the Diplomatic Security Service, their duties or their employees.

Chapter 1

She didn't look like a prostitute. That was the first thing that came to Liam Jones's mind when he saw her standing next to a bench outside the courtroom. He didn't know what he'd expected—not exactly—but it wasn't a fresh-faced woman in her midtwenties wearing a summery dress in pastel swirls of pink and green, bare legs and sandals. Her blond hair was shoulder length, clean and shining, and held away from her face by cloisonné combs in a way that made her look heartbreakingly young.

There was a definite family resemblance to her cousin, Liam's new sister-in-law, Angelina Mateja. So she had to be Caterina Mateja. Which meant looks were deceiving. If he hadn't known who she was, if he hadn't known she was testifying in his brother's human trafficking and prostitution ring conspiracy case, he'd have pegged her as a model—tall, slender, almost delicate in appearance, aloof, with a touch-me-not air. And a definite attitude. She was listening to two men in impeccable dark suits and power ties that shrieked they were the prosecutors on the case—one a dapper man in his fifties, the other younger than Liam. *Prepping their witness?* he wondered idly. *Isn't it kind of late for that?*

And though he couldn't hear what they were saying, he knew damned well Caterina Mateja wasn't at all happy with whatever they were telling her. Two other men wearing identical black outfits, badges and side-arms—all of which Liam recognized—stood on either side of her, obviously providing her with protection.

A longtime Diplomatic Security Service special agent, Liam wasn't there in a professional capacity. Not officially. Officially he was on vacation for the next three weeks. But his brother Alec also a DSS special agent—*not just a special agent,* he reminded himself with a smile of familial pride in his brother's accomplishments, *the regional security officer at the US embassy in Zakhar*—had asked him to meet him at the courthouse this morning for the start of the trial. As a witness Alec had been precluded in a pretrial motion from sitting in the courtroom for the proceedings. But there was nothing stopping Liam from being there, and Alec had asked him to attend as a special favor. Not that Alec had told Liam a lot about the case ahead of time, nor would Liam discuss the trial with his brother while it was under way. But this case was important to

Alec—a career maker—and Liam would do anything for his brother.

Liam glanced at his watch. He was early, but that was par for the course with him. He planned his days carefully—planned his entire life that way, actually—and he didn't like leaving things to chance. Traffic in Washington, DC, was rarely predictable, often troublesome even in the summer, so Liam almost always arrived early for whatever he had going when he was in town. He was *never* late. Not even in New York.

He leaned casually against one of the rotunda's marble pillars, careful to keep his distance as he waited for his brother. Alec had told him US Marshals were guarding Caterina Mateja since she was a crucial witness in this trial, more crucial than Alec, who had orchestrated it all. So even if Liam hadn't recognized their outfits and badges he would have known who the two men were.

Liam was armed—he'd had to display his DSS badge and show the guards his SIG SAUER P229R in its shoulder holster in order to bring a weapon into the building past the metal detectors—and he had no intention of making the marshals think he was a threat to their witness.

But even from this distance he couldn't help notice how beautiful she was. How graceful her hands were as she tried to make some point to the prosecutors. How altogether classy and patrician she looked standing there arguing with them but never losing her cool. Anyone less like a hooker he'd yet to see.

Movement out of the corner of his eye had Liam

turning sharply in its direction, then he grinned. "Hey," he said as Alec came up to him.

"Thanks for coming."

"Told you I'd be here."

"Yeah, but sometimes things crop up, so I'd have understood if you couldn't make it. When did you get in?"

"Late last night. Thought about taking the train down from New York, so at least I'd get a little sleep on the way, but decided to drive after all. I'd have been here earlier, but there was a screwup with the guy covering for me at the UN."

Alec grimaced. "Speaking of screwups, I hate to tell you this, but the trial won't actually start until tomorrow—I just found out or I'd have called you. The jury was supposed to be seated this morning, and the trial was going to open with the big guns—Caterina Mateja's testimony—but it's been put off for a day. Last-minute pretrial motions. Sorry I got you down here a day too soon."

Liam shrugged. "Not a problem. I didn't have any other plans."

"So you're really on vacation? For three whole weeks? How'd you wangle that?"

"Three whole weeks," Liam agreed, then affected a pious air. "Clean living."

"Yeah right," his brother scoffed.

"Well, it might have something to do with the fact that I haven't taken any vacation at all so far this year, and my boss would like me to use up some of it before he sends me out of the country."

"That's sounds more like it."

Liam grinned. "So are we on for dinner tonight? Or do you have to rush back to your blushing bride?" He made a sound like a squawking hen, devilishly teasing his brother the way they'd done to each other since they were kids.

Alec cursed him genially, fake-punched his shoulder, then grinned, too, and said, "Angel's given me the night off—she's having dinner with her cousin." He tilted his head in Caterina Mateja's direction. "I'm off-limits there. I'm not supposed to have any contact with her—the trial judge was quite clear about that. But the restriction doesn't include Angel since she's not a witness in this trial. And Caterina will need her moral support."

He shook his head regretfully. "The defense attorneys will rip her to shreds if they can. They'll paint her as black as the judge will let them get away with. A vengeful prostitute is what they'll call her, out to get her former lover—so they'll say—any way she can for dumping her. Even lying to convict him."

"Any truth to that?"

Alec bent a hard stare on his brother. "I'm going to pretend you never asked me that question."

Liam shook his head. "Look I know she's your wife's cousin and all that, but—"

"But nothing," Alec said in a steely voice. "You don't know what Caterina's been through. If you had any idea…if you knew the courage it's taking for her to face these men—*especially* Aleksandrov Vishenko—and testify in open court, you wouldn't—"

The chatter of submachine gunfire and screams from civilians echoing through the cavernous rotunda interrupted whatever Alec had intended to say next. Both brothers spun toward the gunfire, reaching simultaneously for their SIG SAUERs. And both brothers saw immediately they were shielded from the gunmen's sight by the marble pillar they were standing behind.

How the hell did they get Uzis past the metal detectors? Past the guards at the door? were Liam's first thoughts, but he didn't waste more than a couple of seconds on those questions. His gaze swung toward the woman he was pretty sure was the intended target. The marshals had her down on the floor, covering her body with theirs as they tried to return fire. Both prosecutors were also down—but not voluntarily. One was obviously dead, a grim sight. The other was still alive, but for how long was anyone's guess. And the marshals weren't faring much better. One was wounded in the thigh, the other had taken a spray of bullets to his nonshooting arm and shoulder. Both were doing their damnedest to shield Caterina, but they were caught out in the open with only the bench for shelter and no warning. And semiautomatics were a pitiful defense against submachine guns.

"Cover me," Alec said, darting to his right, not even waiting for acknowledgment. Liam switched his gun to his left hand—*thank God I'm ambidextrous,* he thought—operating on instinct and training that was second nature after so many years, not to mention a lifelong knowledge of his brother. He peered around the marble column, took careful aim and fired a volley of shots at the men with the submachine guns to distract them from Alec circling around behind to get the drop on them. Liam had the savage satisfaction of hearing a scream of pain as one of his shots found its target.

One down, he thought, still on autopilot. *One to go.* He switched his gun back to his right hand, moved in the other direction and fired again from the other side of the column, emptying the clip. His spare clip, which he carried in his jacket pocket, was already in his left hand. Seconds was all it took to eject the empty clip and slam the full one home. Seconds he didn't really have, because one of the Uzis was still firing.

But then he recognized the sound of Alec's SIG SAUER, followed by an agonized scream—*not* Alec's voice. When he slid cautiously out from behind the pillar he saw Alec kicking the Uzis away from both downed gunmen, and he started running toward his brother. But Alec had other ideas.

"They're dead," he shouted to Liam across the rotunda. "Get Caterina the hell out of here. She dies, this case dies, too."

Liam hesitated for only a second. Then he turned in the direction of Caterina and the US Marshals shielding her. "Diplomatic Security Service," he announced quickly, displaying his badge before the men could draw a bead on him. "That's my brother over there with the gunmen. He's DSS, too."

Both marshals were bleeding heavily, but they were still conscious. "Your brother's right," one man gasped. "It might be just those two, but who the hell knows? Get her to safety." He rolled off Caterina as he said this, and Liam—still carrying his gun in his right hand—reached down with his left hand to help her to her feet. Blood had dripped from the wounded men onto the dress she was wearing, and there was blood on her arm, but Liam was glad to see she appeared to be unhurt. Shocked. Dazed. But physically untouched.

He grasped her arm as a courtroom door down the hallway opened and a dozen spectators spilled out, along with the deputy assigned to that courtroom. "Come on," he urged, pulling Caterina behind him, shielding her with his body just as the marshals had done.

It took no time at all for Liam to decide going out the front door was too risky. He didn't know what other exits there were in the building, but he did know there was a garage downstairs. A garage where he'd parked this morning, not knowing that spending the few extra dollars to park beneath the courthouse instead of a couple of blocks away would be a lifesaver.

He hustled Caterina to the nearest stairwell—he knew better than to try for an elevator that could become a death trap—never letting go of her arm. He'd just thrust her through the doorway when he caught sight of two men moving purposely toward them. But the men were on the other side of the rotunda, too far away to catch them if they didn't dawdle.

Time seemed to stretch out in that odd way it does when adrenaline is pumping, and Liam's thoughts raced ahead of his body as they clattered down the stairs. *Garage. SUV. Police station? No, too many unknowns. Uzis in the courthouse. Conspiracy? Those two men. Good guys or bad? No way to tell. Need a bolt-hole. Safe house. Who to trust?*

Alec, of course, but Alec couldn't be a part of this. Not now.

Liam practically threw Caterina into the back-seat of his SUV. "Get down on the floor," he ordered brusquely. He grabbed a blanket out of the emergency pack he kept in the rear, and spread it lengthwise over Caterina's body. "Don't move. Don't even breathe. I don't want anyone to see you, not the parking attendant or anyone else."

He drove out of the garage at a sedate pace, not wanting to raise suspicions if he squealed his tires in his haste to escape. But his eyes were on the rearview mirror, watching to see if anyone exited the stairwell he and Caterina had used. *So far so good.*

He paid the attendant with a twenty, refusing to let himself display the slightest hint of impatience as he waited for his change. He didn't bother with a receipt. He'd just rolled up the window when he saw two men in his rearview mirror. Running in his direction. He couldn't be positive, but they sure looked like the same men who'd chased after them upstairs.

Liam floored the accelerator. Then he was on the streets of DC. He turned left, and left again, then gunned the engine as the light turned yellow, watching sharply to see if anyone ran a red light to follow them. It wasn't likely—the men pursuing them had been on foot, so he didn't really expect a chase car that quickly—but he wasn't taking any chances. No one ran the red light, so Liam drove five blocks, turned right, left and right again, then pulled his SUV onto the freeway heading toward Virginia. Virginia, and anonymity. Anonymity equaled safety. At least for now.

Traffic was light on the freeway out of the city in the middle of the morning, and Liam made good time. He only needed part of his attention to drive, and he returned to ponder the question he'd asked himself earlier. Who to trust? His fellow DSS agents at the Bureau of Diplomatic Security? His boss? The State Department? The FBI?

Though he knew better than to text while behind the wheel, Liam suddenly pulled his cell phone out and hit speed dial two for Alec—his SUV's Bluetooth capability would allow him to talk hands-free.

"It's me," he said when Alec answered. "Just wanted you to know we had two pursuers on foot." He quickly described what the two men looked like and how they were dressed. "Could have been Fibbies, but I doubt it. They just didn't have the *look*, if you know what I mean. Didn't see any guns, but that doesn't mean anything. If they were bad guys they're probably long gone by now, but just in case..."

"We'll check it out. You got clean away?"

"Yeah. Heading out of the city as we speak."

"You got a destination?"

Liam laughed a little. "Anywhere but here, bro."

"Caterina okay?" The concern in Alec's voice was obvious. And just as obviously, his concern wasn't all professional.

"Not a mark on her."

"Keep her safe."

"You know I will."

There was silence on the other end. Then, "Call Cody when you get the chance," Alec said.

"You read my mind. What's the situation there?"

"Both shooters are dead, but you already knew that. No ID, nothing to say who they are. The serial numbers on the Uzis were filed off, but the FBI thinks they might be able to raise them—we might get lucky there."

"What about the people they shot?"

"The lead prosecutor's in the morgue, the other one's critical. I think the marshals are going to make it. Hey, gotta go. The FBI's bearing down on me again, and I don't want them to hear this conversation."

After Alec hung up, Liam's thoughts kept circling back to the events as they had unfolded. *Uzis in the courthouse,* he reminded himself. He knew they were Uzis—the sound was unmistakable. This hadn't just *happened.* Someone had plotted and planned very carefully. *How did they get Uzis past the metal detectors and the guards?* he asked again, still without an answer. At least not a palatable answer. Because the answer was— they couldn't. That meant a conspiracy. A conspiracy that included someone with enough authority, enough clout, to smuggle the submachine guns in. Someone with a lot at risk. Someone who would do anything to keep Caterina from testifying.

Liam dismissed the idea that the prosecutors had been the targets. They were collateral damage, nothing more. Caterina was the one they wanted dead. He only knew the bare bones of the case she was testifying in, the few bits and pieces Alec had shared with him, but he knew one thing for sure—she was lucky to be alive.

Damned lucky. And even luckier she'd fallen in with someone who could protect her now that her US Marshals bodyguards were out of the picture.

Liam had been driving in silence for fifteen minutes when he suddenly realized something and cursed softly. Despite the fact that Caterina had to be smothering underneath the blanket on the floor even with the SUV's A/C blasting on max power, she hadn't moved, hadn't complained, hadn't asked if she could come out from beneath the blanket yet.

In fact, Caterina hadn't spoken one word since this whole thing began. Not a single word.

Chapter 2

Cate had escaped into a self-induced fugue state. She'd learned how nine years ago, how to disassociate her mind from her body so that what was happening to her body was as remote as if it was happening to someone else. It was the only way she'd been able to survive those two years with Aleksandrov Vishenko. The only way she'd been able to bear the pain—mental and physical. The only way she'd been able to stay sane in a world that had gone sickeningly insane.

But she hadn't had to escape this way for years. Not since she'd physically escaped Vishenko's clutches, not since she'd regained possession of her own body...her own soul. But she hadn't forgotten how. Just as she would never forget what Vishenko had done to her, she would never forget the coping mechanism that had allowed her to survive those two hellish years.

She floated in darkness beneath the blanket, remembering the rosebushes in the garden at her cousin's house. How she'd envied her cousin living among all that beauty! Angelina's mother's prized rosebushes, which she'd nurtured as if they were all the other babies she could never have after Angelina was born. Red roses, yellow roses, roses with fancy blended colors and even more fanciful names, like Fire and Ice and Dream Come True. But Cate had always preferred the white roses. Plain. White. Pure. Like a young girl in her First Communion dress. Untouched. Cleansed of mortal sin.

She'd been that girl a long time ago. A lifetime ago. But she'd never be that girl again. She could never undo what had been done to her. Could never undo what she'd done to survive.

Suddenly she wasn't floating anymore. Suddenly she was remembering what she'd long-ago sworn she would *not* remember, waking or sleeping. The memories her brain had successfully blanked out for years, until Alec Jones had erupted into her life and forced her to remember. Alec, who'd convinced her to testify against Vishenko and the others about what she knew, about the evidence she'd secreted away. Alec, who was married to Angelina now.

He hadn't judged her. Not the harsh way she judged herself. Neither had Angelina. They'd treated Cate tenderly, lovingly, but with a matter-of-factness that allowed her to retain that mental disassociation from her past. As if those things had happened to someone else. Not to her.

Now that she was aware of her surroundings, Cate realized she could barely breathe beneath the blanket. It was hot, stuffy, smothering. She was also aware of the steady rumble and vibration caused by the engine and the SUV's wheels as they ate up the miles. Putting distance between themselves and the men who'd tried to kill her. Vishenko's men. She had no doubt about that.

The SUV slowed. Then veered to the right. Then stopped. Cate heard the driver's door open and close, but she didn't move. Didn't speak.

Suddenly the side door opened. "Sorry," a deep voice said above her as the blanket was abruptly removed. "Why didn't you say something?"

Strong yet gentle hands helped Cate rise and come out of the SUV to stand next to it, and for a moment the world swung dizzyingly around her as she regained her equilibrium. Then she steadied and was able to focus on the man in front of her.

He looked so much like Alec Jones that he could be his twin brother. But there were differences, and though Cate couldn't have said exactly what those differences were, she knew in an instant this man wasn't her cousin's husband. He was tall and broad-shouldered, just as Alec was, with a muscular compactness that spoke of a man who kept himself in fighting trim. Close-cropped auburn hair, also just like Alec. And soft brown eyes. *Is it his eyes that are different?* she wondered distractedly. Not the color, no. But the expression in them. An expression that told her plain as words he found her attractive. Man-woman attractive. Alec had never looked at her that way. Alec had known she never wanted any man to look at her that way…ever again.

But there was something else in this man's expression that bothered her even more. Gentleness notwithstanding, Cate knew he'd made a snap judgment about her…and found her wanting. It wasn't obvious from his manner, but she had a sixth sense about these things.

"Who are you?" she asked abruptly. "You're not Alec."

"Liam. Liam Jones. Alec's my brother."

She glanced around now, taking in their surroundings. They were in a rest stop on the highway. Not deserted, but not overly crowded, either. There were no other cars in the parking area, but there were a couple of tractor-trailer trucks on the other side of the divider. "Why have we stopped here?"

He smiled ruefully, and Cate caught her breath. That smile changed his whole face from pleasantly masculine to something extraordinary. "You were so quiet I forgot you were under the blanket in the back," he said in a deep voice that sounded like Alec's in a way, but was also different somehow. "When I remembered, I was kicking myself for not letting you out sooner. I stopped the first chance I had."

His hand went to brush back her tousled hair—a perfectly natural response under the circumstances—but Cate shied away. Then despised herself as a coward when the smile faded from Liam's face.

"Sorry," he said again, but there was a watchfulness in his eyes now. A guarded expression she couldn't read. Not exactly. But she knew he hadn't missed her reaction to his innocent gesture. His gaze dropped from her face to her dress and then to her arm, and when she looked down she realized the blood had already dried. Not her blood, of course. The blood of the men who'd risked their lives protecting her. Men like this man.

She didn't know how she knew Liam was a bodyguard, too. There was just something about him. She had only vague, disjointed memories of their flight from the courthouse—she'd already entered that escapist fugue state almost the moment the first shots were fired, the moment the two US Marshals had thrown themselves on top of her to shield her with their bodies. But Liam had carried a gun, she remembered that now. And he would have used it, she remembered that, too. Had he already used it? Was that how the machine guns targeting her had been silenced?

"Did you kill them?" The question popped out before she could stop it.

He obviously knew to whom she was referring. "I killed one of them," he said quietly. "Alec got the other one. But there could have been others around—backup killers—there was no way to know. So Alec told me to get you out of there."

She culled her memory, trying to recall the frenzied voices around her during and after the attack. Then she said slowly, "'She dies, this case dies, too.' That was Alec, yes?"

"Yeah. I didn't like leaving him in that situation, but he was right. I had to get you to safety. That was more important."

"Who are you?" she asked in a voice barely above a whisper.

"I told you. I'm Alec's brother Liam."

She shook her head impatiently. "No, I mean, *what* are you? Are you a US marshal like the men who were guarding me?"

"Diplomatic Security Service. DSS. Like Alec. The DSS is responsible for a lot of things, including protecting foreign dignitaries when they visit the US, and I've done my share of that. In fact, I was on the detail guarding your Princess Mara when she first came to this country. Alec and I both were. So yeah, I knew what to do when bullets started flying. That's my job."

"So what is next? Where do I go?"

"We," he told her. "Where do *we* go. I'm not sure. I've got to call a man." He pointed to the dried blood on Cate's arm, then indicated the restroom a short distance away. "You might want to wash up a little and use the facilities while I do that. My call will take a while."

When Cate agreed, she was surprised he led the way to the ladies' room but prevented her from entering until he'd checked it out. "It's clear," he told her when he returned. Then he moved away from the doorway a couple of paces, pulled out his cell phone and hit speed dial.

He was still on the phone when Cate came out of the ladies' room. She'd washed the blood from her arm and done her best with the dress—which was still damp in places, although she'd blotted as much of the water from it as she could—but anyone who looked closely could still see the faint discolorations that would probably never go away completely. She didn't care. This dress didn't really belong to her, it was a dress designed to present a certain appearance for the jury. Well-to-do, but not too expensive. Not the Mayflower Madam, but not a street hooker, either. The dress had been picked out by the prosecutors, who wanted her to look young and wholesome. The girl next door.

Cate *was* young. In years, if nothing else. But she wasn't wholesome—she was damaged goods. She would never be wholesome again. But the jury didn't have to know that, and she had no intention of telling them how she felt about the two-year nightmare when she'd been Vishenko's prisoner. *Stick to the facts,* the prosecutors had hammered home, *don't volunteer opinions.*

Angelina had said the same thing. But she'd also advised Cate to let her emotions show just enough so the jury empathized with her, believed her implicitly. If she was too cold the jury wouldn't like her. And the jury needed to like her, Angelina had said. Angelina, who had at one time been a prosecutor herself long ago, but who had also been a bodyguard for Zakhar's Queen Juliana. Angelina, who now headed the queen's security detail, but who had come over to the States to be there for Cate during the trial.

"Okay," Liam was saying to the man on the other end of the phone. "Call me back as soon as you can. I'll be waiting." He listened for a minute, then laughed and said, "Yeah, you're right. It's a hell of a way to start a vacation." Then he disconnected.

"Who were you talking to?" she asked.

"Let's sit in the SUV," he told her. "I don't want you out in the open if I can help it."

He held the passenger door for Cate but didn't touch her at all, as if he knew she couldn't bear to be touched in a personal way. Then he got into the driver's seat, saying, "That was Cody Walker. My brother-in-law. At this point he's about the only person who can help us that I *know* I can trust. He was already working on it—can you believe it?—he'll call me back when he has something definite." He chuckled softly, shaking his head. "Alec called Cody a half hour ago, told him I was in trouble and I'd be in touch. Even before I talked with Alec. Damn! Alec's always one step ahead of me—he can read my mind."

"I know him," she said. "Your brother-in-law. I met him when I first met your brother. You told him where we are?"

Liam shook his head again. "The first thing you have to learn about security, Ms. Mateja, is a concept called 'need to know.' At this point Cody doesn't have a need to know where we are, so I didn't tell him. When and if he needs to know, I will."

Cate waited for one heartbeat, then two, before she said, "Cate. Please just call me Cate. I... I don't like Caterina." She couldn't suppress the little shiver as she said the name. "And I don't use Mateja anymore." *Not for seven years.* "Except in court, of course. I must use it there—it's my legal name."

"What last name do you go by, then?"

She laughed a little. "Would you believe... Jones?"

"You're kidding."

"No, I'm not." She darted a look at his face. "I wanted an American name so common no one would be able to trace it…or me. The only names I could think of like that were Smith and Jones."

"'Alias Smith and Jones,'" he murmured under his breath.

"Pardon?"

"Nothing. Just an old TV western Alec and I used to watch on cable." He looked as if he were going to explain more, but changed his mind.

She waited, but he didn't say anything, so she continued. "Cate Smith sounded too much like Kate Smith, the singer—I didn't want anyone to remember me for any reason." Her smile faded. "The book I read in the library about going underground advised not changing your first name too much, especially the first letter. Too easy to slip up and say your real name—or at least *start* to say your real name—if you're taken unaware. Same thing for signing your name. So I became Cate Jones."

"Cate Jones." He tilted his head to one side as he considered it. "Not bad. And most people who heard you say it would think *K* not *C*, making it even less likely they'd recognize your name." Then his soft brown eyes hardened. "So why were you going underground in the first place?"

She wanted to look away from that hard, uncompromising stare, but she couldn't. "Alec knows," she said finally. Painfully.

"But you don't want me to know, is that it?"

Cate shook her head. "You don't have a 'need to know,'" she reminded him.

"Touché," Liam said with a little huff of laughter. "Touché."

* * *

"Escaped?" roared Aleksandrov Vishenko in Russian to the two men who were the bearers of bad tidings to their boss. "What do you mean, she escaped?"

"It wasn't supposed to happen," said one man as he tried to placate his boss. "But there was interference from an unexpected source—Diplomatic Security Service agents who happened to be in the courthouse... armed. Both of our men are dead. At least they cannot talk."

"They would not have talked anyway," insisted the other man.

"Perhaps. Perhaps not," the first man said, glancing at him. "They are dead, so it no longer matters." Then he faced his boss again. "The courthouse is swarming with FBI agents and men from the US Marshals Service—both marshals guarding the woman were wounded. One of the federal prosecutors is dead, the other could die any moment. And the woman was spirited away by one of the men who foiled the initial attempt on her life. We do not know where he has taken her. Not yet."

"Find out," Vishenko hissed at his men. "Find out where she is and take care of her. Permanently. If she lives to testify, we are all dead."

Liam's cell phone shrilled, interrupting his conversation with Cate, and he grabbed it. "Hello?"

"It's me," said Cody Walker, Liam's brother-in-law. "I spoke with my boss, Nick D'Arcy, in Washington."

"Was that necessary?"

"Not unless I wanted to have a job tomorrow," Cody said dryly.

"Sorry," Liam apologized. "I guess I'm not thinking clearly at the moment."

"D'Arcy can be trusted. There are only a few absolutely incorruptible people in the world, people I'd trust with my own life, and Nick D'Arcy is one of them. He's also one of the most brilliant minds in the business, not to mention eerily omniscient. Didn't I ever tell you his nickname is Baker Street?"

"Yeah, you mentioned it once or twice. Keira, too. Sherlock Holmes, right?"

"Right," Cody said. "So do you want to hear the plan he came up with, or not?"

"Let's have it."

"The agency has a safe house in Fairfax, Virginia. Got a pen and paper?"

"Hold on a sec." Liam pulled both from an inner jacket pocket, and balanced his cell phone as best he could on his shoulder. "Shoot."

"Go to this address first." Liam jotted down the address Cody gave him, then repeated it back. "Right. Someone from the agency will meet you there and exchange vehicles—just in case they know who you are, just in case they've got your license plate number and are tracking you that way."

"Make it an SUV, okay? I'm more comfortable with that kind of versatility and power under the hood."

"Sure thing. You won't have any complaints. And he'll have a new cell phone for you, too. Encrypted. Untraceable. At least I think it'll be untraceable. Alec had to tell the FBI who you were, so of course they've got your cell phone number. They can locate you by triangulating on the cell towers your phone pings off."

Liam hadn't thought of that, hadn't thought he needed to hide from law enforcement as well as from the men out to kill Cate, but apparently Cody had. "For now, make sure your cell phone is off unless you're using it. Once you've got new wheels and a new phone, go to this safe house." And Cody recited another address.

"Okay," Liam said, after he'd confirmed he had the second address correct. "So we go to the agency's safe house. Then what?" He looked at Cate as he said this, but her expression gave away nothing of what she was thinking.

"You stay there with our witness, at least for tonight, while the agency opens an investigation—or rather, reactivates the one we already had going with Trace McKinnon and Alec. You *did* know the agency had a hand in this case, didn't you?"

"I didn't, but I do now."

"Talk to Alec, once you get to the safe house. He'll bring you up to speed on everything you need to know. Tell him I said the agency trusts him to use his discretion."

"Will do."

"And, Liam? I know technically you're on vacation, and maybe I shouldn't even be asking, but…"

"But what?"

"D'Arcy wants to know if you'll stay on this assignment…at least for the next few days."

Puzzled, Liam said, "Sure thing. But why?"

"There was a case a few years back—before your time—when D'Arcy was working for the US Marshals Service. They were infiltrated by a domestic terrorist organization, and a witness D'Arcy was responsible for was almost killed. Later, your sister discovered the FBI had been infiltrated at the same time, by the same group. A group with ties to the Russian Mafia."

"Holy crap."

"Yeah. Information was leaked, and three people died when the terrorist organization tried to torture the whereabouts of the witness—a former cop who'd gone undercover for the FBI—out of his partner. The partner would have given the witness up if he'd known where he was—one of those killed was the man's own baby son, and the other was his wife—but he honestly didn't know where the witness was, so he was killed too, to send a message. That's why D'Arcy doesn't want to take any chances. He doesn't want the FBI or the US Marshals Service to know where our witness is…at least for now."

"He's dead wrong, at least where those marshals are concerned," Liam said hotly. "I saw them. They were covering her like a blanket, taking the bullets meant for her. If either of those men betrayed—"

Cody cut him off. "It wouldn't necessarily have been one of them. It could have been anyone who knew where she would be, all the way up the line. In the US Marshals Service or the FBI. Hell, it could have been the US Attorney's Office for all we know. But someone smuggled those guns into the courthouse. And until we know who, D'Arcy wants the agency to play it close to the vest. So are you in?"

"Sure, but for how long? I've only got three weeks."

"Hopefully not that long, but the agency will clear things with the DSS either way—you'd better believe D'Arcy has that kind of pull. That's one of the reasons I wanted him involved. He'll call in a favor if that's what it takes—and just about every federal agency owes him one...or a dozen."

"Okay. Then I'm in." He almost disconnected then, but Cody stopped him.

"One more thing." Liam could sense Cody's hesitation before he said, "Do what you need to do to keep Caterina Mateja safe." Liam glanced at Cate, but again her expression conveyed nothing that gave him a clue to her inner thoughts. "We had another witness in her case," Cody continued, "one who could corroborate much of her testimony, but she's dead. It happened over the weekend. Caterina doesn't know it yet—the prosecutors didn't want to frighten her, but I got the report last night. It was made to look like a traffic accident, but—and keep this to yourself—she was murdered. Despite the fact she was being guarded by US Marshals, too, same as Caterina."

Liam carefully schooled his face so Cate—who was watching him intently—wouldn't be able to read anything from his expression, and Cody continued with barely a pause. "The FBI is still trying to piece together exactly where the protection on the other witness broke down. The agency was politely told to butt out. But they did confirm it was murder. Just like whoever killed her tried to murder Caterina this morning. Only with Caterina, they weren't trying to hide anything—and they were willing to take out anyone to get to her."

Liam swore under his breath. Just when he thought things couldn't get worse…they did. "I get it," he told his brother-in-law. *Alec knew the other witness was dead—he had to,* Liam thought. "After it all went down Alec said, 'She dies, this case dies, too.' That's pretty much it, isn't it?"

"Yeah. In a nutshell. We've got other evidence against Vishenko and the conspirators, but nothing like what Caterina has to say. And some of the physical evidence needs Caterina to validate where it came from—it's useless without her.

"D'Arcy told me the death of the other witness was the main reason the trial was delayed a day. The prosecution made a motion first thing this morning to use this other witness's grand jury testimony and her deposition, since she's no longer alive to testify in person. The defense, of course, fought that tooth and nail, citing the defendants' rights under the Sixth Amendment to confront the witnesses against them. No one knows how the judge will rule—the motion is still pending—but I wouldn't make book on the ruling going our way unless the prosecution can prove the defendants are the ones who killed the witness. Of course, everything's on hold for now, with one prosecutor dead and another in intensive care. The judge granted the prosecution a one-month continuance."

"What about the marshals who were wounded?" Liam asked. "Alec said he thought they'd make it. Do you know anything more?"

"Holding their own, that's the last I heard."

"Better than nothing. Thanks for checking. Keep me posted if you hear anything."

"Sure thing. And, Liam…be careful, okay? I don't want to be the one to tell my wife her brother's dead and I knew it might happen."

Liam smiled to himself. "Don't worry. I'm a big boy. And you should talk. You and Keira both. There's no bullet out there with *my* name on it."

After Cody hung up Liam sat staring into space for a few seconds. Thinking about what Cody had said… and what he hadn't. Then he glanced over at Cate, who was watching him with blue eyes so pale they looked gray inside the SUV's shadowed interior. Who was sitting still as a statue in the seat next to him—he'd never known a woman who could be as still and silent as she. And he wondered exactly what—out of all the things Cody had said—he was going to tell her.

But that wasn't all he was wondering. *Be honest,* he told himself. *You're wondering what the hell Alec knows that she doesn't want you to know. You're wondering how a woman like her—good background, intelligent, obviously educated—ever ended up as a prostitute. And knowing that about her, you're wondering why she acts as if she can't bear being touched by a man. By you.*

The last one hurt. He didn't know why, but it did. Badly.

Chapter 3

A nondescript SUV was waiting for them in the church parking lot Cody had directed Liam to, and it took only a few minutes to make the swap. "So what will you do with my SUV?" he asked the agent as he moved his GPS and emergency overnight case into the agency's vehicle and they exchanged keys.

"We'll take good care of it, don't worry," the man assured Liam. "It'll be ready and waiting for you the minute you need it. *And* we'll deliver it to your door-step, no charge."

Liam eyed the replacement SUV dubiously, wondering about its roadworthiness given the exterior, and the man said, "It looks a little worse for wear on purpose. The agency doesn't like its vehicles to attract attention. But it's got brand-new tires and everything under the hood is new, too, so don't worry about that. And the plates are untraceable."

"Good deal," Liam said. He handed over his cell phone and took the replacement offered. After he'd tucked it in his pocket, the agent handed him something else—a zippered case. "What's this?"

"Maintenance kit and ammo clips. Fully loaded. SIG SAUER P229R, right?"

Liam hadn't been expecting it—*but maybe I should have,* he thought. The agency was damned efficient, and he might need the additional firepower—he was already operating on his spare clip after the firefight this morning. And his own maintenance kit had been left with his luggage in his hotel room. He took the case in his left hand and shook the other man's hand with his right. "Thanks."

"No problem. Good luck," the agent added sincerely.

They'd driven for ten minutes, following the automated voice of the GPS, when Cate suddenly said, "I have nothing with me. No clothes other than the ones I'm wearing. No purse. I don't even have a toothbrush."

Liam glanced over at her for a second, realizing she was right. She didn't have her purse with her. She must have dropped it in the courthouse, and of course he hadn't been worrying about that then. He returned his gaze to the road and said, "I doubt that will be a problem. If I know Cody, everything we need will be at the safe house, including clothes."

"How will they know my size?"

Liam laughed abruptly, thinking about the ammo

clips the agency had provided him with at the same time he'd been given the SUV and new cell phone. Ammo clips that were a perfect match for his SIG SAUER. "You'd be surprised what the agency knows."

A long silence followed. All of a sudden, Cate said, "She's dead, isn't she?"

Liam was instantly on alert. Cody had told him not to mention it. "Who?"

"The other witness." Her voice was soft, and he caught the faintest trace of an accent that reminded him of Princess Mara of Zakhar, whose bodyguard he'd been for six months in Colorado. But Cate's English was less formal than the princess's, more idiomatic. Maybe because she'd spent eight of the past nine years in the US. And despite the softness, there was a layer of steel beneath it, just like the princess. This woman was no pushover, either.

When Liam didn't answer, she explained, "The woman who was going to back up my testimony. She's dead. That's why the trial was delayed. That's why the prosecutors were so insistent this morning I needed to come in for another prep session with them this afternoon, even though we'd already spent so many hours preparing last week I was sick of it. That's why your brother said, 'She dies, this case dies, too.' So the other witness must be dead."

It was the longest speech Liam had heard Cate make to date. He made a judgment call, then admitted, "Yeah. Cody told me a little while ago."

"Vishenko murdered her." A flat, cold statement.

"Maybe. There's no proof of that. Not yet."

"There may never be proof. But I know." She tapped a hand against her breastbone. "I know it here. Just as I know he's the one who tried to have me killed. He is ruthless. Amoral. An animal. He'll do anything to prevent me from testifying."

"But you're going to testify anyway. Why?" he asked, curious to understand what drove her to take the risk when so many men had refused to flip on Vishenko in the past.

"Because Alec and Angelina are right. He is evil, and he must be stopped. No matter the cost." Her voice dropped to a whisper as if she was reciting an oft-repeated mantra, so that Liam had to strain to hear her next words. "'I am only one, but I am one. I cannot do everything, but I can do something. And I will not let what I cannot do interfere with what I can do.'"

He recognized the quotation with a sense of shock, mentally adding the last sentence, *"And by the grace of God, I will."* The entire thing was carved in wood over the fireplace mantel at home, a maxim his parents had instilled in all their children from an early age. It was the driving force that had led him and all his siblings into the US Marine Corps and then into public service. "Edward Everett Hale," he said blankly. "How do you know that quotation?"

She drew a deep breath, then exhaled slowly. "Your brother said that to me. I was afraid—so terribly afraid I ran and hid for six years. Then Alec found me. He is *such* a good man, your brother—I could not let him down. He made me realize I have a duty to do whatever

I can do to stop Vishenko. 'I am only one.' But if all the ones band together, we can defeat him."

Liam was shaken. Cate had divined the kernel of wisdom out of the quotation, had pinpointed his own *raison d'être*—his reason for being. Yes, he was only one. But sometimes one person *could* make a difference.

Right and wrong. Good and evil. He couldn't remember a time when the differences between these things weren't important to him, same as they were for Alec. For all his siblings. Maybe it was old-fashioned nowadays. Maybe the dividing lines had become blurred for many. Not for him. But that didn't mean he saw the world only in black-and-white. It didn't mean he didn't recognize and accept that a thing could be both right and wrong.

He'd killed a man today. Some would say that killing was *always* wrong. Not in his book. There was a higher *right*—saving lives—that trumped the *wrong*. Did he regret killing that man? Liam glanced away from the road for a second toward Cate sitting so still and quiet, looking even younger in repose…until one looked in her eyes.

No, Cate was alive now because the men who'd tried to kill her were dead. The only thing he regretted was that he and Alec hadn't somehow prevented the entire incident from occurring. So that no one had died. So that no one had been wounded. Impossible, of course. But otherwise he didn't have any regrets.

Except the way Cate had shied away from him. From his touch. That still bothered him. *And while you're at it, might as well admit something else is bothering you,* his inner voice nudged into his consciousness.

He so didn't want to go there. Didn't want to examine his reaction too closely, but… *It is what it is,* he admitted to himself. He'd never been jealous of Alec—not since the day he turned eighteen and joined the Marine Corps anyway, which Alec had done the year before him. From that point on their friendship had been untainted by anything as destructive as jealousy on either side. Each was the other's cheerleader, and the accomplishments of one were a source of pride to the other. Liam had even followed his brother into the DSS. *Not* because he was jealous of what Alec was doing, but because he believed wholeheartedly the DSS was his true calling, same as it was for Alec.

But that's exactly what he was feeling right now. Jealousy. Hot, harsh, unreasoning. He didn't like it one bit, but he couldn't refuse to acknowledge it. He was *jealous*— of the admiring way Cate spoke Alec's name. As if…

"At the end of the road, turn right," said the GPS. And when Liam had dutifully done so, the GPS said, "You have reached your destination."

Twilight covered the earth, and there was a delicious smell of roast chicken wafting through the house. The agents who ran the safe house—a husband and wife team in their fifties, but who continued to instill confidence in their abilities—had told them dinner would be ready in thirty minutes. Lunch had been so delicious Cate was looking forward to dinner with an appetite she hadn't had since Alec had found her. Since he'd convinced her to testify against Vishenko.

In addition to feeding them, the agents had made sure Cate and Liam had everything they needed—from clothes, to toiletries, to bedrooms, to information. What little information they had, anyway, which wasn't much. Cate remembered how the first question Liam had asked was the status of the marshals who'd been wounded in the attack on her, and the other prosecutor, too. As if he really cared about men he didn't know. As if it *mattered* to him.

She'd wanted to know, too, of course. She hadn't had a lot to do with the prosecutors other than prepping for trial, but the two marshals were part of a team guarding her for the past month since she'd returned to the US from Zakhar, and she'd gotten to know them. Both men were married. One had two young boys already and his wife was expecting their third child in a couple of months. The other had just become a father for the first time six months ago. If Cate still believed in a just and merciful God, she would have prayed for the men, prayed they would recover completely and their families would get through this terrible time in their lives without too much grief.

But Cate didn't believe. Not anymore. Vishenko had killed her faith in God as surely as he'd killed her faith in the goodness of mankind. So she no longer prayed. Not for herself. Not for others.

Angelina still believes. And Alec, she told herself wistfully as she sat on the bed in the bedroom assigned to her—a delightfully feminine room she would have loved when she was sixteen. Now it did nothing for her.

Cate had spent more than six of the past seven years running. Hiding. Living off the grid. Taking temporary jobs where they'd pay her in cash. Living hand-to-mouth at times, barely able to scrape up enough money to rent a room in a halfway decent boardinghouse. Skipping meals on occasion, when her money wouldn't stretch to cover a roof over her head *and* food. Always looking over her shoulder. Always terrified. Always moving on to somewhere new after a few months, somewhere Vishenko's men couldn't find her.

No friends. She couldn't afford friends, and not just because they might accidentally betray her. She couldn't take the chance—if Vishenko's men finally ran her to ground—that one of her friends would get caught in the cross fire. She knew Vishenko's men wouldn't care who else was killed so long as she was. She was almost more terrified of causing someone else's death than she was of dying.

Like the prosecutor today. Dead because of her. One minute he'd been alive and she'd been arguing with him, the next minute he was dead at her feet and her bodyguards were plastered over her, taking those bullets meant for her. Vishenko's revenge for her daring to oppose him. For daring to escape. For daring to testify. The prosecutor wasn't a friend, but she'd still caused his death. And if anyone else who was shot this morning died, that was her fault, too.

Don't think that way, the rational part of her brain told her. *It's not your fault, it's Vishenko's.* But her conscience didn't want to listen. If she'd stayed in Zakhar all those years ago, if she'd listened to Angelina…none of this would have happened. *You would probably be married by now,* she thought, *to a strong man of good character.* A man who would treat her with respect. A man with high moral standards—like the ones she'd had herself when she was sixteen. A man like...

She shied away from that thought, the same way she'd shied away when he'd tried to touch her hair. Liam. He hadn't meant anything by it. Hadn't intended to give her cause for alarm. And he certainly hadn't been going to strike her. Abuse her. Terrify her. She knew that. Her brain knew that. But her body had reacted without thinking. Would it always?

She would never marry. Not now. What respectable man would want her? And even if—miracle of miracles—she found one who did, could she ever bear to be touched...*that* way? If she couldn't even let an obviously decent man like Liam brush her hair out of her eyes—an innocent gesture—how was she ever going to let a man touch her in more intimate ways?

She sighed, suddenly so worn-out she could barely sit up. She laid down on top of the bedspread and pulled a corner of it over her. *Fifteen minutes,* she promised herself as she closed her eyes. *Just fifteen minutes.* She shivered a little in the air-conditioned room and clutched the bedspread closer, huddling beneath it. She wasn't used to air-conditioning. And she was too thin.

Does Liam think you're too thin? The question came at her out of nowhere, and it surprised her. Even more surprising was the answer. *No, he doesn't. Remember the way he looked at you? The way his eyes said he found you attractive?*

Such a good man, despite the fact he'd already judged her. She didn't fault him for that—his opinion of her was no worse than her opinion of herself. It made no difference in the way he treated her, though, and that touched a secret place inside her. Even thinking the worst, Liam was so protective, like Alec. But Alec was Angelina's, heart and soul.

Hovering between waking and sleeping, Cate's thoughts winged back to Angelina. Sometimes it seemed as if her memories of long ago, her memories of her cousin were the only things that still belonged to her. Angelina, who'd treated Cate like a little sister…spoiling her a bit, making much of her. Calling her *dernya*, which meant *little treasure* in Zakharan. Never making her feel unwanted the way her parents had made her feel unwanted because she wasn't a boy.

Cate smiled sadly, remembering happier times with her cousin…when they were both determined to succeed in their own way. When they both believed in the power of prayer the way they believed in hard work. Back when she'd idolized Angelina and wanted to be exactly like her—even though she'd known she couldn't be. She'd known she'd never excel academically, the way her cousin did. She'd been twelve to Angelina's seventeen, but she'd known even then that if she excelled it would have to be in a different arena.

When had she decided to become a model? Was it when she'd shot up four inches between seventh and eighth grades, adding another three inches in ninth? When the other girls in her school had gazed enviously at Cate's luxurious golden hair, her face, her slender figure, her graceful walk? The desire to excel at *something*—to stand out from the crowd—the way Angelina always had and always would?

Cate hadn't been jealous of Angelina, but she *had* wanted to impress her—easy to see that now. But Angelina had stayed safely in Zakhar—accepting the limitations staying there placed on her as a woman, yet working within the system to effect change. Cate had been impatient with those limitations, those restrictions, especially the ones placed on her by her parents. Restless to break free, to escape the tedium of school—where even her popularity with her fellow students hadn't been enough to satisfy her—and seek fame and fortune as a model.

And when her parents had died unexpectedly in a car accident, sixteen-year-old Cate suddenly saw it was possible. She'd thought the promised modeling contract in the US was her one-way ticket out. Had believed the work visa provided by the US embassy—but paid for by the man who'd dangled that modeling contract in front of her starstruck eyes—was her escape from middle-class mediocrity. Who could have known she would escape…into hell.

Dinner was still twenty minutes away and he'd already meticulously cleaned his SIG SAUER, so Liam called Alec again. He'd spoken with his brother twice since he and Cate arrived at the safe house, but both times had been strictly business. Now he needed to talk to his brother about Cate—and the things Alec knew that Liam knew nothing about. He told himself it was important to the case, and maybe it was. But in his heart he knew that wasn't why he was asking. There was just something about Cate he couldn't shake off. Cate…and her relationship with Alec. His brother. His newly married brother.

Come on, he rallied himself. *You know Alec inside and out. There's no way he's fooling around. Not Alec.*

Cate was a different story. He knew almost nothing about her, and what he did know wasn't…encouraging. So his attraction to her was unexpected, unwanted and totally out of character. He'd always been drawn to sweet young things, ever since the transition from junior high to high school, when he'd first noticed girls were different. Wonderfully different. But he'd always gone for the wholesome girls back then, the girl-next-door type. And when he'd grown up, things hadn't changed all that much. He was still attracted to women he wouldn't be ashamed to introduce to his family.

He didn't know how or why Cate had become a prostitute, but even when he'd been in the Marine Corps stationed overseas he'd never picked up a hooker. Never paid for sex. He had a healthy libido—okay, more than healthy to tell the truth—but he drew the line at paying for sex. It was degrading to both the man and the woman.

Besides, even though he and Alec didn't have the looks in the family—Shane and Niall had a corner on that—they did have something even better. Charm. Charisma. And a way with the ladies that had become almost legendary in the DSS, though neither brother was the kind to kiss and tell.

So the fact that he was attracted to Cate—and damn

it, he *couldn't* shake it off—meant he needed some answers from Alec. Fast.

"So tell me about Cate," he said as soon as his brother answered the phone.

"Cate? You mean Caterina?"

"Yeah. But she says she doesn't go by that name anymore. Except in court."

Silence at the other end. Then, "When did she tell you this?"

Liam let out his breath long and slow. "This morning. When she told me she doesn't use Mateja anymore, either. When she told me about going underground. About picking an alias."

"Must have been quite the conversation."

"Not really." Liam laughed ruefully. "When I asked her why she went underground, she told me that you know, but I don't have a 'need to know.' Right after I explained the concept to her."

"And *do* you have a need to know?" Alec asked pointedly.

Liam thought about it for a minute. "Yeah, I think I do."

Silence hummed between them, and Liam knew his brother was reading between the lines, hearing what he *wasn't* saying. Finally Alec said, "Not a good idea, Liam. She needs protection. Not some guy hitting on her."

"I'm not 'some guy,' and I'm not hitting on her." Liam held on to his temper…barely. It was so unlike him, it gave him pause. "And I know she needs protection. That's why I'm here."

"As long as you remember that."

"You don't have to tell me how to do my job." His

temper threatened to get away from him again, and Liam knew his brother could hear the edge he couldn't keep out of his voice. "That's what she is. A job. That's all," he insisted, but an insidious little voice in his head asked, *Are you trying to convince Alec? Or yourself?* He ignored the little voice and said harshly, "Just tell me what I need to know, damn it."

"Where do you want me to start?"

"Why did she go underground? What was she running from?"

"Not what. Who. Aleksandrov Vishenko. One of the defendants in the case."

"She mentioned him. Said he was the one trying to kill her."

"With good reason. She can put him away for life. Not to mention what her testimony can do to the other defendants."

"What does she know?"

"It was a three-way conspiracy. A group of Zakharian criminals were luring young, pretty Zakharian women to the US under the guise of modeling contracts. The previous two regional security officers at the embassy—the one I replaced and the one before him—and several Foreign Service officers were fraudulently providing US visas for the women. Many of them underage girls, really. And Aleksandrov Vishenko's branch of the Russian mob was taking delivery of the women and forcing them into prostitution. Making a fortune selling some of them to gangs across the country, or pimping them out themselves." Alec paused for a moment. "Caterina saw it all. She lived it. And she had evidence."

"How'd she get the evidence?"

"If you believe Vishenko, she was his willing mistress for two years."

Something cold and hard gripped Liam. "And if you don't believe him?"

"She was his prisoner for two years. His personal sex slave."

"Oh, Christ!"

"Yeah," Alec said dryly. "That's what I said when I first heard about it. Made me sick to my stomach. Literally. Then I wanted to cry. For her." He didn't say anything for a minute, letting that sink in. Then he added, "I can't tell you any more than that. It's her story. You would have heard all about it in court tomorrow—if Vishenko hadn't tried to kill her. But for now, you'll have to get the rest from her. If she wants you to know… she'll tell you. But let me say this. You really *don't* want to know. I wish I didn't. Because knowing what I know, well…it makes me think vigilante justice might not be such a bad thing after all."

Guilt slammed into Liam as he realized he'd made assumptions about Cate based only on what little he thought he knew about her…most of it false. He tried to figure out why he'd been so quick to judge her, then shook his head when it dawned on him he'd *wanted* to think the worst of Cate…to counteract his totally unexpected strong attraction to her. It hadn't worked. And now he could add guilt to the equation.

Chapter 4

A voice from the bottom of the stairs called Liam and Cate to dinner, and Liam started down the staircase. But when no sound came from Cate's bedroom he turned around and tapped on her door, thinking maybe she hadn't heard the call. When she didn't respond he rapped harder, but still no answer.

He tried the doorknob and it wasn't locked, so he twisted the knob and opened the door a few inches. "Cate? Dinner."

The room was shrouded in darkness, and there was no movement, nothing to suggest she was even in there. Suddenly concerned—*she wouldn't just take off, would she?*—he pushed the door open all the way. That's when he saw her huddled in the center of the bed, the bedspread pulled around her slender body. Fast asleep.

He trod quietly over to the bed, hesitated for a second, then touched her arm lightly. "Cate." She jumped as if he'd shot her, jerking upward so quickly Liam was startled back. "Hey, sorry. Didn't mean to scare you. Just wanted to tell you dinner's ready."

She pushed her hair away from her face and blinked at him. Then she rubbed her eyes—tired eyes, he saw now. Sad eyes. Ancient eyes that were the window into a soul in torment. How had he missed it before? "It's okay," she said finally. "I didn't mean to fall asleep. I was just resting my eyes, and…" She stared at Liam through the shadows in the room. "Thanks for waking me. I wouldn't want to miss dinner." She smiled, a slight movement of her lips that came and went so quickly it almost couldn't even be called a smile. "I've been smelling that roasted chicken for hours, it seems."

Any other woman Liam would have offered a hand to help her off the bed. But Cate wasn't any other woman. And now that he knew—well, he didn't know exactly what he *knew*, but his imagination was working overtime, supplying details he didn't want to think about. Not about Cate, or any woman. So no way was he going to touch her. It made sense now why she hadn't wanted him to touch her before. It wasn't personal. It wasn't *Liam Jones* she was rejecting—she didn't want *any* man touching her. And he didn't blame her. Not one bit.

Dinner wasn't the silent affair Liam had expected. The agents, who went by the last name of Morgan, carried on a conversation between the four of them by sheer will. They refused to let Cate withdraw within herself, and asked a series of innocuous questions designed to put her at her ease. She answered haltingly at first—as if she wasn't in the habit of carrying on dinner conversation—then with increased confidence. And Liam was convinced that whatever else she was, whatever else she'd been, she was well-read. *Self-educated?* he wondered. Cate let something slip that made him suspect libraries were her only recreational outlet…in large part because they were free.

Liam answered when questions were addressed to him, but in between he watched Cate. Surreptitiously. He remembered watching her that morning—was it only that morning?—arguing with the prosecutors. Her hand gestures graceful and fluid. Now he watched her hands close up, fascinated by everything she said and did. And that's when he saw it. It wasn't obvious—just a slight darkening of the skin. But it shouldn't have been there. Not twin bands circling both wrists in almost exactly the same location. And suddenly he knew what they were. And how she'd gotten them.

Scars. Scars left by something bound tightly around her wrists, bindings she must have fought against until her skin was raw and bleeding. Repeatedly. Then he heard Alec's voice saying, *"…Made me sick to my stomach. Literally. Then I wanted to cry. For her…"*

Bile welled up in his throat as his stomach churned violently and he wanted to cry for her too, despite his deceased father's long-ago strictures on crying. But more than that he wanted punish the man who'd done this to her. He wanted to pummel him into a bloody pulp, wait a few minutes, then come back and do it again. And again. Until the man had paid for those scars, and what they had to mean. As if he could erase his own mistaken thoughts about Cate by exacting two years' worth of vengeance. For her.

Shaken more than he cared to admit, Liam swallowed hard and glanced away. His eyes caught those of Dave Morgan across the table, and knew the other man had spotted the same thing he had. Was having the same kind of reaction any decent man would have to the knowledge that Cate had been abused. Bound. And most likely raped—repeatedly.

Guilt slammed into him again. Guilt that he'd judged her from the beginning, that he'd wondered how and why she'd become a prostitute. That he'd been baffled by his attraction to a woman of the streets, even one who looked like her.

Now he knew that whatever she'd done, it hadn't been by choice. She hadn't *chosen* her life any more than she'd *chosen* to have those scars inflicted on her by Aleksandrov Vishenko. *Has to be him,* he reasoned. *Who else it could be? No wonder she despises him. No wonder he's afraid of what she'll say on the witness stand and tried to have her killed. And no wonder Alec wishes he could exact a little vigilante justice. I do, too.*

Liam's new cell phone suddenly shrilled, startling him out of his reverie. The ringtone wasn't his usual one, so it took him by surprise. He quickly excused himself from the table to answer the call.

"Yeah?"

"It's me. Cody. Just wanted to let you know we were right. The agent you gave your cell phone to used it, on my orders, just to see what would happen. And sure enough, someone in the FBI was triangulating on the signal."

"Shit."

"No kidding. Doesn't necessarily mean anything bad. Could be they're just trying to locate you to bring you in for routine questioning in the shooting—you'd be cleared of course, but they have to follow procedure. Get your statement and match it to the statements of the other witnesses, not to mention Alec's statement. Do ballistics tests on your gun. The whole nine yards. Or it could be they just want to bring Caterina in for safekeeping—she's still a key witness in the conspiracy trial. On the other hand, it could be someone trying to track down the two of you…for Vishenko."

"Yeah, I get that."

"So D'Arcy wants to change the plan a little. We've got Alec and his wife in protective custody—and boy, the FBI was pissed about *that*, especially when D'Arcy refused to divulge their location to them. We want to ensure the same for Caterina and you—but the FBI knows about the agency's safe house in Fairfax. Don't ask how—it's a long story. So D'Arcy wants to move you to another safe house, one outside Fayetteville, North Carolina. If you leave now you can be there in just under five hours."

Liam was tired—he'd had a long drive yesterday from New York to DC, today had been another long day and his body had used up its store of adrenaline already—he wasn't looking forward to a five-hour drive.

But now wasn't the time to worry about that. Safety was the primary concern. Cate's safety.

Cody was still talking. "Don't use your credit cards to get there—pay cash. The Morgans will give you enough cash for anything. And new identification and credit cards for both of you will be waiting at the next safe house, just in case we have to move you again. Oh yeah, and swap GPS units with the Morgans."

Surprised, Liam blurted out, "They can track us by my GPS? I didn't think that was possible, not without—" He stopped abruptly, realizing that law enforcement was constantly coming up with new and improved surveillance techniques, some of which the public was completely unaware. And if it could be done at all, the FBI would know how.

Silence at the other end. "Think about it," Cody said finally. "But don't think too long. We want you out of there in the next fifteen minutes."

"What do I tell Cate?"

"At this point I think you're going to have to tell her the truth. At least some of it."

"I already told her about the death of the other witness."

"I told you not—"

"She knew," he said flatly, cutting Cody off. "She figured it out, so there was no reason not to confirm it."

"How's she holding up?"

"She's keeping it together, at least on the surface. I don't know what she's feeling inside, but it can't be good."

"She's still planning to testify, right?"

Liam grunted. "Don't worry. Whatever Alec told her, it must have resonated. So yeah, she's still planning to testify. No matter the cost."

They drove through the night, a night that—thanks to the full moon and the steady stream of traffic—wasn't all that dark. But it was anonymous, and that's all Cate cared about. She hadn't hesitated when Liam told her they had to move on to another safe house. Moving on was something she did on a regular basis, so it wasn't unusual for her. She'd packed the few clothes and other essentials the Morgans had given her into a small suit-case—also provided by the Morgans. She'd been ready in less than five minutes.

Now, as she watched Liam driving at a steady pace— the speedometer just barely nudging the legal limit— she considered asking him the questions that had been percolating in her mind since his sudden announcement right after receiving the phone call. *Who called you? Was it Alec? He's a witness too, so is he safe? And Angelina. What about my cousin?*

But she wasn't in the habit of asking too many questions. When you started asking questions, people had the unfortunate response of thinking that gave them the right to ask questions in return. And Cate didn't answer questions. Not as a general rule. The less people knew about her, the less chance there was that Vishenko's men would find her.

Alec had asked questions. So had the FBI and the men from the US Attorney's Office. She'd had no choice but to answer those questions. And she would answer any and all questions put to her in court. Honestly. But for some reason she didn't want Liam asking her questions. Especially about her past—she didn't want him to know. Anything.

And why is that? a little voice inside her head asked. The answer was one she didn't want to acknowledge. *You don't want him to think badly of you. But you don't want him to think of you as a victim, either. You just want him to think of you as a woman. A woman he's attracted to. Admit it.*

"You're awfully quiet over there," Liam said. "You okay?"

"Fine. I'm just thinking."

"Worried about this move?"

She shook her head, but realized his eyes were on the road and he couldn't see it. "No. Not really. I'm used to it." *I'm used to moving from place to place,* she thought. *Whenever I got the feeling Vishenko's men might be close, I always moved on. Why do you think I'm still alive?* But she didn't say any of this to Liam.

The long silence that followed was broken when Liam said, "Cody—my brother-in-law—said the FBI knows about the safe house we were just at. That might not mean anything, but Cody's a damn good poker player. First rule of thumb—never give away anything, especially an edge. Not if you don't have to."

"'Need to know,'" she said. "I understand."

"Exactly."

"So where are we going now?" she asked.

Liam hesitated.

"I do have a need to know," she said softly, but putting determination behind it. "It's my life—not only do I *need* to know, I have the *right* to know."

"Okay, yeah," he agreed finally. "The agency has another safe house in Fayetteville, North Carolina. Cody and his boss think we'll be safer there than at the one in Fairfax."

"Why?"

He told her. Flat out. Not trying to sugarcoat anything. When he was done she said, "Thank you for being honest with me." She considered everything he'd said, then asked, "So Vishenko has the FBI infiltrated?"

Liam shook his head. "We don't know that. It's only one of several possibilities they're considering. But in the meantime, the agency doesn't want to take any chances. Not with you."

Cate thought of something. "Alec is a witness, like me. And Angelina. Are they being guarded, too?"

She could tell her question bothered Liam somehow—it wasn't anything he said, just a feeling she got. *Is he worried about his brother's safety?* she wondered. *As I am?*

"Don't worry. The agency has them in protective custody," he said curtly. Then he asked, "What do you mean Angelina's a witness, too?"

"Not a witness in this case—the conspiracy. But she would be a witness against Vishenko if he's extradited to Zakhar."

He glanced at her for a second, as if puzzled, then shifted his attention back to the road. "I don't get it."

"For the attempted assassination of the crown prince," she explained patiently. "Don't you know?"

She added a few specifics regarding the assassination attempt in St. Anne's Cathedral in Drago during Crown Prince Raoul's christening ceremony the year before, an assassination attempt foiled by her cousin, Angelina and Liam's brother. "If Vishenko gets off in this trial, he still has to face justice in Zakhar. Alec told me the extradition paperwork has already been processed on Zakhar's end. They're only waiting for the outcome of the conspiracy trial here before pressuring the State Department to turn Vishenko over to them for Zakharian justice."

"Alec didn't mention it." And there was an edge to Liam's voice that said he was upset he'd been kept in the dark.

Cate put a hand out to touch his arm in commiseration, then drew it back. Instead, she said, "At first I asked Alec why I needed to testify. Why I needed to risk my life to put Vishenko behind bars in the US when he will be tried in Zakhar for what he nearly did to the crown prince. One of the shooters has already confessed, naming Vishenko as the man behind the attempt. The man who supplied the money." She breathed deeply. "But Alec made me see it is not just Vishenko, although he is key. All the men in the conspiracy must face justice—the Zakharians who lured the trafficked women and the men from the US embassy who provided the false visas are just as guilty as the men from the *Bratva*. We cannot bring them down unless Vishenko goes down."

Cate was silent for a moment. "Whenever I'm afraid— and I'm often afraid—I remind myself that even if Vishenko escapes justice here he will be tried in Zakhar. And the courts in Zakhar are much quicker than they are in the US. Justice is swift. Punishment harsh." Her voice dropped a notch. "Even if he kills me he will not escape. And that is a very comforting thought."

"He's not going to kill you," Liam asserted. "Not if I have anything to say about it."

Warmth from out of nowhere filled Cate at Liam's words. Not so much the words themselves as the tone of voice in which they were uttered. Coolly confident in his own abilities. Determined. And she knew he meant it. She was safe in his hands, as safe as it was humanly possible to be…which was a tremendously relieving feeling.

They arrived at the new safe house before midnight. As he'd done at the first safe house, Liam didn't pull into the driveway, walk up to the front door and knock. He reconnoitered first, driving past the house and around the block slowly, then circling back again. It was a little thing, but it emphasized to Cate he wasn't a novice at this. And that extra caution only added to her feeling of safety. Vishenko might still succeed in killing her—anything was possible—but Liam wouldn't make it easy for him.

Just as before, Liam parked on the street a few houses away, and Cate knew he didn't want to announce to anyone who might spot the SUV or who might have been following them which house they were actually in. Not that they'd been followed—Liam had made sure of that, too, long before they'd arrived at the safe house. Another little detail.

So many details, Cate thought. Between the US Marshals who'd guarded her before and Liam now, she realized just how much she *hadn't* done to safeguard herself those six years on the run. Vishenko's men hadn't found her, so she must have done *something* right. *But some of that must have been luck. Blind luck.*

Liam handed Cate's suitcase to her and grabbed his duffel bag with his left hand. He guided her down the sidewalk toward the safe house without actually touching her, his right hand tucked inside his jacket. And Cate knew why. He'd killed for her before. He would again, if necessary. And somehow, instead of making her afraid of that ruthless side of him the way she feared Vishenko, the thought helped her breathe easier.

It was after two in the morning, and Liam still couldn't sleep. He was exhausted—more than exhausted after a long, adrenaline-packed day capped by a five-hour drive through what seemed an endless night. And he hadn't been able to let Cate share the driving for two very good reasons. First, she had no ID at all on her, since she'd left her purse behind in the courthouse, so of course she wouldn't have a driver's license or other state-issued ID with her. And second—more importantly—she didn't know how to drive.

He'd been dumbfounded when she'd admitted as much to him when they'd stopped for gas and he'd asked her if she wanted to take a turn behind the wheel while he rested. Except for a few anomalies, such as residents of New York City, what US citizen over the age of sixteen didn't know how to drive? He'd held back the question with an effort, but then realized he should have known. *Duh,* he'd told himself when she'd flushed with shame at her deficiency. *Cate wasn't born and raised here. And if she's been living off the grid for much of the past seven years, what chance would she have to learn to drive? To practice?*

Now as he laid in bed, moonlight streaming through the window across the room, he wondered what else Cate had missed out on besides the teenage rite of passage of obtaining a driver's license. *Don't go there,* he warned himself. But it was already too late. His thoughts winged to the scars on her wrists he'd noticed at dinner, and what they meant. What they *had* to mean. He gritted his teeth as he heard Alec saying, *"You really* don't *want to know. I wish I didn't."*

But he did want to know. He wanted to know everything. And he wanted Cate to be the one to tell him. He wanted her to trust him as much as she trusted Alec, and he wanted her to confide in him the way she'd confided in Alec.

Jealousy reared its ugly head again. It made no sense. Cate didn't belong to him and he had no right to feel possessive of her. No rights at all where she was concerned. Especially when it came to his brother. His married brother. But that didn't stop Liam feeling as if he did. As if somehow…someway…as if saving Cate's life gave him the right to care about her. Not just her future, but her past, too.

Liam's older brothers Shane and Niall used to tease

Liam when he was little, saying Liam had been born in the wrong time. That Liam should have been a knight-errant in the twelfth century, roaming the world saving damsels in distress. He'd hated that designation as a boy—hated being teased—but as a man Liam had to admit there was more than a little truth to it.

Wasn't that why he'd been so upset when it seemed as if Trace McKinnon was taking advantage of Princess Mara back when the three of them—McKinnon, Alec and Liam—were guarding her? Wasn't that why he'd wanted to confront McKinnon about how obviously in love with him the princess was, even though he'd let Alec talk him out of that confrontation?

And wasn't that why—when he and Alec had drawn straws to see which one of them got to tell McKinnon what the princess had left behind for him when she'd unexpectedly returned to Zakhar—he'd almost decked Alec when Alec had won the draw? Because he'd wanted to be the one defending the princess. Because he'd wanted to be the one making McKinnon pay for hurting her so grievously.

Liam sighed and turned over restlessly, the sheets rustling softly around him. "You can't escape who you are, Jones," he muttered, punching up his pillow. And on that note he finally fell asleep. But his sleep was rocked by dreams. Dreams of Cate. Dreams of saving her from a fire-breathing dragon…a dungeon…the black knight, who bore a strong resemblance to Aleksandrov Vishenko in armor. Dreams of riding off with Cate on horseback, her slender body cradled protectively in his arms. Even in his dreams he knew it was ridiculous—he didn't know how to ride. But that detail wasn't germane, because in his dreams he was invincible—he could damn near do anything he wanted to…in his dreams. And what he wanted to do more than anything was keep Cate safe. No matter what he had to do.

Chapter 5

Aleksandrov Vishenko jerked awake, his heart pounding, shreds of a nightmare still lingering in his mind. He sat up and reached for the ever-present water bottle he kept beside his bed and drank deeply.

A body stirred beside him. "What is it?" the young woman asked drowsily.

"Nothing. Go back to sleep," he answered in harsh tones.

She obeyed, resettling her blond head on her pillow—*they always obey*—he told himself contemptuously. *Whores always obey.* Only one woman had defied him. One woman had fought him for more than a year, as if she was still the virgin she'd been the first time he'd taken her. Her desperate struggles had added immeasurably to his excitement, and he'd relished conquering her. Each time. Every time.

Caterina hadn't cried after the first night. Hadn't begged him to let her go. Hadn't begged him for *anything*. But her eyes…her eyes had betrayed her. He'd still been virile enough then to lust after her at least every day. Overpowering her futile struggles—laughing even, when she fought him—his ultimate victory ramping up his sexual prowess in a way he hadn't achieved since his teenage years. Every time he forced her to admit defeat he walked away feeling like a king. Like a god.

Then she'd surrendered—or seemed to—and that conquest had been even sweeter. Infinitely sweeter. Knowing she acknowledged him as her master. Knowing, too, she hated his touch despite her surface acquiescence—ahhh, that had kept his excitement flowing. He'd known she tried to escape him in her mind, but he hadn't cared…so long as her body belonged to him.

Then she'd escaped in truth, taking all the evidence of his crimes she could lay her hands on. And his life had never been the same. At first he'd tried to find her because he was afraid she'd take her evidence to the authorities. But when the arrest he'd expected almost hourly failed to materialize, his motive for finding her changed. Then he'd thought it was because she'd dared to run, diminishing him in his men's eyes. In the first year after her departure he'd been forced to put down two attempted takeovers of his empire by men within his organization who'd thought he was losing his touch…just because Caterina had made him look foolish by escaping.

But after his empire was secure again, after he'd killed a few men to prove himself still the most powerful, the most ruthless of men in the *Bratva*, he realized the real truth. He wanted to bring her back to him—to *force* her back into his bed where she belonged—because sex without Caterina had lost its zest.

Even though he had his pick of the young women brought into the US by the human trafficking ring, even though his men singled out the prettiest, youngest, most virginal-looking blondes for him to deflower before putting them to work as prostitutes, it still hadn't been enough. The tears of the women he raped did nothing for him—he'd craved the hate in Caterina's eyes. The hate…and the immensely powerful feeling it gave him to know she couldn't stop him taking her…despite her hatred.

But eventually…after all these years without her… he'd adjusted. The fire to possess her, control her, conquer her, had dimmed. Then he'd merely wanted her dead. Not just to ensure the evidence she'd stolen never fell into the wrong hands—though that had been a concern—but to have his revenge on her for depriving him of the sexual pleasure she'd given him. Pleasure he'd never been able to recapture with another woman no matter how hard he tried.

What was money, after all? he'd reasoned when he raised the price on her head. A means to an end. A million dollars was worth it. Oh yes, Caterina Mateja had been worth a million dollars to him…dead.

She still was. That hadn't changed. With Caterina dead, the case against him would fall apart like a house of cards with one card removed from the bottom of the stack. *So close!* he raged suddenly. His men had been so close.

Vishenko no more believed in miracles than he believed in God. But if he *did* believe in them, then Caterina's escape had been one. He'd used nearly every tool in his arsenal, had called in markers from a half dozen of his fellow crime bosses within the *Bratva*, had bought the best law enforcement officials his money could buy—the plan should have been foolproof.

But at least her near-death experience would make her reconsider testifying. Wouldn't it? Changing her mind about that wouldn't save her life—she still needed to die—but it would buy him a little time.

Cate woke late. She knew it by the angle of the sun's rays coming through her bedroom window. She laid there for a moment, trying to remember where she was. *Fayetteville,* her brain finally supplied. *Safe house. With Liam.*

Liam. She turned over and tucked her hand beneath her cheek as she thought about him. He reminded her so much of Alec in the way he looked, the way he talked, even his mannerisms. But—and it seemed almost sacrilegious to admit after Alec had rescued her from a life on the run and convinced her she had a purpose in life far greater than just continuing to live—she *liked* Liam even more than she liked Alec…and that was saying a lot. Maybe it had something to do with the fact that

Alec had eyes only for her cousin, Angelina...but she didn't think so. Not entirely.

There was just something special about Liam—his heart-stopping smile, the way his eyes smiled even before his lips did, the flashes of self-deprecating humor that told her even though he was a serious man in many respects he didn't take himself *too* seriously. She liked that about him. And then there was the way he so carefully *didn't* touch her if he could help it, as if he knew— *well, perhaps he does,* she admitted with a little pang of pain. *Perhaps Alec told him. Or perhaps I told him when I flinched away from his hand yesterday. He's a very perceptive man. It wouldn't take much for him to figure out I can't... I don't...*

She hadn't wanted him to know. Silly, she realized now. She couldn't keep who and what she was a secret from him—he already knew, at least in part. And eventually the whole world would know everything...when she testified. Hadn't she already had this discussion with herself, when Alec had convinced her to testify? "'I am only one,'" she whispered, reminding herself why she was here. Why she was putting herself through this. "'But I am one.'"

It was cold comfort. Especially with thoughts of Liam fresh in her mind. What wouldn't she give to be able to come to him—whole, clean—and see where their attraction took them? If nine years ago had never happened. But that was stupid. If nine years ago hadn't happened, Liam would never have entered her life. She wouldn't have been in that courthouse yesterday morning. No one would have attempted to kill her. And Liam wouldn't have been forced to come to her rescue. To save her life.

She rose eventually and made her way quietly, cautiously, to the upstairs bathroom, taking along the plastic bag with the toothbrush and other essentials the Morgans had given her at the other safe house—the one in Fairfax. No one else seemed to be around, so either they were still asleep—not very likely—or they'd all awakened far earlier than she had and were already downstairs.

Finished in the bathroom, Cate returned to her bedroom, dressed quickly in one of the three changes of clothes the Morgans had supplied her with, then made her way downstairs. She followed her ears to the kitchen, where she could hear faint deep voices, though she couldn't make out the words. She crept silently nearer, then checked abruptly in the doorway when she spotted a stranger sitting at the kitchen table with Liam drinking coffee.

When the two men saw her, they both put down their coffee cups and stood. The tall black stranger reached her first, his hand outstretched. "Good morning, Ms. Mateja," he said in his booming voice. "You don't know me, but I've been following your case very closely. I'm Nick D'Arcy."

She shook his hand. "Are you Liam's boss?"

"No, ma'am. I'm the head of the agency. But we've been involved in this case from the beginning. One of my agents put this case together with Liam's brother," he said, indicating Liam standing on the other side of her in his shirtsleeves, his gun in its shoulder holster clearly visible. "And I'm the one who arranged this safe house for you." He smiled gently. "I hope my people have made you comfortable here, Ms. Mateja."

"Oh yes. I—" *wasn't expecting a lot,* she almost said, but then realized that might come across wrong. *I'm used to making do,* didn't sound right, either. She smiled perfunctorily and settled for saying, "Very comfortable, thank you. But please call me Cate."

Liam took a step closer to her, his hand outstretched as if to touch her…but he didn't. "Cate, D'Arcy was just telling me he has another plan for us—if you agree."

She looked from one man to the other. "Another plan?"

"Why don't you sit down," Nick D'Arcy said, "and we can discuss it." He moved to the coffeemaker on the counter. "Want some coffee?"

"No thank you." Cate didn't drink coffee. She'd been too young to acquire the coffee habit before she'd first come to this country, and for six of the past seven years coffee had been a luxury she couldn't afford, even if she'd wanted to…which she didn't.

Liam opened the refrigerator and took out a carton of orange juice, offering it to her. "Juice?"

"Yes, please."

He grabbed a tumbler from the cabinet and filled it before handing it to her. She accepted it with a simple, "Thank you."

D'Arcy had refilled Liam's coffee cup and his own, and they settled around the table. "Here's the situation, Ms.—Cate," he corrected himself smoothly. "I don't know how much Liam told you about this case, but—"

"Very little." She glanced apologetically at Liam. She didn't want to seem critical, but he really hadn't said all that much. *Need to know,* she reminded herself now. He'd told her only what she needed to know…no more, no less. "I know another witness is dead," she admitted, glancing down at her hands. "I knew her," she added, almost to herself. Then her eyes met D'Arcy's. "Not friends, you understand. But I met her when we were first brought to this country nine years ago. She was a year older than me." She could have said a lot more, but anything she revealed about the other woman would be far too revealing…about herself. About what had happened to them both.

"I'm going to tell you a little story," D'Arcy said. "And afterward I think you'll understand why I'm not willing to take chances this time around. Did you want some breakfast before I start?" he asked, shifting gears. "This could take a while." When she shook her head, sipping at her orange juice, he took a deep swallow of coffee. He placed the cup back on the table, arranging it just so, as if he was mentally arranging exactly what to tell her in the few seconds it took him. Then he looked at her, all softness gone from his face.

"Aleksandrov Vishenko's branch of the *Bratva* was collaterally associated years ago with a domestic terrorist organization called the New World Militia, founded and run by a man named David Pennington. Ever heard of him?" Cate shook her head. "Pennington was briefly married to Vishenko's sister, Mariella. They had one child, who they named Michael…born with a birth defect that left one leg shorter than the other. Not crippled. Just not perfect. And Pennington was a perfectionist."

His brows twitched together. "Mariella subsequently divorced Pennington, resumed her maiden name—Vishenko—and changed her son's last name at the same time. Then tried her best to forget she'd ever been married to Pennington. But apparently her brother didn't share her aversion to her ex-husband. Either that, or Vishenko didn't care about the personal aspect so long as his relationship with his ex-brother-in-law remained profitable. Which it did. Very profitable, for both men. Arms dealing, including the theft of military grade weapons. And drugs, of course—Vishenko was an up-and-coming member of one of the most powerful drug cartels in the country. He was young, but completely amoral even then."

Amoral. A word Cate knew firsthand in relation to Vishenko. She managed to suppress a shiver at the memories, but she couldn't do anything about her eyes. Couldn't hide the sudden flash of revulsion the memories evoked.

D'Arcy had seen her reaction, she knew—his eyes betrayed him—but thankfully he didn't comment on it. He went on with his story. "The *Bratva* bought themselves an FBI agent, the best their money could buy—a man who eventually became the special agent in charge of the FBI's New York Field Office Criminal Division. At roughly the same time, the New World Militia infiltrated the US Marshals Service when I was still working there."

He smiled grimly. "That brings us to where I come

in. Five years earlier the FBI had approached a New York City cop named Ryan Callahan, recruiting him to go undercover with the New World Militia. To gather evidence against Pennington and bring down his organization. Callahan did that, all right. Then testified against Pennington and a host of others in the New World Militia. I was assigned to guard him. Not just until the trials, but afterward, to give him a new identity through the Witness Security Program."

"Some people refer to it as the Witness Protection Program, Cate," Liam threw in. "That's one of the things US Marshals do—protect witnesses who need protection, like they were protecting you. And in some cases provide them with new identities, new lives."

"Like me," Cate said, remembering all at once what Alec had promised her—that after she testified against Vishenko and the other members of the conspiracy, a new life would be created for her in some little backwater town in some out-of-the-way place. Where she would be safe from reprisals. Where she could live without always looking over her shoulder. Even if she chose to return to Zakhar, the plan was for her to disappear.

"Right," D'Arcy agreed. "I created a new identity for Callahan—Reilly O'Neill. I stashed him in a little town in the middle of nowhere—Black Rock, Wyoming—for reasons you don't need to know. To make a long story short, three people died when the New World Militia tried to torture Callahan's whereabouts out of his partner, something Josh Thurman—the partner—couldn't tell them because he didn't know. But when he and his family were murdered we knew the militia was getting close, so we faked Callahan's death as Reilly O'Neill, and I moved him to another location."

His eyes narrowed and his expression sharpened. "When Pennington's conviction was overturned, I was forced to reveal Callahan was still alive and still able to testify to the prosecutors in the case, and I sent two men to retrieve him—Larry Brooks and Trace McKinnon."

Cate's eyes grew big. "I've met him… I've met Mr. McKinnon. He came to see me once with Alec."

"Yeah, I figured you'd make the connection. McKinnon was clean, but Brooks was dirty. He was secretly a member of the New World Militia. He set a firebomb that almost killed Ryan Callahan—Reilly O'Neill—and the woman who is now Callahan's wife. They escaped by the skin of their teeth. Then Callahan and another man laid a trap for Pennington—with my help. A trap Pennington walked right into," he said with satisfaction.

He didn't come right out and say it, but Cate guessed from his expression that whatever trap Pennington had walked into, he hadn't walked out of…ever.

"Four years ago," D'Arcy continued, "Pennington's son, Michael Vishenko—née Pennington—tried to get revenge on the six men he held responsible for what he considered his father's murder. Ryan Callahan was one of those men. I was another."

"My sister was involved in that case," Liam offered. "She almost died when she stepped in front of a bullet to protect someone else."

"Special Agent Keira Jones was—and still is—one of the best agents I have," D'Arcy agreed. "Although her last name is Walker now." He pursed his lips, as if debating whether or not to reveal something, then said, "She was instrumental in locating you last year. She made the connection between a name she was asked to investigate by her former partner in the agency—McKinnon—and what seemed to be a totally unrelated case regarding someone the agency had been keeping tabs on for years, Aleksandrov Vishenko."

D'Arcy smiled slightly. But it was the kind of smile, Cate realized, that boded ill for whoever was on the receiving end. Not her. Vishenko. D'Arcy went on to explain, "It was the contract he had out on you that tipped her off—a contract whose price was upped from a half million to a million dollars. With the agency's blessing she helped her brother track you down. He never would have found you without her. Never would have rescued you in time."

"Alec's sister." She glanced at Liam. "Your sister. Yes, I've met her, too. She was very kind to me." So kind, she remembered now. And not at all judgmental. Just like Alec. Like Angelina.

"That pretty much brings you up-to-date," D'Arcy said. "I've got deaths on my conscience, the Thurman family among them. But I've never lost a witness I was responsible for," he told her. "I don't want you to be the first."

Cate glanced from him to Liam, then back again. "So what is this new plan?"

"Callahan," D'Arcy said. "Nobody knows of his connection to the agency, which is more important than I can explain right now. And he has more lives than a cat.

He should have been killed at least a half dozen times I know about—and probably a few I don't—but somehow he's cheated death time and again. That's why I want to put you in his hands, Ms. Mateja—Cate. If anyone can figure out a way to keep you safe until the trial begins, it's Ryan Callahan."

A cold, sinking feeling washed through Cate. And she knew the face she turned to Liam was ashen, her eyes stricken, unable to hide how betrayed she felt—a betrayal she had no business feeling. She knew logically Liam didn't owe her anything. He'd kept her safe thus far, but only to help his brother. To help salvage the case against Vishenko and the rest of the defendants. Not because he cared what happened to her—twenty-four hours ago he hadn't even met her.

Twenty-four hours? she asked herself, shocked at the answer. Dismayed. Because it seemed as if she'd always known him. Always trusted him to keep her safe.

The idea of losing Liam's protection cut her to the bone, and for a fleeting moment she imagined if she looked down she'd see herself bleeding somewhere. Then she carefully wiped all expression from her face, pulling back within her internal borders. She was alone…as she'd always been nearly her entire adult life. As she always would be. No one but herself to count on. Liam wasn't hers, not in any way. Not even in this. *And you'd better accept it,* she told herself harshly. Savagely. *You're on your own. Again. Still.*

If Cate had stabbed Liam she couldn't have wounded him more than she had with that one stricken expression…followed by that deliberate blankness. As if she thought he was abandoning her. As if she expected it.

His anger built quickly. What had he done to give her that impression? What kind of a man did she think he was? Then he remembered Alec telling him Cate's story had literally made him sick, that she'd been Vishenko's prisoner for two years. Two hellish years. Helpless. At the mercy of a man like Vishenko, who had no mercy in him. Those scars on her wrists told their own story. She'd eventually escaped…on her own. No one had helped her back then. Or all the years since then, except for much of this past year. She'd been on her own and on the run for six years until Alec found her. So it shouldn't come as a surprise to Liam she expected the worst from the men in her life. Except maybe Alec.

Still…it hurt. Just as it had hurt when she'd shied away from his innocent gesture yesterday. He wanted—perhaps unreasonably—for Cate to trust him, the same way she trusted Alec. *And where did that come from?* he asked himself. He wasn't sure he was ready for the answer, but he couldn't pretend it wasn't there. Couldn't ignore how he felt.

"I'm not leaving you, Cate," he explained, forcing himself to gentleness despite his anger and hurt. "Earlier this morning—before you woke up—D'Arcy was laying out his plan to stash you with Callahan. But that doesn't mean I'm out of the picture. Not by a long shot."

"I don't understand." She strove to shield her emotions from him—that was obvious—but Liam thought he saw something in her eyes. Those pale blue eyes looked almost gray—a trick of the light, he knew—

and eventually she lost her internal struggle, her eyes beseeching him to explain.

His dreams of last night came unexpectedly to mind. Dreams of saving Cate, rescuing her from any and every danger that threatened. And all at once he knew it wasn't just in his dreams he felt that way. He wanted to keep her safe. *Needed* to keep her safe. No matter what he had to do.

He'd already killed once for her—his protective instincts kicking in even before he knew her, because he couldn't let anyone be murdered in front of his eyes, not if he could prevent it. But this wasn't the same thing at all. Now he knew her. Now it was personal. Now he knew just how much she needed him, even though she thought she didn't. Even though she didn't believe she could count on his protection.

I'll prove her wrong, he vowed to himself. *She doesn't know it yet, but she can trust me to keep her safe. Always.*

Chapter 6

D'Arcy broke the silence when he said abruptly, "Callahan lives in Black Rock, Wyoming—that little town in the middle of nowhere I was telling you about—with his wife and three children. He's the sheriff there. But he's also done some covert work for me—nothing you need to know about, but I'll tell you this—I'd trust him with my life. I can't make the decision for you, though. I can't force you to go there. I can only offer you some options, and Callahan is one of them."

Cate's gaze shifted away from Liam's face, blankness descending again. "What are the other options?"

D'Arcy's expression betrayed he didn't much care for the other options, but he said, "The US Marshals Service is one option, but it's not a choice I'd make. Not after what happened yesterday. Don't get me wrong. Those men who were guarding you—"

"How are they doing?" she asked quickly.

"They're going to make it."

"Thank God," Liam interjected, meaning it sincerely. As a bodyguard himself in the DSS, he knew the often thankless job the marshals performed, keeping witnesses alive.

"Yes," D'Arcy agreed. "Thank God. But just because those men guarding you did their jobs doesn't mean the Russian Mafia hasn't infiltrated the US Marshals Service. Or the FBI. Or the US Attorney's Office. We don't know who, and we don't know how. But somehow Vishenko's men were able to get to the other witness and kill her. They made it look like an auto accident, but we know it was murder. Despite being guarded by marshals, same as you," he said grimly. "And someone orchestrated the attack on you yesterday morning— not hard to figure out where you were going to be," he said. "But it had to be an inside job because someone smuggled guns into the courthouse."

"Uzis," Liam clarified. "I could tell by the sound, and Alec confirmed it yesterday. The serial numbers were filed off, but he said the FBI is hopeful they can raise them." When Cate's expression betrayed her ignorance of the importance of this, he explained, "Serial numbers that have been filed down to hinder investigation can sometimes be restored by applying an acid solution to the metal. Then they can be tracked—guns with serial numbers leave a paper trail. And no one is better than the FBI at following a paper trail." He glanced at D'Arcy. "Sorry, I know your agency's pretty damn good at that, too."

"True." One corner of D'Arcy's mouth twitched into a ghost of a smile. "We think we're better, but perhaps you're right." He turned back to Cate. "As I started to say, you could return to the US Marshals Service. They'd do their best to keep you alive until the trial, but…"

"What are my other options?"

"The agency could keep you. My agency. It's not our federal mandate—keeping witnesses safe. Temporarily, yes. Yesterday. Today. Not a problem. But at some point I'd have to justify the expense." He smiled wryly. "My agency's not exempt from government bureaucracy, much as I'd like it to be. The taxpayers expect oversight, and the GAO—the Government Accountability Office—can get downright nasty about the damnedest things," he said, trying to interject a little humor into the situation. "Those are just about your only options," he concluded.

"What about Liam's agency?" she asked, displaying her ignorance about this, too.

"I work for the Diplomatic Security Service," Liam explained. "The DSS. Yeah, some of us are bodyguards, but as I told you before, we guard diplomats, not federal witnesses." He caught D'Arcy's eye. "I'm officially on vacation, as D'Arcy knows." His gaze returned to Cate's face, willing her to trust him. "Which means I'm on my own time. Which means I can choose to stay with you until my vacation runs out—and I do. I will. Even if I have to extend my vacation indefinitely. I have no intention of leaving you, Cate," he said softly. "Not until I *know* you're safe."

She sat there for a minute without saying anything. Without moving a muscle. So still. So quiet, Liam realized. Just as she'd been yesterday. "I need to think about this," she said finally.

"Don't think too long," D'Arcy told her. "If you want marshals protecting you, I've got to let the FBI know where you are. Arrange to have the marshals pick you up. If you choose Callahan, I've got to arrange to get you there safely."

"Who knows where I am now?"

"Besides you? Five people, four of whom are in this house. The other is Cody Walker, Keira Walker's husband. The head of the Denver branch of the agency. Not even Alec Jones and his wife know where you are right now—all they know is that you're safe." He smiled again, another smile that didn't reach his eyes. "Need to know, Cate," he reminded her. "Liam says he explained that concept to you. It's crucial you understand just how serious it is."

An expression flickered over Cate's face that Liam couldn't decipher…until she said, "I survived on my own for six years, Mr. D'Arcy, with a price on my head. Vishenko's men didn't find me until he raised the price to a million dollars. I think I understand how serious 'need to know' is."

Cate wandered into the backyard. The flower beds were past their prime this late in the summer, but still retained enough color to draw her attention. She found a small wooden bench under a silver maple tree, and seated herself on it to consider her limited choices.

She wished she could speak with her cousin, Angelina, and her cousin's husband, Alec, but she knew what they would say. Nothing that had happened yesterday changed anything—she still needed to testify. And to do that, she needed to survive long enough to make it possible. This meant either returning to the custody of the marshals…or putting herself in the hands of a stranger in Wyoming.

On the one hand she knew nothing about Ryan Callahan. Just because Nick D'Arcy trusted him didn't mean she would…or should. On the other hand, was it possible the US Marshals Service had somehow been infiltrated by Vishenko, as D'Arcy had suggested? Or by another branch of the *Bratva*? She knew the various branches of the Russian Mafia traded favors with each other from time to time, so even if Vishenko himself didn't have someone on the inside, that didn't mean she hadn't been set up by someone in the US Marshals Service. Or the FBI. Or the US Attorney's Office.

She twisted her hands together in her lap, the thumb of her right hand absently brushing over the scar on her left wrist as she had a habit of doing when she was stressed. *Who to trust? Who to trust?*

Liam found her there. She hadn't heard him approach, but suddenly he was standing there in front of her. So reassuringly protective. So much like his brother Alec…and so different at the same time.

"Have you decided?" he asked.

Cate shook her head. "Not yet." Her eyes met his. "If it was you…what would you do?"

He went down on his haunches, holding her gaze. He looked as if he'd like to take her hands in his, but refrained…because he knew she didn't like to be touched. "I can't tell you what to do," he told her. "All I can tell you is three people I trust with my life trust Nick D'Arcy's judgment—my sister, Keira, her husband, Cody, and Trace McKinnon. If it was my decision, I'd go with D'Arcy's recommendation."

"So you think I should go to this Ryan Callahan in Wyoming?"

His expression was solemn, earnest. "I don't know him. I only know *of* him—from the same three people I trust with my life. But what I do know about him is reassuring. I think any other choice is a risk I wouldn't take. Not if I were you."

She decided in that instant. "Then I will go there."

He stood up and automatically held his hand out to help her rise. The kind of gentlemanly gesture that came naturally to him, she could tell. Like yesterday, when he'd innocently tried to brush back her hair. Before she could stop herself, she placed her hand in his. Trusting Liam as she trusted his brother.

Even more than you trust Alec, she told herself silently. *Be honest, at least.*

And if she was honest—completely honest—she was also attracted to Liam…even more than she was attracted to Alec. For a long time after Alec had exploded into her life, she'd had something of a crush on him. Harmless, because not only did she know he was in love with Angelina, she didn't want any kind of physical relationship with him…or any man. She just admired him tremendously. Tried to pattern herself after Alec's moral strength and inner convictions, the same way she tried to pattern herself after her cousin.

But that's not what she felt for Liam, and it disturbed her. Because what she felt *wasn't* harmless. Or at least it wouldn't be…if she was the kind of woman who could respond sexually to a man. If she could shed her past like a snake shedding its skin. If she didn't cringe at a man's touch.

Then she realized she was touching Liam…or he was touching her…and she wasn't cringing. Wasn't getting the choking, panicky feeling that usually overwhelmed her when a man got too close.

And why is that? she marveled. Liking the sensation of Liam's hand holding hers. No, more than liking it. Enjoying it. Responding to the firm, yet gentle way his hand enveloped hers as he pulled her to her feet. A tiny shiver of awareness—*good* awareness—coursed through her body. How she knew it was good she had no idea. But it was…and it confused her.

To cover her confusion, she asked, "How will I get to Wyoming?"

"I'll take you there."

"You knew I would say yes?"

He shook his head. "No, but D'Arcy is a man who plans ahead. Whichever choice you made, he had plans in place. He'd already asked me if I would take you to Wyoming, and he had a backup plan ready in case I said no. He also had a plan to get you back in the care of the marshals, if that's the route you preferred. We'll fly to Aurora, Colorado, in a military plane out of Pope Air Force Base—it's not that far from here—then drive up to Black Rock."

"Why a military plane?"

"First, D'Arcy wants you in safekeeping as quickly as possible, which means driving is out. If we flew commercial, there'd be pictures of you at the airport that would end up in a government database. D'Arcy told me that's how Keira found you in the first place. She matched your picture when ICE—Immigration and Customs Enforcement—arrested you to the picture on your expired work visa with face recognition software. And the FBI has the same software.

"Second, in order to carry my gun on board the aircraft I'd have to declare it and prove I was authorized to do so. While the agency has the pull to arrange something like that for the false identity they'll be giving me, using it at the airport would leave a record, which would mean there'd be pictures of me in that database as well that someone might access—not a risk D'Arcy wants to run. And third, arranging things so I can be armed at all times even when I fly would take time, time D'Arcy doesn't want us to waste. He wants us to vanish. Now."

Liam paused for a second to give Cate a chance to speak, but when she didn't he continued. "The US Air Force plane we'll be taking isn't flying to Colorado just for us—we're hitching a ride, as it were. But D'Arcy pulled some strings to get us seats on the first plane heading in our direction, which is scheduled to take off just after three this afternoon.

"When we get to Colorado, the agency will provide us with a completely untraceable vehicle—like the one they gave us yesterday. It's roughly six hours from Aurora to Black Rock by car. I don't know about you, but I'm still recovering from yesterday and last night, so I thought we'd check into a hotel tonight and start driving north first thing in the morning. We'll have plastic—credit cards," he explained at her confused expression. "But D'Arcy doesn't want us to use them, even though they'll be in our fake names. He doesn't want us to leave *any* kind of a paper trail, if possible. We'll have enough cash for the trip...unless something disastrous happens. The credit cards will just be backup in case of emergencies."

"I see." And she did. Wasn't that what she'd always done since she'd escaped from Vishenko seven years ago? Disappear into thin air? Travel as secretly as she could, insisting on being paid in cash and paying cash for everything so as not to leave a record someone could trace?

"D'Arcy will be glad you took his recommendation."

"Not his," she said quickly. "Yours."

Liam drew a sharp breath. "Does that mean you trust me...a little?" he asked in his deep voice. "That you know I won't just abandon you, after all?" The expression on his face was a dead giveaway she'd hurt him earlier with her assumption that she was on her own... again.

"I'm sorry," Cate said, contrition in her tone as they

walked toward the back door. "I shouldn't have assumed the worst. I should have known you wouldn't do that to me...any more than Alec would."

Liam stiffened beside her. It was almost imperceptible, but Cate—who'd learned the hard way to read body language and react to it—could tell. And she wondered what she'd said that would have caused a negative response in Liam. *I apologized. I told him I was wrong for not trusting him. What is negative in that?*

Then it came to her out of the blue as Liam opened the back door into the house and held it for her, and the realization startled her. *He didn't like you mentioning Alec's name. His own brother. His own brother whom he loves. He didn't like it, and that means...*

She told herself she was imagining things. But deep down she knew she wasn't. Liam was attracted to her. No, it was beyond that. He was becoming territorial where she was concerned.

Vishenko had been territorial, keeping her for his exclusive use for two nightmare years. Putting her on display in his Long Island mansion for certain of his associates who came there to meet with him. Glorying in his power over her. Knowing she was frighteningly aware of the punishment he would inflict once they were alone if she repulsed him in front of his men. However she fought him in private, he didn't care. In fact, he enjoyed it. But she was not to cause him to lose face.

Cate had learned that lesson the hard way. And to her shame, she'd eventually complied. Letting him control her with threats instead of beatings after the first few months when she'd literally been his prisoner. Letting him control her…in front of others. Conceding him the power he insisted on…in public.

Then…pretending to concede even in private after the first year. She'd fought that battle with her self-respect, but Vishenko had broken her resistance enough so that she knew the only way to escape was to pretend. To loosen the stranglehold he had on her. To lull him into a false sense of security where she was concerned. Hating him, despising him—and herself—she'd submitted. Then she'd escaped. She would never submit again. Not just to Vishenko, but to any man.

Liam wasn't like Vishenko. She knew that. In her heart she knew that, but…she didn't want him to think she belonged to him, either. She would never be a man's *possession* ever again. Even if she died for it.

After they found D'Arcy in the living room and told him Cate's decision, Liam watched Cate walk away from them without another word, up the stairs to her bedroom, quietly but firmly closing the door behind her.

"Did she take much convincing?" D'Arcy asked him.

Liam dragged his thoughts away from Cate and turned to the other man, shaking his head. "Not really. She's smart enough to know what's best for her. It's just been a lot for her to take in. Including everything that happened yesterday."

D'Arcy's face reflected his regret…and his frustration with himself. "I should have expected something like that…and have been prepared for it. Especially after the other witness was killed. But I'll be honest. I thought she was safe in the courthouse. Which just proves I can make mistakes—bad ones—like every other man out there. I just don't happen to like it."

One corner of Liam's mouth curved upward in a half smile. "Baker Street. Isn't that what Keira and Cody call you? And McKinnon, too? Because you're so omniscient?"

"Yeah, I have that reputation," D'Arcy said, returning Liam's partial smile. "But maintaining it takes constant vigilance. And this proves I'm not really omniscient— otherwise Vishenko would never have been able to get this close to taking her out." He sighed, looking his age for once, before his face hardened. "Don't let anything happen to her, Jones. I know I don't have to tell you that—you and your brother did a damned fine job in the courthouse yesterday, and you got her safely all the way here. But this case now rests on the slimmest of threads. Without Cate…forget it. Vishenko and his cohorts walk free. Again."

"What about the extradition to Zakhar? Cate told me Vishenko is facing unrelated charges there, as well."

"Yes, and the US has an extradition treaty with Zakhar. But Vishenko's lawyers will fight it. It could drag out for years. And Vishenko will be free on bail in the meantime, just as he is now. Do you really think he'll meekly let himself be dragged off to Zakhar for a trial that will be little more than a formality given how the Zakharians feel about the monarchy?" D'Arcy shook his head. "I don't think so. If this conspiracy trial tanks, Vishenko will fight extradition all the way, and in the end I'll bet he skips bail rather than go to Zakhar, extradition or no. He has the money…and the connections, to go anywhere in the world. There are countries *without* extradition treaties with the US and Zakhar that would harbor him as a refugee…for a price."

Liam stood just inside the closed door to his bedroom, with his back to it. At first he thought about what D'Arcy had said about Vishenko. Then his thoughts moved inevitably to Cate, and the need to keep her safe. Not just for the trial…for himself, as well. And wasn't *that* a kick in the teeth. He hadn't seen it coming. Not at all.

He needed to get himself under control. Cate wasn't his woman, and he had to stop the damned knee-jerk reaction every time she mentioned Alec's name. So she had a thing for Alec. So what? Alec was a prince of a guy, and she wouldn't be the first woman attracted to him. What the hell business was it of his anyway?

Problem was, Liam wanted it to be his business, and that was crazy. He'd known Cate a day. Just a day. Twenty-four hours, maybe a little more. Okay, it was a jam-packed twenty-four hours, with dead assassins, a dead prosecutor and three others in the hospital. Closely confined with Cate—in his SUV, then in the first safe house, then driving to where they were now.

Watching her shy away from him yesterday, as if he would ever—*ever*—strike a woman. Watching as she turned those betrayed eyes on him in the kitchen this morning, an expression that tore his heart out. Then watching as she placed her hand in his. Touching him voluntarily for the first time. Trusting him…at least a little.

Then she'd withdrawn. Oh yeah, he'd sensed it immediately. She didn't like him acting as if she belonged to him. *Has to have something to do with Vishenko,* he told himself roughly. *Vishenko...and those scars on her wrists.*

So he needed to get himself under control. Especially if they were going to be in close proximity from here to Wyoming. On the military plane…then sharing a hotel room tonight—or a two-bedroom suite if they could get one—because it would be dangerous not to have Cate constantly under his eye, constantly under his protection. Dangerous for her.

But that would be dangerous for him. Not the same kind of danger she faced, but dangerous just the same. Because the knight-errant in him was already infatuated with her—any more time in her company could push him right over the edge. And that was crazy. Just crazy.

But true.

Love at first sight was a fantasy, not a reality. Sexual attraction—yeah, he wouldn't deny a man could see a woman and instantly be drawn to her sexually. He'd been physically attracted to Cate from the beginning, despite thinking the worst about her. But love? Wasn't possible. Love was a combination of many things, all of which took more than twenty-four hours to come to fruition. Liam had never been in love, but he knew that much at least. He'd been in lust—heavy lust, on occasion—but no amount of lust for a woman had ever turned into love.

The closest Liam had ever come to being in love had been the six months he'd guarded Princess Mara with his brother and Trace McKinnon. He'd been drawn to the princess from the beginning, despite his assignment as one of her bodyguards, but he'd quickly nipped that in the bud for two very good reasons: he couldn't let himself be distracted from his duty guarding her... and he'd seen the way she looked at McKinnon from day one.

He'd even taken McKinnon to task for being so hard on her—telling the other man to cut her some slack— wondering in the back of his mind if something would eventually develop between the two of them...and it had. Liam had taken it well, mainly because he hadn't let himself grow to care for the princess too much since he'd known there was no future in it. But he still had a soft spot for her.

Oddly enough, Cate reminded him of the princess. Not in looks, but in that innocent way she had. Even though he knew she'd been through hell, even though those scars on her wrists told their own sickening tale, there was still something untouched about her. Something pure. Inside, where nothing that had happened to her could really touch the woman she was. A core of untarnished steel.

Which brought Liam right back around to the realization he was falling for Cate. Hard. And that was crazy. Wasn't it?

Chapter 7

Liam and Cate left right after lunch. D'Arcy had already departed to catch his flight back to DC, but before he went he gave Liam detailed instructions for the trip, including how to contact Callahan once they arrived in Black Rock.

Liam was amazed at how quickly the agency had provided everything he and Cate needed, especially the false identification, credit cards and gun license in his new name. Not to mention the wad of cash he'd been handed, which they didn't even make him sign for. "Receipts if you can," was all they'd said, and he'd nodded as he folded half the bills into his wallet and tucked the other half into the duffel bag he'd received at the first safe house.

Liam had already programmed the GPS for Pope Air

Force Base, so all he had to do when they got themselves situated in the SUV was plug the GPS in, turn it on and select his preprogrammed destination. He glanced over at Cate sitting so quietly in the seat next to him, and smiled. "You ready?" She nodded. "Then let's go."

He waved at the couple who ran the safe house, and in no time at all they'd left the safe house behind.

Even though the drive would be short, Liam turned the radio on and fiddled with the selection until he found a National Public Radio station. Then he realized Cate might prefer something else—music possibly—so he quickly asked, "Do you mind? I'm not much for music when I drive. I'd rather listen to NPR. But if you'd rather…?"

Cate shook her head. "No. Whatever you want to listen to is fine with me. You're the one driving."

After that she lapsed into silence. She didn't say another word until they drove into the entrance of the base. She was so quiet and still, if Liam wasn't so attuned to her—to everything about her, including the way she breathed—he would scarcely have known she was there. Although he was focused on his driving and listened to NPR with a fraction of his brain, the rest of him wondered about that. About why she didn't talk the way most women did, needing to fill the silence between themselves and the man they were with. About why she kept herself so motionless. Then it came to him. Cate didn't want to draw attention to herself…in any way. She wanted to be invisible.

* * *

They settled into their seats across the aisle from one another in the very rear of the Beechcraft C-12 Huron twin-engine turboprop plane that would take them to Colorado. The plane was only half-full, but Liam wanted distance between the four officers who were also taking this flight and the woman he was guarding, so he'd steered Cate into the back of the plane. He hadn't missed the marked interest on the faces of the other passengers, all male, as they passed through. Cate's natural beauty—which she did nothing to enhance—meant she would always draw male attention wherever she went. And there wasn't a damned thing she could do about it. *Not a damned thing I can do about it, either,* Liam told himself. *Except keep the wolves at bay as best I can.* Keeping the wolves at bay might turn out to be an even tougher mission than keeping Cate alive.

They'd been flying for nearly half an hour and Cate hadn't spoken one word. Liam hadn't either, other than to ask her if she was comfortable, to which she'd nodded. Then she'd turned her face to the window, effectively shutting him out.

He knew he should respect her right to privacy. Knew he shouldn't try to force the issue. But he wanted to know her better. *Needed* to know her better. And since she wouldn't volunteer information, that meant he had no choice but to ask. He searched for an opening, one that would be innocuous enough to start with, and he settled on, "Tell me about your cousin. About growing up with her in Zakhar."

Cate turned away from the window to look at him. "Angelina?" Warmth colored the one word, and her lips curved in a reminiscent smile. "Angelina was wonderful. Like a big sister. I adored her. I still do."

"She's what? Five years older than you?"

"Almost. When I was little I wanted to be like her. But then I knew I couldn't—she was so much smarter than me, you see. So I decided to do something else." Her breathing quickened, and she turned away to stare out the window in silence, and Liam knew somehow she'd gone down a path in her mind she didn't want to talk about.

Feeling as if he was treading in a field of land mines, Liam asked, "What's your earliest memory of your cousin?"

At first Cate didn't answer, then she turned toward him and said, "I must have been about three. Angelina would have been eight, I guess. We were in the park, and she was rolling this large ball for me to chase. I wasn't very good at it, but she didn't mind. Now that I look back, I see she was very patient with me, always. Very protective. This huge dog came rushing up to me, barking—wanting to play, I imagine—but he scared me and then knocked me down. I started crying. Angelina was like a whirlwind. She chased the dog away, then picked me up, dusted me off and soothed away the tears. Then she bought me a big red balloon to distract me." The reminiscent smile was back. "It probably cost her all the pocket money she had, but that didn't matter to her. She tied the string around my wrist, tucked the ball we'd been playing with under one arm, took my other hand and walked me home."

Cate glanced at Liam, her eyes bright. "I have not thought of that day for years. Thank you for making me remember a good memory."

"What other good memories do you have of your childhood?"

"Oh many. Too many to recount. But looking back, remembering how protective Angelina always was, it's easy to see why she went into her line of work. When she told me she began her career as a prosecutor, then joined the Zakharian National Forces when the king opened them up to women, I was surprised at first. Not that being in the Zakharian National Forces isn't an honorable job," she quickly explained, "but a prosecutor—even starting out—makes more money than a soldier. Even when she was selected as one of the queen's bodyguards, that job still wouldn't have paid as much as her starting salary as a prosecutor."

"It's not always about money," Liam threw in.

"I know that. For people like Angelina—and Alec, too—the jobs they do mean everything to them. They are protectors. It's in their nature." Her voice dropped. "You too, Liam. I haven't thanked you for saving my life. I should have thanked you yesterday, but I…"

"I'm not looking for thanks."

"I know you're not. But I'm grateful anyway." She drew a deep breath. "I don't want you to think I take you for granted. That I take your protection for granted.

I… I don't. Even though it may have seemed like it this morning."

Liam wasn't sure what to say. Part of him wanted to tell Cate the truth—that she'd hurt him immeasurably when she'd assumed he was abandoning her. And that he was falling for her. But another part of him knew it was best not to say anything about that. She was starting to trust him. Trust was a huge step for Cate. He didn't need to throw anything else at her. Not now. Not yet. Time enough for that later…assuming what he was feeling was the real thing, and not some crazy, misguided knight-errantry.

So all he said was, "I understand. So long as you understand me. So long as you understand I care about keeping you safe."

"I do."

"Okay then."

Another long silence was broken only by the voices from the front of the plane. Then Cate said, "Tell me about your family. About your brothers and sister."

"What do you want to know?"

Her tone was wistful. "I was an only child, and after her brother's death so was Angelina. That's one of the reasons we're so close, I think. It must be nice being part of such a large family."

Liam chuckled. "Well, when I was little I wanted to be an only child, so what does that tell you?"

"You did?"

"Don't get me wrong," he said. "I love my family. But sometimes a kid can feel as if he's lost in the shuffle when there are so many." He caught the quizzical expression on her face. "I wasn't the baby of the family. That was Keira, my younger sister. But I *was* the last boy out of four boys. It seemed as if anything I wanted to do had already been done by my older brothers. Better than I could do it, too."

"I don't believe that."

"It's true. And being as I was only eleven months younger than Alec, we were always competing with each other when we were younger." He laughed abruptly as a cherished memory rose in his consciousness. "I can't tell you how thrilled I was the day I gave Alec a black eye."

"You *fought* with your brother?"

"Hell yeah, all the time." He cast her a rueful grin. "Shane and Niall—my two oldest brothers—were constantly at each other's throats, despite the fact that they presented a united front to the world if an outside threat should arise. Alec and I were the same way. *We* could fight with each other, but woe betide anyone who tried to take on either of us one-on-one. He had my back and I had his in that situation."

She shook her head in disbelief. "But if you love your brother, how could you fight with him?"

Her disbelief amused him. "It's what boys do, Cate. And in a large family, competition for attention and affection can get pretty fierce at times. Studies show that sometimes children act out—misbehave—if that's the only way they can get their parents' attention."

"Is that what you did? Misbehave?"

"No more than any normal kid. I won't try to tell you I was an angel growing up, but neither were any of my brothers. Our parents grounded us occasionally, but we deserved it—even if we would have denied it at the time. And there were times we deserved it that we skated by."

Her face crinkled in puzzlement. "Grounded? Skated? I don't think I—"

"Skated means we got away without punishment, kind of like an ice skater scooting away from trouble. Grounded is a type of punishment that can be particularly effective for kids—it means being confined to the house, or your room, or something like that, except for school and church."

"Oh."

"I'll bet you were a perfect little angel growing up," he teased. "You probably were never grounded."

She laughed. "No, I wasn't perfect, but I never gave anyone a black eye, either."

He laughed, too. "Alec and I don't fight like that anymore. Actually, I don't think we physically fought each other once we entered our teens. But competing—yeah, we continued to compete until the day I turned eighteen and joined the Marine Corps. After that, we only competed against ourselves. The Marine Corps has a way of turning a boy into a man despite himself."

She was quiet for a moment as she digested this. "So tell me about them, about your brothers and sister. What are they like?"

Liam considered this. "Shane—he's the oldest. He was the first to enter the Marine Corps, and stayed the longest. He rose through the ranks the hard way, starting out as a buck private and rising to the rank of colonel. He'd still be in the Corps if not for a domestic terrorist incident that happened a few years back. Shane was home for Christmas on leave—pretty rare for him. He was at the shopping mall with my sister the day after Christmas when a pipe bomb went off in a bookstore. Shane threw himself between the explosion and a woman who was seven months pregnant at the time. He suffered a brain injury—not debilitating, but bad enough for the Marine Corps to give him a medical discharge. Pretty devastating for him—the Corps was his home."

Cate blinked rapidly, and Liam suspected she was moved by the story but didn't want him to know it. He continued. "Shane knocked around for a couple of months afterward, unsure what he wanted to do with himself. Then he went into politics, heart and soul." He couldn't repress the pride he felt in his oldest brother when he said, "He's Senator Shane Jones now."

If Cate was the type to say "wow," Liam knew she would have said it. Instead she said softly, "You must be as proud of him as I am of Angelina."

"Yeah."

"What about the next brother after Shane? Niall, yes?"

"Niall," he confirmed. "I can't really tell you what he does because none of us know. He spent four years in the Corps—same as Alec, me and then Keira. After he left the Corps he went into... I guess you could call it black ops, although that's not really the name for it, and you didn't hear it from me."

"Black ops?"

"Covert operations on behalf of your government. But not something the government wants the world to know about. Deniable. Governments do it all the time. In fact, Zakhar carried out several covert operations in Colorado a few years back, when I was one of Princess Mara's bodyguards." Cate turned startled eyes on Liam. "Oh yeah," he told her. "I can't tell you the details, but trust me, they happened. All in the name of protecting Princess Mara."

Including a fake kidnapping attempt on the princess led by none other than King Andre Alexei IV in order to test Trace McKinnon, he thought to himself. *Including really kidnapping McKinnon and taking him by force to Zakhar.*

But that was all water under the bridge. Only a very few people in the government knew what had happened. Officially deniable across the board.

Cate was silent for a minute, then said, "So what about Alec and Keira? I've met your sister—she was very sweet to me. And I've known your brother for almost a year—not to mention everything Angelina has told me about him. But she's in love with him, so of course…"

Liam wanted to ask Cate—*really* wanted to ask Cate—about her own feelings for Alec. But he couldn't figure out a way to ask that wouldn't come across wrong. Instead he examined his conscience and said honestly, "Alec is…special. You probably already know that. I grew up both admiring him and competing with him. Sounds kind of strange, I know, but…anyway, I followed him into the Diplomatic Security Service not because I wanted to outdo him, but because I knew if it was right for him, it was right for me. Does that make sense?"

He glanced at Cate and caught her nod. "Working with Alec for six months guarding Princess Mara—that was a real privilege. I learned a lot from him—from McKinnon too, of course, but—"

"I've met Mr. McKinnon."

"Yes, you said that this morning."

"He was once your sister's partner, isn't that what Mr. D'Arcy said?"

"Yeah, funny how these things work out sometimes. McKinnon got tapped to guard Princess Mara because he'd once been a US marshal *and* because he spoke Zakharan like a native."

"So tell me about Keira. I only met her the one time, but…as I said, she was very sweet to me. And I met her husband, too. He came to the safe house with Alec and Angelina last year."

"Keira's special, too. I didn't realize just how much she meant to me until we almost lost her a few years back. That Edward Everett Hale quotation—the 'I am one' quote you said Alec told you? It applies to all of us, but in slightly different ways. Keira's interpretation of what it means led her to take a bullet meant for another man, and she almost died as a result. As a matter of fact, the man whose life she saved was Ryan Callahan—the man D'Arcy is sending you to."

"No," Cate said, shaking her head. "That's too much of a coincidence to be true."

"I kid you not. I don't know the whole story—Keira

and her husband would never say exactly what all was involved, and trying to get anything out of McKinnon is like pulling teeth. But it's true."

"You must be very proud of your sister." The wistfulness was back in her voice, and she suddenly turned away, staring out the window. "I could never be that brave," she said under her breath.

"Are you kidding?" The words came out rougher than Liam had intended. "You were walking into a courthouse ready to testify against one of the most depraved, most vicious criminals in this country. A man who has never hesitated to kill witnesses against him. A man who tried to kill you to keep you silent. And you're still willing to testify. Do you know what kind of guts that takes?"'

"But I'm afraid," she explained, as if that made all the difference. "To do what your sister did, to do what Angelina did when she killed the man who would have killed your brother—I'm not brave that way. I'm not brave at all—I'm a coward. Without Angelina, without Alec, I could never face Vishenko."

Liam cursed under his breath at how she was putting herself down, how she was minimizing her own valor. "You think Keira wasn't afraid? You think your cousin wasn't afraid?" He wanted to shake some sense into Cate, but knew he couldn't touch her. Not when anger was spilling through him. "Yesterday morning when we heard the Uzis, you think Alec and I weren't afraid? Hell yes, we were afraid. What do you think bravery is, Cate? It's conquering your fear and doing what you have to do in the instant you have to do it. Anyone who says they're never afraid is a liar, or a fool."

The fingers of Cate's right hand touched her left wrist, and Liam suddenly realized she had a habit of doing that. A habit that betrayed her inner turmoil. He hesitated, then reached over across the aisle and placed his hand on hers. "You're not a coward, Cate. A coward wouldn't have these scars." She averted her face, as if embarrassed, but he wouldn't let her look away. He caught her chin with his hand and turned her to face him.

"Do you know how much it tears me up inside to see these scars?" he told her, his voice rasping like sandpaper, but so low he knew he couldn't be overheard by the men in the front of the plane. "But I'm awed by your courage at the same time. Knowing what these scars mean, knowing what Vishenko did to you, and you're still willing to face him in spite of everything. That's courage, Cate. Courage far beyond anything I can claim."

The color drained out of her face. "Alec *told* you?" she whispered.

He shook his head. "No. He only told me who you were running from when you went underground. He said anything else had to come from you. But I'm not blind, and I'm not stupid. It didn't take much for me to figure out what caused these scars."

He lifted the hand he held and kissed the delicate skin on the inside of her wrist, where he could feel her pulse racing. "They're nothing to be ashamed of," he told her. "They're badges of honor."

She tried to pull her hand away, but he wouldn't let her. "You don't know," she said in a shamed little voice. "You don't understand. You think you do, but you don't."

"Can't you tell me?" he asked, his voice as gentle as he could make it given his anger at Vishenko. "I want to understand, Cate. I really do."

"No." Her voice wobbled at first, then she repeated the word, more firmly this time. "No. Please don't make me tell you."

Another dagger to his heart. Liam let Cate's hand go, but not until he'd kissed the palm. "No," he said, and it was as fervent a promise as he could give. "I'll never *make* you do anything you don't want to do, Cate. Never."

Chapter 8

Aleksandrov Vishenko bent his cold, hard gaze on one of his brigadiers. "Where is she?" he demanded. He didn't have to specify a name. There was only one woman on Vishenko's mind now, and all of his men knew it.

"Vanished."

"That answer is not acceptable."

The brigadier shrugged. He had been with Vishenko for many years, almost since the beginning, and his loyalty was unquestioned—as far as anyone in Vishenko's position could count on loyalty. Which meant the brigadier could be brutally honest, instead of telling Vishenko what he wanted to hear. "It is what it is, *Pakhan*. She is not to be found. It is as if she crawled into a hole and pulled it in behind her."

He waited for that to sink in, then added, "The usual methods will not work. Not this time. Especially since time is so critical. Our sources say they do not know where she is." He named no names, but Vishenko knew who those sources were, knew just how highly placed they were in the various branches of law enforcement. If they didn't know where Caterina Mateja was, then there could only be one agency guarding her.

Which meant Vishenko had no options left—except one. He would have to bet his last chip on one roll of the dice. A chip he'd never gambled with before. A chip so valuable it could only be used once.

After Cate and Liam's military plane had landed and they'd been met by one of the agency's agents with the promised SUV, they drove to a hotel not that far from the base. Cate wanted to wait in the SUV while Liam checked in, but he refused. "I need to keep you in sight at all times," he explained. "I don't think there's much of a risk here, but I can't take that chance." He smiled at her in fading daylight. "It won't take long."

Ten minutes later Liam had the keys to a two-bedroom suite. The clerk had wanted to swipe Liam's credit card for incidentals, even though he'd paid cash for the suite, but a two-hundred-dollar cash deposit took care of that. There wouldn't be any incidental charges—no long-distance phone calls from the room, no movies rented, nothing taken from the honor bar. But the clerk couldn't know that. *He probably thinks Cate and I are having an affair,* Liam thought with a touch of amusement, *since I don't want to give him my credit card.*

Fifteen minutes after that they were in the room, luggage stowed away. "I know it's not that late here, but my body is still on East Coast time," Liam said, "and I'm starved. What do you say to having dinner in the restaurant downstairs? It's not a four-star restaurant, but it's convenient."

One corner of Cate's mouth turned up in a little smile. "Anything is fine. I'm not in the habit of eating out at all, much less four-star cuisine. I doubt I'll be able to tell the difference."

Cate was touched by how Liam put himself out to keep her entertained over dinner—and to keep everything light. After this afternoon's conversation, she'd been afraid he would try to question her again, but he didn't. He kept her laughing with the misadventures of Alec and Liam in their tween years. "All I can say is, your poor mother," Cate gurgled.

"She's forgiven us." Liam crossed his heart and held his hand up. "Honest."

"What's she like, your mother? The way you talk about her, she sounds wonderful."

"She is. We're lucky to have her. She wants a few more grandchildren—and don't think she hasn't thrown out hints! But so far Alyssa—Keira and Cody's little girl—is it. Although Alec says he and Angelina are trying."

Cate beamed. "Yes, I know. Angelina told me. I would be so happy for them if it happened."

"So it wouldn't bother you?" Liam put his fork down. "Forget I said that."

Cate put her own fork down, her smile fading, and wiped her mouth on her napkin. "Why would you ask me that question?" In the back of her mind was a suspicion, one she'd had ever since this morning.

"Forget it."

"No, I want to know why you think it would bother me if Alec and Angelina had a baby."

Liam stared at her for a minute, his mouth tightening. Then he said, "Because of the way you feel about Alec."

She started trembling. She couldn't help it. She clasped her hands in her lap so he wouldn't see them shake. "Because of the way I feel about Alec?" she asked. "What way is that?"

"You…care about him," Liam said roughly. "I'm sorry, Cate, but it's obvious whenever you say his name. He's something special to you. He's my brother, and I love him—I know he's a hell of a guy. But he's married. And he loves his wife very much. So…"

Cate went hot and cold with embarrassment and something more. Hurt. Hurt that Liam would think badly of her when she wanted so much for him to… She quashed that thought, as ruthless with herself as she could be.

Although she was embarrassed, she wasn't ashamed. Not about this. "I care about Alec, yes," she said very quietly. "Meeting him changed me for the better. But I'm not in love with him. I never was. I never will be." Her breath caught in her throat. "And you have no right to question me about this. About him. About what I feel for him. I have never done or said anything that gives you the right." She placed her napkin on the table and stood. "Even if he is your brother."

With her head held high, she walked out.

Liam started to go after her, then realized he needed to pay the check first. He frantically signaled for the waiter, and curtly asked for the check when he arrived. He peeled off a couple of bills, saying, "No change." Then he headed for the exit Cate had taken, and rushed into the hotel lobby.

He was too late. The elevator was already on its way up, and Liam hoped like hell Cate was on it. That she was heading for their suite. And that his stupidity hadn't put her in danger. He cursed himself under his breath as he stabbed at the elevator button, waiting impatiently until the bell dinged and the doors opened.

As the elevator ascended to the eleventh floor, he tried to think of the best way to apologize. He'd put his foot in his mouth. *No, both feet,* he told himself with brutal honesty. Cate had every right to be angry, and he didn't blame her. He'd be angry at himself, too, if the situation was reversed. His only excuse was that he cared about her. Too much. And that he was *jealous* of what she felt for Alec. But Cate was absolutely correct—she'd never said or done anything that gave him the right to criticize her actions. To condemn what she felt for Alec. To act as if she belonged to him.

Shame crawled under his collar as he exited the elevator and headed for their suite, only to be brought up short at the sight of Cate standing by their door, her face a mask that revealed nothing. "I don't have a key," she said when he got closer.

"I'm sorry. Not about the key, but for what I said downstairs. I was out of line, and I know it." The apology made him feel a little better.

But Cate didn't acknowledge his apology, and that made him feel even more of a heel than he'd felt before. She waited for him to insert the keycard and open the door for her, then slipped past him without a word. She went into her bedroom and closed the door. Firmly. Then he heard the unmistakable click of the lock.

He sighed and bolted the door to their suite before heading to his own bedroom. *Great going, Jones,* he told himself as he got ready for bed and brushed his teeth. *You're a prince of a guy, you know that?*

He placed his SIG SAUER on the nightstand, hesitated, then picked up the cell phone the agency had given him and dialed a number. "Hey," he said when his brother-in-law answered the phone. "It's Liam."

"You and Cate made it in safely, I take it?"

"Yeah. No trouble with our flight."

"SUV okay?"

"What? Oh yeah, it's fine," he reassured Cody. The SUV the agency had delivered was just like the one the agency had supplied before. Not new. Nothing that would draw attention. Though he'd known the minute he'd stepped on the gas that under the hood—where it counted—the SUV was top quality. But he wasn't thinking about that.

"So tell me about Callahan," he demanded now.

"What's to tell? Didn't D'Arcy fill you in?"

"Yes and no." Liam wasn't really sure what he was asking, except that tomorrow he'd turn Cate over to a stranger for safekeeping. And despite what he'd told her this morning—that he trusted Nick D'Arcy's judgment—he wanted to know a little more about Callahan before he did that.

Cody seemed to read between the lines. "Callahan's the best," he said quietly. "He saved my life a few years back, when he had every reason to hate my guts. Officially he's the sheriff of Black Rock now—a position I held way back when—but he's also done some jobs for D'Arcy and the agency. All hush-hush. If I told you I'd have to kill you," Cody joked, forcing a laugh out of Liam. "Seriously, though, I'd trust him with my life. Even more, I'd trust him with Keira's life."

Liam knew the sun rose and set with his sister as far as Cody was concerned, so that statement said a lot. He breathed deeply and let go of the tension that had dug its tentacles into him. Cate would be safe with Callahan. That was the bottom line. He needed to know she'd be safe.

"After you turn Cate over to Callahan, why don't you come down and spend a few days with us? We've got the room, and you know you're always welcome. Seems a shame not to, since you're already in the area, and technically you're on vacation. Your mom would like to see you, I know. Not to mention Keira and Alyssa."

Despite feeling a little more reassured about Callahan, Liam wasn't ready to commit to anything. He'd promised Cate he wouldn't leave her until he *knew* she was safe, and he had no intention of going back on his word.

But that's not the only reason you don't want to leave her, his conscience taunted him. *You don't want to leave her because you're fall—*

"I'll let you know," he told Cody quickly, trying to quiet the voice in his head that refused to be silenced.

Cate slept restlessly, then woke a little after midnight. She watched the minutes click by on the digital clock on the nightstand next to her bed, desperate to get back to sleep but unable to do so. She tucked her hand beneath her cheek and realized she couldn't sleep because she couldn't stop thinking of Liam. Couldn't forget his accusation in the restaurant that she cared too much for Alec. That somehow she wanted to come between Alec and Angelina. *As if that was possible even if I wanted to,* she thought angrily. *Which I don't.*

Then her anger turned to sadness. Not sadness that she couldn't have Alec. But that Liam would think she was the kind of woman who would try to break up a marriage. "That tells you exactly what Liam thinks of you," she whispered in the darkness. Despite all his encouraging words this afternoon. Despite the gentle kiss he'd placed on her wrist that had made her catch her breath at the wondrous sensation, realizing—miracle of miracles—she didn't cringe from his touch, she actually enjoyed it. Heat had bloomed inside her, and she'd longed to have him hold her in his strong arms. Wanted to know what his lips would feel like on hers.

But all that meant nothing. Because in his heart of

hearts Liam believed the worst of her. Maybe he even believed she'd voluntarily stayed with Vishenko from the start, despite what he'd said on the plane about how the scars on her wrists affected him. How could she know what he *really* thought? And that was the most hurtful thing she could imagine. That Liam—*Liam*— would think she'd chosen a life of shame.

The backs of her eyes ached, but the tears she'd sworn she'd never cry again were denied her. She turned her pillow over, seeking a cool spot, and tried to force herself to sleep. But it was useless. Finally she got out of bed, belted her new terry cloth robe around her waist and crept into the other room for a glass of water.

She'd just put the glass down on the counter when a slight sound made her turn around sharply. Liam stood there in the shadows, wearing nothing but a T-shirt and boxer shorts, his hair rumpled from sleep. With a gun in his hand.

"Sorry," he said. "I didn't mean to startle you." He glanced down at the gun he held, and made a face. "I heard a noise and thought I should investigate." He disappeared back into his bedroom, then returned without the gun. "Couldn't sleep?" Cate shook her head. "My fault," he said in his deep voice. "I wasn't sleeping all that well myself. I apologized…but I know it wasn't enough." His eyes were sad. "Please forgive me."

At nearly one in the morning, with darkness surrounding them like a blanket, Cate could speak honestly. "It hurt me," she admitted. "It hurt that you would think I was the kind of woman who…"

"I didn't. I didn't think that." He sighed. "I don't

know why I said it. I just… I wanted to be the one you felt that way about, and I… Jealousy is an ugly, destructive emotion, Cate. Especially when it's your own brother you're jealous of."

"You don't have to be jealous of Alec." Her voice was low but intense. "I care for him. I admit that. But I never wanted him to touch me…*that* way." There was a long pause fraught with things they'd both left unsaid. Until she whispered, "I never wanted any man to touch me *that* way…until I met you."

Liam took a step toward her, his face betraying both disbelief and a desire to believe. Warring emotions written plainly. "Do you know what you're saying?"

Cate took a step back. "Yes, I know. But just because that's how I feel, doesn't mean I can. I can't. You have to know that about me." She squeezed her eyes shut for a moment, then looked at him with all the despair nine desperate, lonely years had engendered in her. "There's nothing I want more than to be able to come to a man clean and whole. But I can't."

"Why can't you?"

She turned away so Liam could only see her profile. "Nine years ago I was brought to this country to be a…" She swallowed. Hard. But she couldn't get the word out. "Vishenko saw me in that house where I was taken." She turned back to face him. "He *picked* me, you understand? Out of all the women in that room. All weeping with terror and fear of what by then we knew would happen to us—all but me. I don't know why I wasn't crying, but he told me that was why, out of all those women, he picked *me* to be his toy," she said in a bitter voice. "His personal plaything."

Liam's brows drew together in a frown. "Nine years ago? You couldn't have been more than—"

"Sixteen. I was sixteen." Self-mockery crept into her voice. "I wasn't forced with repeated beatings, threats and drugs to service hundreds of men, like the other women. Oh no! I was Vishenko's chosen one. He raped me, and then he kept me for himself…for two endless years." Her voice dropped to a whisper. "I would rather have been among the other women."

Cate's despair ate at Liam, fueling his anger at the man who'd done this to her, who'd forced her into feelings of shame and worthlessness no woman should ever have to endure. He reached out to touch her, to comfort her somehow, but she shied away. "Please don't," she whispered. "I can't. Not after what he did to me."

"Cate…"

"You don't understand," she cried out, pain and self-loathing in her voice. "The scars you've seen—they're nothing. Nothing!" She fumbled with the tie on her robe, then the buttons of her pajama top, her fingers clumsy in her haste. "At first he would just rape me," she panted in a desperate undertone. "But it wasn't enough for him." Then the last button pulled free and she turned, exposing her bared back. "This is what he did to me," she told him, her voice breaking. "When I refused to cry, when I refused to submit, this is what he did to me—to make me beg him for mercy. To make me beg him to let me go."

"Oh God." Liam closed his eyes and averted his face for a moment, fighting the sickness that rose in him. Not the sight of the scars themselves, but the realization of the agony Cate must have endured when each and every scar was inflicted.

Then he turned his gaze back to her. Gently, so gently he didn't know he had that much gentleness in him, he pulled the pajama top up and turned her around. He drew the edges of the top from her unresisting grip and pulled them together. Then he buttoned the buttons with fingers that trembled slightly.

Her breathing was ragged as she tried to drag in enough air. "You wanted to know what Alec knows. I didn't want that. Didn't want you to know." Her face was stony, her eyes bitter. "I wanted to keep my shame a secret from you as long as I could, but you wanted me to tell you." Her next four words dropped like hard little pebbles thrown into a pool of water as smooth as glass. "So now you know."

Liam couldn't bear it. Those words were uttered as if she believed he'd turn and walk away from her now, as fast as his legs could carry him. As if she believed that would be any decent man's normal reaction to her revelations. As if she was responsible for what happened to her.

He drew Cate into his embrace—taking her by surprise so she had no chance to pull away—and held her close, rocking her like a little girl. Comforting her the only way he knew how, the way his mother had comforted him when he three…four…five. Then he heard it, a sound he'd never expected to hear from Cate. Weeping. Soft, heartbroken sobs that ravaged his heart to hear.

He bent and caught her knees, sweeping her into his arms, cradling her against his chest as he carried her into his bedroom. *Oh God, oh God,* he begged. *What do I do? What do I say? How can I make this right for her?*

He laid her gently on the bed, then followed her down, still holding her—just holding her—as she wept. And every sound she made was a lash against his heart. It seemed like forever, but when her tears finally subsided, he reached over a grabbed a handful of tissues from the box on the nightstand. He wiped her face, then held the tissues for her as she blew her nose.

"I'm sorry," she said between little huffing sounds as she tried to catch her breath.

"Don't be sorry, Cate. That was coming for a long time, I think."

"I didn't cry—after the first time," she told him brokenly. "Tears didn't soften his heart." She didn't have to name him for Liam to know who she meant. "He *enjoyed* hurting me—tears would only have added to his pleasure." She was silent for a long, long time, then added so softly he had to strain to hear, "I have not cried for nine years."

His heart slowly tore in two, knowing what she'd endured in silence for two years. And knowing, too, there wasn't a damned thing he could do to take her remembered pain away, no matter how much he wished it.

She made as if to pull away from him, but he refused to let her go. "Don't," he told her after he cleared the obstruction in his throat. "Just let me hold you the

way someone should have held you nine years ago."
What had happened to Cate should never have happened—not to her, not to any woman. The knight-errant
in Liam wanted so badly to *do* something—avenge her.
Make Vishenko pay in blood. But that wasn't what Cate
needed now. She needed to be held. Comforted. Not a
sexual embrace, but a loving one.

She didn't resist, and Liam marveled at that. But he
wasn't going to question it. Not now. Not when she was
willing to accept comfort from him, the comfort he'd
longed to give her since the moment he'd seen those
scars on her wrists. No, to be honest, he'd wanted to
comfort her since the moment she shied away from him
yesterday morning.

Was it only yesterday? It didn't seem possible. Too
much had been crammed into too few hours, and he was
still reeling emotionally. But the only thing that mattered right now was Cate. Letting her know how much
he hurt for her. How much he cared.

As he held her close, many things started to make
sense to him, things he hadn't really understood before. Cate's desire to be invisible, to not draw attention
to herself, for one. Her feelings for Alec, another. Alec
had rescued her from a life on the run. Gratitude was a
natural response. And as he'd told her, Alec was a hell of
a guy. Admiration—the same kind of admiration he felt
for his brother—was another perfectly natural response.

But she wasn't in love with his brother, and inside
he heaved a sigh of relief. What had she said earlier?
*"...I never wanted him to touch me...that way... I never
wanted any man to touch me that way...until I met you."*

And Cate thought she wasn't brave. How many women would have admitted that to a man they barely knew? How many women would trust a man they'd just met to hold them in an intimate embrace on a bed and not push for more after the woman admitted her attraction to him?

She trusts you, he realized, the shock reverberating through his system. *She doesn't know it, but she really does trust you.* He'd wanted her trust, and now he had it—at least up to a point. But suddenly he knew it wasn't enough. He didn't just want Cate's trust in this way. He wanted more. He wanted it all.

Chapter 9

Cate woke first. Liam must have pulled the covers over them at some point during the night, and she was lying with her head pillowed on his shoulder. His other arm was snug across her body, as if to hold her safe.

She couldn't believe it. She'd slept through the night in Liam's arms, and no nightmares had invaded her dreams. She hadn't woken in a panic, either, with that choking feeling and a runaway pulse. Liam holding her wasn't like Vishenko holding her. When Vishenko had held her he'd wanted to hurt her, and she'd fought him until her strength had given out. It was different with Liam. He was holding her to comfort, to heal. To shelter her from anything that might hurt her. To place his body between hers and danger.

She raised her head to see what time it was, but when

she moved Liam woke immediately, his hand already reaching for the SIG SAUER on the nightstand. Then his eyes focused on her, and he subsided back onto the bed, leaving the gun where it was. "Morning," he told her. And the guarded tone in his voice told her he wasn't sure what her reaction would be to having spent the night in his arms.

"Good morning." And it *was*, she realized. It *was* a good morning. She smiled at him. A tentative smile, but a real one. "Thank you."

"For what?"

For not forcing me, she wanted to say, but she knew he wouldn't understand. He'd be insulted—no, he'd be hurt to think she believed he could do to any woman what Vishenko had done to her. She hadn't. Not really. But how to explain? "For holding me," she settled on.

His chest rumbled with soft laughter. "My pleasure, Cate," he told her. There was a light in his eyes that warmed her, and he repeated, "My pleasure."

While Cate dressed and packed her few things, Liam called Callahan on the cell phone. "It's Liam Jones," he identified himself when Callahan answered. "I assume you were expecting my call?"

"Yeah." He didn't say anything more, and Liam realized Callahan was a man of few words.

"We're still at the hotel, and we're going to have breakfast before we leave. But we should be there in about seven hours. D'Arcy said I shouldn't go to the sheriff's office—"

"Yeah, Nick asked me to meet you someplace safe,

where no one will see you. My office is out—too many people. And I'd rather you not come to the house—my wife wouldn't say anything, but I can't guarantee my children won't accidentally reveal we have a guest staying with us—they're too young to know better."

Liam frowned. "Then where—"

"You know how to get to your brother-in-law's cabin near Granite Peak?"

"I think so."

"I'll meet you there. I'll be the one with the Smith & Wesson."

Aleksandrov Vishenko's private airplane landed on the single runway of a local airstrip in Arlington, Virginia, then taxied toward the hangar. Once there, the pilot turned off the engines, then he and the copilot exited the plane and entered the office to arrange for refueling and to file a new flight plan. As always, Vishenko wanted to be ready for anything, including a quick getaway if necessary.

He was early for his meeting, but he'd planned it that way. The government official he was there to see— his most dangerous gamble—would not arrive for another hour. But the stage would be set and Vishenko's men—who'd arrived earlier and were waiting inside the hangar—would search the bureaucrat for weapons and listening devices when he arrived, before allowing him to board Vishenko's plane. Then, and only then, would Vishenko offer his bribe in absolute secrecy…to the man he feared most. To the man who'd been after him for years and who was one witness away from putting him behind bars for life. To the man who had a reputation as an incorruptible man…but Vishenko had learned differently.

"Every man has his price," Vishenko reassured himself now as he reviewed the details in his mind. Overtures had been made—through an intermediary, of course—and the government official had proved… amenable. Corruptible after all. But greedy. He had not named his price—but all indications hinted the price would be steep. If that was the price of his freedom, though, Vishenko would pay it. Gladly.

Cate and Liam had a leisurely breakfast, during which they talked about nothing in particular, then loaded their things in the SUV. As she buckled her seat belt Liam asked her, "Is there anything else you need before we get on the road to Black Rock? I know the agency provided you with a few changes of clothes and toiletries, but they might have overlooked something. There *are* stores where we're going, but your choices might be limited."

She shook her head. "I'm used to making do."

Liam sighed softly. "That's not the point, Cate. If you need something, now's the time to speak up."

She hesitated. "How long am I staying with Sheriff Callahan?"

"Hard to say. The trial has been postponed for a month, that's all I know for sure. The way D'Arcy was talking yesterday, though, I got the feeling he doesn't plan to produce you until the last minute. So at least a few weeks."

"I'll go crazy with nothing to read," she said finally. Reluctantly. "If there's a library…"

"I'm sure there are libraries in Buffalo and Sheridan, if not in Black Rock itself. But unless Callahan or his wife checks the books out for you, you're out of luck—no local address to apply for a library card, remember?" He turned the key in the ignition, then put the SUV in gear. "We have time. We'll stop and get you some books to read."

Liam pulled into the parking lot of the first Walmart he came to, then led Cate inside, grabbed a shopping cart and headed over to the book aisle. Once there she glanced around, picked a book off the shelf and read the back cover, then put it down again. She did that numerous times, he noticed, before finally settling on one book.

"This one," she said. But her eyes stared longingly at the last book she'd set down.

Liam shook his head. "Come on, Cate. One book won't last several weeks." He already knew from the conversations he'd had with her that she was well-read. One book might have been good enough for some people, but not her. He went back down the aisle, selected the books she'd picked up but rejected and tossed them into the cart.

"Liam, no!" Her protest wasn't loud, but it was insistent.

He ignored her. When he had a dozen books in the cart he turned around and faced her. "If there's something you really don't want—fine. Put it back. But if you want to read it, then I'm buying it. This is my money, Cate, not the agency's, so you don't have to worry."

"But, so many," she said faintly. She glanced at the price of the paperback in her hand. "I can't let you—"

"I want you to have the books you want to read," Liam said, cutting her off. He knew his face was set in stubborn lines, but he wasn't going to back down on this, no matter how much Cate protested.

"But I—"

"No arguments, Cate," he said. His left hand came up of its own volition and cupped her cheek. She didn't flinch away, so his thumb brushed gently over her lips the way his lips longed to do. "Let me do this for you," he said softly. "My way of apologizing for what I said last night."

"You already apologized." And her eyes told him she'd already forgiven him.

"Yeah, but this will make me feel better." He grinned his most engaging smile at her. "And besides, there are a couple of books here I wouldn't mind reading myself. I'll borrow them if you don't mind."

She didn't say anything more, just added the book in her hand to the pile in the cart and followed Liam to the checkout. As the cashier rang up their purchases, Liam noted absently Cate's taste in reading was eclectic, but the majority of books were fiction. Women's fiction. Or at least that's what his mother called the genre. Liam still thought of it as romance—books most guys avoided like the plague. All of a sudden, though, something occurred to him, bringing her choices into sharp focus. If Cate read romances, then that meant—in her heart of hearts—she still believed in love.

A rush of excitement swept through him, which he was hard-pressed to keep off his face. Cate still believed in love. Still believed men could have tender feelings for a woman as well as baser urges. Still dreamed dreams, despite what she'd been through. Which meant there was a chance for him. Unbelievably good news, since he was halfway to being in love with her already.

Vishenko's men swarmed around the government official the minute he entered the airplane hangar. The pat down one of them gave him was much more thorough and intimate than any airport screener, but he didn't protest. Another man ran a metal detector over him that pinged on his artificial left knee—he was forced to roll up his pants leg and show them the vertical surgical scar, then take out his wallet to display the ID card he used when he went through the metal detector at the airport, the one with a graphic X-ray picture of what his knee looked like now. A third goon ran an electronic scanner—a scanner that would detect any listening device he might be wearing—over his entire body with the exception of the artificial left knee that had already set off the metal detector. His heartbeat was a little faster than normal, but that was only to be expected…given what he was about to do.

In a long-ago era he'd been a US marshal. He'd protected witnesses with his life, and had the scars to prove it. But it had been years since he'd handled field assignments, since he'd put his life on the line. Not since he'd assigned himself to the team backing up Reilly O'Neill—aka Ryan Callahan—and Cody Walker when they confronted David Pennington. *How long ago was that?* he wondered, mentally trying to add up the years.

It had never been about the money. Even at his level within the government, his salary and benefits paled in comparison to what he could have earned elsewhere, so money had never been a motivating factor for him. *But every man has his price,* he reminded himself with grim smile. *Every man has something he will risk everything for.* He was no different.

Incorruptible. Everyone who knew him believed as much in his incorruptibility as in his omniscience. So no one would suspect what he was about to do. No one. And that dovetailed nicely with his overall plan.

"If you need a rest stop," Liam told Cate when they were back on the road, "don't hesitate to tell me. I know guys tend to forget women usually need to stop more often."

"Okay." There was a hint of reserve in her voice, a little shyness, and Liam guessed this probably wasn't a conversation she was used to having. She glanced down at the bag in her hands—the one she'd refused to let Liam put in the back with their limited amount of luggage—then over at him. "Thank you. You have no idea how much I appreciate this, and I…well…thank you."

"My pleasure." And it was, he realized—just as much a pleasure as holding her had been last night. He'd never given a woman a gift that brought him as much joy as seeing the warm glow in her eyes at the thought of *own-*

ing so many books. If he'd given her expensive jewelry it wouldn't have meant as much to her.

They whiled away the next hours talking about books they'd read. Liam was surprised and yet not surprised to learn they'd read some of the same books, and had similar takes on them.

"Wasn't it unbelievable how Isaac Cline played such a critical role in two of the worst natural disasters in US history?" Cate asked, referring to both Erik Larson's *Isaac's Storm: A Man, a Time, and the Deadliest Hurricane in History* and John M. Barry's *Rising Tide: The Great Mississippi Flood of 1927 and How It Changed America*. "And because of him, because of his actions so many years apart, both disasters were immeasurably worse than they could have been."

"I know what you mean."

"Both times he did the wrong thing," Cate said softly. "But with the best intentions. It had to be heartbreaking for him." She was silent for a moment. "That's why I feel responsible for what happened the other day—the prosecutor who was killed, the men who were shot."

"You're not responsible," Liam insisted, taking his eyes off the road for a few seconds to make sure Cate understood. "Vishenko—assuming he's behind the attempt to kill you, which is a pretty fair assumption—is responsible. For all of it. Not you."

Cate shook her head. "But I am. Because I was a coward for so many years…until Alec convinced me otherwise. If I had—" She broke off, and Liam wondered what she'd been about to say. She finally continued. "If I had gone to the police years ago with what I knew…with the evidence I had…who knows? Things could have been so different."

Liam was sure this wasn't what she'd originally been thinking, but all he said was "You can't second-guess yourself like this. That's the first thing you learn when you become a bodyguard. All you can do is the best you can do *at the time*."

"That's what Alec and Angelina said."

"They're right." Cate still didn't look convinced, so Liam added, "Remember what D'Arcy said? That Vishenko was working hand in glove with Pennington back in the day? They could have stopped him then, same as Pennington, if they'd known. But they didn't. Everything that happened to you at Vishenko's hands could have been prevented…if they'd stopped him years ago. Same goes for what happened in the courthouse. But they didn't know. D'Arcy, Callahan and my brother-in-law, Cody, did the best they could with what they knew *at the time*. That's all any of us can do. If we clutter up our minds with what-ifs and might-have-beens, we'll be frozen with fear of making a mistake. Then at the critical moment we won't do *anything*. And that's worse than doing the wrong thing for the right reasons."

The GPS beeped at that moment, announcing a rest area five miles ahead. "Do you need to stop?" he asked her.

"No, I'm fine for now."

Liam thought for a moment. "The past is the past, Cate," he said finally, returning to their original conversation. "It is what it is, and we can't change a single thing. Would I change things I've done over the years if I could? Sure. I don't think anyone can say they've never made a mistake they'd give anything to fix. But we can't fix it. We can only learn from it, and try not to make the same mistakes in the future."

He took his right hand off the steering wheel and laid it over her left one. Once again she didn't flinch away from his touch, and Liam drew courage from that lack of negative reaction. He drew a deep breath. "Last night you said there's nothing you want more than to be able to come to a man clean and whole, but you can't because of what Vishenko did to you. If that's the only thing holding you back—because he made you feel broken and unclean—don't. Don't let the past color your future. Don't let him win."

"That's what Alec said when he was trying to convince me to testify against Vishenko. He said, 'You can't let him win...not ever again.'" She turned away and stared out the window, her face a mask of repressed emotion. "Do you think I *want* to let him win?" she asked in a desperate undertone. "Do you think I *want* to remember?" She swallowed hard. "I don't want that, but I'm afraid, Liam. Afraid that if I try to...to...do as you say, that I will remember. And I don't think I can bear it."

Vishenko sat back in his leather seat in the cabin of his private Learjet, and stared across the short distance at the government bureaucrat he was attempting to bribe. Despite the fact that it was early afternoon, he'd served them both snifters of Courvoisier L'Essence, his favorite cognac, and both men were savoring it.

Vishenko gave the other man points for being a good negotiator by the simple expedient of saying absolutely nothing. He had not named a price. He had not mentioned a name. He had merely sat silently in the seat he'd been offered…and waited for Vishenko to make the first move. To make the first offer.

"One million," Vishenko said finally.

The man chuckled softly, his teeth gleaming white in his dark face. "That has been offered to others for more than a year. And it got you absolutely nothing."

True, Vishenko acknowledged to himself. "What would you consider a fair offer?" he asked, wanting the other man to state his price…so he could negotiate down from there. If he made the first offer himself, he could easily overshoot the mark and end up paying more than the man would settle for.

The bureaucrat shrugged his shoulders. "I'm here at your request. I'll listen to what you have to say. But that's all. If you want something from me, tell me. Then I'll decide if it's worth it…to me."

"Three million," Vishenko said.

The man smiled to himself, sighed regretfully and shook his head. He put down his cognac, stood up and turned as if to go.

"Ten million, and that is my final offer," Vishenko said on a desperate rush. He *had* to silence Caterina Mateja. He had less than four weeks to do it, so time was of the essence. This man knew where she was hiding, and he was the only one Vishenko knew who knew. Others had to know her location, but Vishenko didn't know their names. It was certainly possible one of the others would accept far less than ten million dollars, but he couldn't afford to wait.

"Ten million." The other man considered the offer. "That is…a possibility. But what exactly do you want for your ten million?"

Vishenko spoke in Russian. The other man shook his head. "Sorry, but I don't understand."

Vishenko wasn't sure about that. The bureaucrat's reputation was one that led him to believe the man spoke many languages, including Russian. But he wasn't positive. He hesitated, then was reassured their conversation couldn't be recorded. *My men would have found it if he was wearing a wire,* he reminded himself, *just as they would have found a gun if he'd brought a gun.* "Caterina Mateja has been a thorn in my side for far too long," he said. "I want her dead."

The bureaucrat shook his head again. "I'm not a murderer," he insisted. "Not for any price."

The admission reduced him in Vishenko's eyes. Vishenko had ordered men killed over the years, but had never hesitated to kill with his own hands when called upon…if necessary. Early in his career he'd made his reputation as a ruthless, cold-blooded killer, and nothing had changed. He could kill Caterina Mateja himself, despite his one-time obsession with her.

"Then I want to know where she is," he said. "I can take it from there."

The other man nodded slowly. "I'll think about it."

Vishenko cursed foully, but in Russian. Then said in English with more than a touch of contempt, "What is there to think about? I want Caterina Mateja. Now. Do you know where she is or not? Ten million should easily overcome any scruples you might have about her."

The other man smiled, but his smile was as cold as Vishenko's usually was. "I know where she is," he said softly, meaningfully. "But you will never find her... without me."

Vishenko lunged to his feet and grasped the lapels of the man's suit coat. "Give me her location," he shouted as he vehemently shook the other man.

The man crossed his arms, and with a swift movement freed himself from Vishenko's hold. Then he stepped back, and brushed down his crumpled lapels. "I will think about it," he said once more. "Do that again, however, and I will see you in the courtroom and not a minute before." He turned his back, opened the plane's door and walked down the stairs.

Vishenko moved to the doorway and watched the other man stride across the tarmac. He cursed again in Russian, relieving his anxiety and frustration by calling the other man every derogatory name he could think of. Then he stomped back into the center of the cabin and knocked the other man's snifter against the wall with a tinkling sound of splintering glass.

When he finally calmed down, he picked up his own snifter and refilled it, then dashed off the contents in one abrupt move. "Every man has his price," Vishenko reminded himself. Ten million dollars was more than most men dreamed of, even this government bureaucrat. "He'll be back," he asserted, believing it because he wanted to believe it. "He'll be back."

Chapter 10

Liam pulled the SUV into the clearing at the end of a dirt road and parked with a small sigh of relief. He hadn't been absolutely sure he knew the way to Cody's cabin near Granite Peak—he'd been here only once before, shortly after Keira had married Cody—but he wasn't about to call his brother-in-law for directions. And he would have called Callahan only as a last resort. He smiled ruefully. Why did guys have a thing about asking for directions anyway? A GPS was different. He didn't mind relying on the GPS, which had gotten him most of the way here. The rest had been trial and error, a little blind luck and a sudden memory of what the turnoff looked like.

The good news was that even if someone knew Cate was here in Cody's cabin, unless that person had specific directions and a better GPS than Liam's, they'd be hard-pressed to find it. And even if that person got as far as this dead-end road, there was still the issue of finding the cabin itself. It wasn't visible, no matter which direction you looked. And there were several openings that looked like paths, but if he remembered correctly, those led to nothing but hiking trails—and not easy hiking trails, either. None of those paths led to the cabin.

Liam got out and quickly unloaded the back of the SUV. He slung his duffel bag over one shoulder and handed Cate's small suitcase to her, leaving his gun hand free. Then he slowly rotated around the clearing. If he didn't miss his guess...yes! There it was. It didn't look like a path, and as he recalled there would be places they'd have to walk single file, but eventually the rough path would widen out and lead to the clearing where Cody's cabin stood.

"Come on," he told Cate, leading the way. He wasn't worried too much about their safety at this point. While he wasn't familiar with the Big Horn Mountains in general and Granite Peak in particular, his family had a cabin the Rockies, and he'd spent a lot of time in the mountains growing up. Sound carried. Especially manmade sound—such as a car engine. His ears were already attuned, and he knew if anyone followed them he'd hear it.

A little more than fifty yards later a clearing materialized, and there in the center stood Cody's split-log cabin. Liam started forward, then turned around. "Wait here," he told Cate. "Let me check it out first."

"Do you have the key?"

"Don't need a key," he told her. "Cody doesn't keep it locked."

She looked startled. "He doesn't?"

He shook his head. "Cody said he doesn't keep anything valuable here, anything worth stealing. Other than nonperishable food, that is. If someone needed his cabin, he'd rather they just walk in instead of break in. There's a generator out back—that runs the pump for the well in addition to electric lights, so he's got running water. It's a great place to hole up, and I'm not surprised Callahan suggested it. My sister, Keira, told me the Callahans have used this place more than once in an emergency."

Cate's eyes asked a question, but all Liam said was, "Long story. I'll tell you sometime, but right now I want to check the place out and make sure no one's inside. Once I know you're safe there will be time for other things. Stay here, okay? If something happens, drop your suitcase and run like hell."

Liam strode across the clearing, but paused halfway. "Callahan?" he called. He didn't think Callahan was inside—the fact that no other car had been parked at the dead end in the road was a good indication they'd arrived first. But just in case...

When there was no response after a minute, he mounted the steps, then reached for the door latch, opened the door and walked inside. The cabin had that disused smell. Not rank or moldy, just...uninhabited. A thin layer of dust on the Spartan furniture told him no one had been at the cabin for quite some time, which was just fine with him. He dropped his duffel bag on the kitchen table, then went back to fetch Cate.

"All clear," he told her. Then, "Here, I'll take that." He took the suitcase from her right hand, but let her carry her bag of books.

Once inside, Liam bolted the front door, then went and did the same for the back door. "I'll go out in a little bit and start the generator," he told Cate, "but let me show you around first."

The cabin was one large room. He placed Cate's suitcase on the double bed that stood in one corner, half-screened from the rest of the room by a large carved wooden folding screen that Liam recognized as having once belonged to his mother. A rocking chair held pride of place in front of the fireplace, and a child's bed stood against another wall. *For Alyssa, no doubt,* he acknowledged, thinking of his young niece. The one and only time he'd been here before, he and his brothers had all brought sleeping bags, and they'd bunked down in front of the fireplace.

That had been before Alyssa was born, shortly after Keira had married Cody. Cody had invited the Jones brothers to stag it with him at the cabin, as a way of getting to know each other. Even Shane had made a point to get leave from the Marine Corps, Liam remembered, and he chuckled softly to himself.

"What is it?" Cate asked. "What's so funny?"

"Nothing," he told her. "I was just remembering the last time I was here." When she lifted her eyebrows in a question, he added, "I told you this cabin belongs to my brother-in-law. He married my only sister, and boy! Were we tough on him at first!"

"What did you do?"

"Put him through the wringer, that's what we did. Cody's a couple of years older than my oldest brother, Shane, which means he's quite a bit older than Keira—eight years. We gave him the benefit of the doubt because he was a US Marine at one time, same as us. Same as Keira. But we were all pretty ticked off he'd let her get shot when they were working a case together for the agency—you know the agency I mean. Keira threatened us all with dire consequences if we did anything to her new husband, but…" Liam spread his hands out. "We had to make *sure* he was right for her. Know what I mean?"

Cate shook her head. "Is this some guy thing, like you giving Alec a black eye?"

Liam grinned. "Not exactly, but close. Shane gave him a medium set of lumps, but Cody gave as good as he got, then offered to take the rest of us on. But at that point Shane laid down the law, said anyone who pounded on Cody would have to pound on him first. Shane's the oldest, so…" He shrugged. "We welcomed Cody into the family."

Cate shook her head again, as if she would never understand the workings of the male mind.

"Sorry," Liam said. "I was supposed to be showing you around. This is your bed," he said, pointing to the double bed her suitcase was lying on.

"Where will you sl—" She stopped short, as if she

wasn't sure he was staying there with her, but Liam knew what she'd been going to ask.

"There's a cot in that closet," he said, pointing. "I'll use that while I'm here." He continued as if she'd never interrupted. "That door leads to the bathroom, and that's obviously the kitchen." A kitchen table and two chairs stood neatly in front of the stove and the sink. "And that's the back door. The generator's out there, and I guess now's as good a time as any to crank it up so you can have water. I'll be right back."

He started toward the back door, then reversed course and returned to stand in front of Cate, trying to reassure her with his presence. He very carefully didn't touch her, but he wanted to. And he knew he wasn't entirely successful keeping that out of his expression. "You'll be okay?" he asked. "I'll only be gone a couple of minutes. Feel free to look around."

Cate waited until the back door closed behind Liam, then her curiosity got the better of her and she started on a voyage of discovery where the cabin was concerned. The cabinets in the kitchen contained not only dishes, coffee cups and glasses, but row upon row of canned goods of all kinds and boxes of prepackaged dry food— the nonperishables Liam had mentioned earlier. The closet contained the cot Liam had told her about, and tidy stacks of sheets, pillowcases, pillows and blankets on the shelves. She took one book out of her precious bag of books and put it on the nightstand next to the bed to start reading that night, then stashed the bag out of the way on a lower shelf.

She opened the door to the bathroom and saw a smallish room, with much of the space taken up by a large, old-fashioned claw-foot tub. She wasn't big on baths—when living in boardinghouses a bath meant cleaning out the tub each time, before and after using it. So she was glad to note there was also a shower-head. Towels, washcloths, soap and other toiletries were stacked neatly on the shelves between the sink and the tub. Liam had told her no one actually lived here, but she'd never have known it. Everything they needed was readily available.

She was just closing the bathroom door when Liam returned. "I started the pump on the well," he told her. "There will be water soon." He opened another closet door, one Cate hadn't gotten around to, and made a sound of satisfaction. "I thought I remembered the water heater was in here," he said. He searched in a drawer next to the stove and found a box of kitchen matches. "I'll get the pilot light going so you'll have hot water later on."

When he was finished, he dusted off his hands and tucked them in the back pockets of his jeans. "Is it okay?" he asked her. "I know it's not fancy, but—"

"But it has everything we need," she finished for him. "I already found that out."

"And it's safe," he added. "About as safe as you can possibly get."

The sound of footsteps thudding on the front porch drove the smile from Liam's face, and he pulled his SIG SAUER from its shoulder holster so quickly Cate didn't even have time to draw a breath. Then he was pushing her inside the bathroom just as someone knocked on the front door. "Not a sound," he breathed before he shut the bathroom door with her on the inside, himself on the outside.

Cate strained to hear what was going on in the other room, even going so far as to place her ear against the door, but all she could hear was the rumble of deep male voices. Then the bathroom door opened, and Liam smiled at her.

"False alarm," he told her, indicating the tall, dark-haired man standing just inside the front door, wearing a uniform and a cowboy hat with some kind of insignia on both. "Cate, this is Ryan Callahan, sheriff of Black Rock. Sheriff Callahan, this is Caterina Mateja, but she goes by Cate."

The sheriff moved until he could reach out and shake Cate's hand. "Glad you made it safely," was all he said. Then he glanced at Liam. "So you found the place without any trouble?"

Liam caught Cate's eye, and she knew from his expression he had no intention of telling the sheriff about the two false turns he'd made on the way here, and would prefer she not say anything either. She smiled a little at that. She was starting to read Liam, and she liked that idea. She liked it a lot.

An hour later Callahan rose from the kitchen table where he'd been discussing the situation with Cate, making sure she knew everything he had planned. He pushed in the paddle-back chair, settled his hat on his head and turned to Liam, leaning against the kitchen sink. "I had the propane tank topped off, and stocked the cabinets with enough nonperishable provisions to last a month. But now that the generator's going, I'll bring up milk and eggs and a few other perishables you might need when I come tomorrow morning."

"Thanks."

"I'll check on you at least twice a day. But I don't want to set a pattern someone might get curious about, so I'll vary my times."

"Okay by me," Liam said. "We're not going anywhere."

"Your cell phone will work up here, but coverage can be a little spotty. It works better outside the cabin than inside—just giving you a heads-up. You've got all my numbers, so don't hesitate to call if you need me…but I don't think you will. I think you're safe here because no one knows where you are except Nick D'Arcy and me." He glanced at Cate, then seemed to reach some kind of decision, because he turned back to Liam and said, "I've got some stuff in the back of my SUV to rig an extra security system for you, just in case. It's worked before. But you need to know the location of each trap I set on your perimeter, and how to avoid them. So you'd better come with me."

Liam nodded. "Sounds like a good idea." He looked at Cate. "Stay inside for now, okay? I'll be back in a little while."

Callahan didn't say a word until they reached his SUV, parked next to Liam's. He pulled out coils of rope and wire, several of which he handed to Liam before looping some across his own shoulders. Then he grabbed a box containing what looked to be nothing more than odds and ends, and said totally out of the blue, "Your sister saved my life, you know."

"Yeah, I know." Liam knew the bare fact, but little more than that.

"She took a bullet for me and almost died because of it." Callahan shook his head, admiration coloring his next words. "She's a hell of an agent."

"Yeah, I know that, too."

"I owe her. So whatever you do, don't get yourself killed on this op, okay?" Callahan started walking back toward the cabin without waiting for a response. "I'd never be able to look your sister in the eye again if I let her brother get killed."

"You don't have to worry about that."

Callahan grunted. "Nick asked me to keep Cate safe until the trial, and I will. He also mentioned you were going to hang around for a bit."

"How the hell did he know that? I wasn't even sure myself until this morning."

Callahan laughed, softening his saturnine face. "He's omniscient, didn't you know?"

"Keira and Cody call him Baker Street. McKinnon, too. Sherlock Holmes, you know? But D'Arcy told me maintaining that reputation takes constant vigilance, and even with that he slips up every now and then."

Grimly serious all at once, Callahan said, "Don't I know it." Then he relaxed…or what passed for relaxation for him. "But I'd never bet against him. There's only a handful of men I trust, and he's three of them," Callahan joked. He stopped just outside the clearing and dumped the box he was carrying on the ground, then slipped a coil of rope and one of wire off his shoulder and laid them beside the box. He moved around the clearing's perimeter, then stopped again and dropped the same two coils. Liam followed him. Eventually, when Callahan had dropped his last coils, he took the ones Liam carried, and completed his circuit.

"Special ops?" Liam asked Callahan, his respect for the man growing by the minute.

"A lifetime ago, but yeah. Some things you never forget. You were in the Corps, too, weren't you? McKinnon told me all you Joneses were, including your sister."

"Yeah, but I was just a run-of-the-mill marine. I wasn't special ops."

Callahan bent over and dug into the box he'd left at the first drop. "No such thing as a run-of-the-mill marine," he said flatly as he started forming the first of his traps. "You either *are* a marine…or you aren't. Period. End of discussion."

Liam took Cate on a tour of the cabin's perimeter after Callahan left, making sure she knew where every trap was located so she'd know where *not* to tread. Not that he had any intention of letting her wander around outside without his protection, but just in case…

They opened some cans and heated up the contents for dinner, then ate sitting on the front porch steps. As before, Cate sat silent and nearly still while she ate, but Liam could tell she appreciated the pristine beauty of her surroundings.

He did, too. He'd spent much of his adult life away from the mountains—first in the Marine Corps and then wherever the DSS posted him—but he'd grown up in the Rockies, and he hadn't lost his love for mountain country. He wondered if Cate was as enamored of mountains as he was. She'd grown up in Zakhar—he knew that much from her cousin, Angelina, his new sister-in-law—and Zakhar was seemingly nothing *but* mountains, sort of like Switzerland. Still...

"Have you ever seen the Rockies?" he asked abruptly.

Cate glanced at him, hesitated, then said, "I was living in Denver when ICE arrested me," she said. "Didn't you know?"

He shook his head. "I know almost nothing about the circumstances surrounding your case. Alec didn't tell me much of anything. Not until—" He broke off, unsure how much to reveal.

"Not until you were forced to become my bodyguard?"

Liam stiffened. "I wasn't *forced* to do anything, Cate. I'm here because I choose to be here." He held her gaze. "When it comes right down to it, I'm on vacation—you know that already. I could have just turned you over to Callahan and headed back to Denver if that's what I wanted—Cody invited me to stay with my sister and him. But that's not what I want." He stood up, took her plate and utensils from her unresisting grasp and walked into the cabin before he could add, *Wherever you are, that's where I want to be.* Because he wasn't quite ready to admit that to her.

He placed the dishes in the sink, ran some hot water and added a little dish soap, then took his frustrations out on the dirty dishes. *Hell,* he told himself as he stacked the rinsed dishes on the dish rack to dry, *it's not just that you're not ready to admit to her how much you care. You're afraid she's not ready to hear it. That she'll never be ready to hear it.*

For a man whose own family called him a knight-errant, it was devastating to realize his damsel in distress might not *want* to be rescued…by him.

Night had fallen. Cate showered and got ready for bed while Liam made a perimeter check. She'd known when he told her how long he'd be gone that he was doing it to give her some privacy, and she was touched by his thoughtfulness. The folding screen beside the bed would give her privacy, too. She'd argued with Liam about the cot he'd set up for himself near the fireplace, but she'd known even before she'd started it was a battle she was destined to lose. Despite the fact that he was bigger and taller than she was, he wasn't going to take the bed, and that was that.

She was already tucked under the covers, reading one of the books he'd bought her that morning when she heard the front door open. "Don't worry, it's me," Liam told her in the deep voice that resonated inside her in a way she'd never thought possible.

She tried to concentrate on her book, but she heard him move around the room even though he tried to be quiet about it. When he went into the bathroom she heard the shower running. If she was any other woman—any *normal* woman—she knew she'd be curious. Knew her imagination would be piqued by the idea of a naked man in the shower. No, not just a naked man. A naked *Liam*. Especially since she knew he'd be even more splendid naked than he was clothed…and he was pretty impressive clothed.

But she wasn't a normal woman. And she could never have a normal woman's reaction to a man—she knew that. She wished with all her heart things could be different for her. That she could let herself be touched in intimate ways and not tremble in fear and loathing. Part of her wanted Liam to touch her, kiss her, caress her. Part of her wanted Liam to want her the way a good man wanted a woman—with desire, but also with respect. But she'd told him the truth on the drive up here. She was afraid to try, because she couldn't bear to fail. And even worse, she was afraid she'd freeze up or scream if Liam tried to make love to her. He didn't deserve that. He deserved a woman who could let him touch her without fear.

Cate closed her book, turned off the lamp on the nightstand and tried to think of something else. But her eyes burned with unshed tears as traumatic memories came back to her, memories she desperately wanted to suppress…but couldn't.

Eventually she fell asleep. But her sleep was troubled by nightmares, and she was back in Vishenko's clutches—a prisoner once more. Heard him laugh his coarse laugh as he caught her when she tried to run, then tied her to the bed and laughed again as she struggled against her bonds until her wrists were bruised and bloody. *No!* she screamed in her dreams. *No!*

Liam woke at the first sound Cate made. The first whimper. He almost pulled his SIG SAUER from its holster where it hung from a corner of the cot. But then he realized whatever was troubling Cate wasn't a real threat. At least, it wasn't a *current* threat.

He threw off the sheet covering him and moved swiftly to Cate's bedside. She was thrashing around on the bed, little moans of distress catching in her throat as she fought off the sheet and blanket entangling her. He flicked on the bedside lamp and called her name— softly at first because he didn't want to scare her, then louder when she didn't seem to hear him. "Cate! Cate!"

He touched her shoulder to wake her and she shot up in bed, fighting off his hand with both of hers and screaming, "No!"

Liam backed away, both hands up, palms facing her. "It's okay, Cate. I won't hurt you. I promise. You were having a nightmare, and I wanted to wake you, that's all."

Her eyes suddenly focused on him and she choked on his name. Then she covered her face with her hands and bent over, burying herself in the twisted bedclothes. At first he thought she was crying—any other woman would have been. But not Cate.

Pity swept through him. Just as last night, he knew he had to do something to make it right for her, and he didn't stop to question either his need to comfort or hers to be comforted. He bent down and gathered her into his arms—sheet, blanket and all—then trod across the bare wooden floor to the rocking chair beside the empty fireplace. He sat down with her on his lap, her head cradled against his shoulder.

She was trembling inside her blanketed cocoon, but

Liam knew it wasn't from the cold because it wasn't that cold in the cabin. She was trembling because she couldn't shake off the nightmare. Because something had brought the past back to life for her, the past she wanted to forget.

He pushed the rocking chair into motion with one strong foot, crooning softly to Cate the way he remembered his mother doing to him when he was a little boy, as they rocked back and forth for endless minutes. Eventually she stopped trembling and her ragged breathing slowed, but still he rocked. Then he glanced down at her and realized—to his utter amazement—she'd fallen asleep in his arms.

In repose her face was totally innocent...and totally vulnerable. All those emotional fences she put up around herself vanished when she was sleeping, as if they had never existed. And Liam's heart turned over.

Chapter 11

Cate woke to the sound of someone trying to move quietly around the cabin and the smell of coffee. For just a moment she didn't remember where she was—which wasn't unusual for her because she'd often woken in strange places. What *was* unusual was that she had no memory after a certain point last night. Had no memory of how she'd wound up back in bed…but she had a pretty good idea how she'd gotten there. The last thing she remembered was Liam holding her in the rocking chair, which meant—unbelievably—she hadn't been afraid to fall asleep in his arms. He must have put her to bed, tucked her in, then gone back to his less-than-comfortable cot to finish out the night.

The cabin's interior was still shadowed, but there was enough light to see, so she figured it was shortly after dawn. But Liam was already awake. *He must be an early riser like me,* she thought. She laid there for a minute, until she heard the sound of a door open and close in the distance, then total silence. *Liam must have gone outside.*

She slipped out of bed and headed for the bathroom. When she came out Liam was just walking in the back door, and she scurried behind the screen, then grabbed her robe and tugged it on.

"Breakfast?" he called to her from the other side of the folding screen. "You're not a coffee drinker, right? But I am, so I made a pot for me. Let me know if you change your mind and want some." His voice receded and she knew he'd moved into the kitchen area, but she could still hear him clearly. "There's not much in the way of breakfast food, except dry cereal. There's no milk until Callahan comes back this morning. I can make some oatmeal if you want something hot and don't mind eating it without milk."

Cate grabbed her clothes and hurried back into the bathroom—the screen gave her *some* privacy, but not enough to dress. "Oatmeal's fine," she said right before she closed the door. "I'm not picky."

Liam's agency-issued cell phone rang just as he was pouring himself a second cup of coffee. He answered it, but lost the signal before he could find out who was calling, so he excused himself from the table and took his coffee cup and cell phone outside onto the front porch. Sure enough, it rang again almost immediately.

"Yeah?" Even though supposedly no one but the

agency, his brother and Callahan had the number, Liam wasn't about to answer with his name.

"Liam." Alec's voice sounded in his ear. "I'm glad I reached you. Angel's desperate to know how Cate is."

"She's fine."

"Don't tell me where she is, but how safe is she? All Cody would tell me was that Nick D'Arcy has her stashed someplace. But he says he doesn't know where that is."

"Yeah, as far as I know, he doesn't know." Liam laughed a little under his breath at the irony of hiding out in Cody's cabin without Cody's knowledge. "I'm staying with her for now."

"You are? That's good." Alec's voice had betrayed his initial surprise, but it had quickly been followed up with approval.

"Yeah. And you can tell your wife to stop worrying. Even if someone knew where to look, I don't think they'd find us. And if they did, we'd have plenty of warning," he added cryptically.

"That's good to hear." There was a muffled sound, as if Alec was holding his hand over the phone and talking to someone. *Probably Angelina,* Liam theorized. His theory was confirmed when the warm contralto belonging to his sister-in-law spoke in his ear.

"Liam? Please, may I speak with Cate?"

"Sure. Hold on." He stepped to the doorway and called, "Cate? Angelina's on the phone. She wants to speak with you."

He handed Cate the cell phone when she came outside, but as he did he warned her, "Stay out here. Remember what Callahan said, that reception inside the cabin isn't the greatest. He's right—I already had one dropped call inside."

Cate nodded and flashed Liam a grateful smile, then took the phone and moved a little away from him before speaking. He tried not to listen to her end of the conversation with her cousin, but even though she was speaking in Zakharan he couldn't help understanding most of what she was saying. He reached out quickly and grabbed the phone from her just before she revealed their location.

"Need to know," he reminded her, dead serious, holding the phone against his shirt so their voices couldn't be heard on the other end.

"But my cousin...surely it's safe to—"

"I didn't tell Alec. Don't tell Angelina. Especially not over the phone. You don't know who's listening."

Cate's silvery-blue eyes were huge in her suddenly pale face. "I thought we were safe here."

"We are," he explained patiently. "For now. But in order to stay safe, we have to think safe. Act safe." He lifted the phone and spoke. "Put Alec back on, will you?" And when he heard his brother's voice he said, "Cate was just about to tell Angelina where we are." He winced at the curse from the other end, followed by staccato reminders. "Yeah. I know. I *know.* And she knows, too. She just didn't realize—look, you don't have to tell me how to do my job. Just tell Angelina I won't let anything happen to Cate, okay?"

"I'll tell her," his brother said.

"And, Alec? Do we know anything about how the guns were smuggled into the courthouse?"

"The FBI is working on that. The agency, too, but separately."

"I'll bet. I got the impression D'Arcy doesn't trust the FBI at this point, and from what he had to say I don't blame him. I just hope it wasn't them. Or the US Marshals Service. Or...oh hell, you know what I mean. Keep me posted if there's something I need to know, okay?"

"Will do." Liam started to disconnect but Alec stopped him. "Oh wait, I forgot to tell you."

"Tell me what?"

"Remember the two men chasing after you in the courthouse? The ones you thought might be FBI or backup killers?"

"Yeah?"

Alec chuckled softly. "Turns out they're neither. You won't believe this, but they're from the Zakharian National Forces."

"What? How...why...?"

"Long story, but they were trying to help you. They weren't armed—no way they could get firearms into the courthouse past security—but they were sent to protect Cate. I just found out, or I'd have told you sooner."

"Thanks. That's one less thing to worry about anyway. Talk to you later." Liam disconnected, then glanced over at Cate, who was standing exactly where she'd been a minute before. And her absolute stillness worried him. "Cate?"

"I'm sorry," she whispered. "I wasn't thinking."

He brought his thoughts back to what she'd almost

done—reveal their location over the phone. "That's why you have me." He smiled to ease her alarm and self-blame. "You're careful, Cate. And like you told D'Arcy, you stayed alive and on the run for six years, even with a price tag on your head. That takes smarts. But you're not a professional at this—I am. This is what I do for a living—keeping people alive."

"You and Alec."

That little imp of jealousy returned when she spoke his brother's name, but he fought it off. "Yeah, Alec used to be a bodyguard, too. But not anymore. Now he's the regional security officer at the US embassy in Drago."

"Yes, I know." She breathed deeply all of a sudden. "But he and Angelina were watching over me in Zakhar, making sure I was safe. And Alec told me he'd never forgive himself if anything happened to me because he convinced me to testify."

"You mentioned before he was the one who got you to testify." He took her arm and led her to the porch steps, then sat down and drew her down beside him. "But I thought you weren't supposed to have any contact with Alec before the trial because he's a witness, too. He didn't tell me you were living with Angelina and him."

"I wasn't. I was living in the royal palace."

"You're kidding!"

She shook her head. "No, the king arranged it. It's kind of an involved story, and I don't know all of it, but…"

Liam glanced around the clearing. "We appear to

have plenty of time. There's nothing urgent we have to do as far as I know."

Cate looked at her hands, then at him. "The king had recruited Alec's assistance in stopping a human trafficking ring that was operating between Zakhar and the US. It also entailed corruption and visa fraud at the US embassy—that's where Alec came in."

"That much I know."

"Yes, well…" She paused to consider her words. "I told you Vishenko was directly involved in trying to assassinate the crown prince, didn't I?" When Liam nodded she continued. "He's also suspected of having the king's cousin murdered in jail." She shivered, despite the sun's warmth. "I don't know where the investigation on that stands. And no one knows just how much involvement Vishenko had in the attempted assassination of the king a few years back, and the woman who is now his queen. But the attempt on the life of the crown prince—responsibility for that has been established beyond a reasonable doubt."

"One of the shooters confessed, naming Vishenko as the man who supplied the money," he remembered. "Isn't that what you said?"

"Yes, but they've nailed down the money trail, and it leads right to Vishenko. If they ever get him in a Zakharian courtroom…"

"Yeah, but D'Arcy told me that's a big 'if.'"

"I don't know about that. The king is…" There was admiration in her voice, and an obvious desire to believe the king would not *allow* Vishenko to escape justice, no matter what he had to do. Then she picked up her story again.

"The king told Alec it mattered just as much to him that Vishenko pay for his role in the human trafficking conspiracy as it did for the part he played in trying to kill the king's son. When the king learned I had evidence against Vishenko and was willing to testify in court about what I knew, he insisted on providing me with round-the-clock protection—the same protection the royal security details provide for the king, the queen and the crown prince."

Now it made sense to him that men from the Zakharian National Forces were in the courthouse, guarding Cate as best they could without firearms, but he didn't say anything because he didn't want to interrupt her.

She smiled softly. "The king was so kind—he said it would be best for me to live in the royal palace while I waited for the conspiracy trial, because it would be easier to protect me there than anywhere else. But of course, every time I came over here—depositions, prepping for the trial, the trial itself—I was guarded by US Marshals."

And Zakharian agents, he added in his mind.

Her smile faded. "I knew Vishenko would stop at nothing to silence me. I tried to warn everyone, especially the prosecutors. I really did, Liam." Her eyes beseeched him to believe her.

"I believe you."

"Alec believed me, too. And Angelina. And the king. They all knew I was the key witness. And they all knew Vishenko had killed every witness who'd ever tried to testify against him. No proof—he was too smart for that—but…" Her voice dropped to a whisper. "I never wanted anyone to die because of me. I should have known…should have expected…"

"How could you know? How could anyone predict what would happen in the courthouse?"

Cate suddenly stood up, and her voice was hard, cold and unforgiving—of herself. "I could have. Because I know him. I should have killed him years ago, but I was a coward. Instead of killing him, I took all the evidence I could lay my hands on…and I ran." Self-recrimination colored her next words. "I told you I was a coward, Liam, but you didn't want to believe it. That prosecutor? The other witness? They're dead because I didn't kill Vishenko when I had the chance."

Before Liam could react, before he could stop her, Cate stormed up the steps and entered the cabin, slamming the door shut behind her.

Liam started to go after her. But he'd only taken two steps when a faint sound from the other side of the clearing had him whirling around, his SIG SAUER in his hand.

Callahan froze in his tracks, but by no other sign did he indicate a gun was aiming at his heart. "Guess I should have called to let you know I was on the way," he said laconically.

Liam chuckled softly and holstered his gun. "Yeah, might have been a good idea." He met Callahan halfway and relieved him of the cooler he was carrying.

"Brought you some milk, eggs and butter. Fresh bread, some cookies and an apple pie, too. Mandy—

my wife—likes to bake when she's worried. And she's plenty worried right now, so we've got more bread and other baked goods than we know what to do with."

Liam honed in on the most important fact as they walked toward the cabin. "What's she worried about? I thought this place was as secret as we could wish for."

"It *is* secret. But no place is perfect. Even though Mandy doesn't know *who* you are, she knows why you're here…and she's remembering the two times we've been holed up here ourselves."

"Keira mentioned you'd used the place for this kind of thing before."

"Yeah. The first time was before we were married—right after Mandy's home was firebombed by men trying to kill me. The second time was right after our nearest neighbor showed up on our doorstep bleeding out, trying to warn me I headed up a hit list—and our kids were with us. Not good memories, either of them."

"But—"

Callahan mounted the porch stairs ahead of him and opened the cabin door. "Mandy's worrying for nothing. D'Arcy's got our backs on this, so we're good."

"Every man has his price," Aleksandrov Vishenko repeated to himself in Russian, as he'd been doing almost hourly while he was awake—and even sporadically during his sleep—ever since he'd met with the government official and made him the offer. A day had passed, and he still hadn't heard back. Not a single word. "Ten million dollars. How can he turn it down? He cannot," he reassured himself. "He is merely trying to see if I will raise the price. He is a cunning one, that man. Oh yes, cunning as a fox. He has tried to bring me down for years, and has failed every time. So now he will join hands with me instead."

He filled his snifter with cognac, trying not to think of how he was drinking more and more these days. How the stress over the impending trial was driving him to rely on the Courvoisier L'Essence he loved but had always drunk sparingly…until now.

He owned the world. His world. But unless Caterina Mateja could be silenced, his world would collapse around his ears. That was *not* going to happen. He'd killed to reach the top, and he'd killed to stay on top. He'd killed small men and great ones. He'd killed men who were nearly as vicious and ruthless as he was, but not quite. Not quite. He had always been the victor. That was not going to change. So one slight woman— a woman who couldn't even prevent him from taking her body wherever and whenever he wanted—was not going to vanquish him. Caterina would die. And Vishenko's empire would be secure again.

After Callahan left, reminding them he'd be back to check on them that evening, Liam told Cate, "We'll go stir-crazy cooped up in this cabin. Let's take a walk."

Cate finished putting away the breakfast dishes from the dish drainer. "Okay."

Not the most enthusiastic response, but Liam didn't care about that. He needed to get Cate talking to him again, to find out exactly what she meant about not killing Vishenko when she had the chance. Not just because his curiosity had been piqued, but because he needed to understand. And at the same time, needed to make her understand something important, too.

Not killing someone—not even someone as evil as Vishenko—didn't make you a coward. Not everyone could kill. Liam didn't have that strict moral inhibition, but that didn't mean he took killing lightly. He didn't.

He'd killed three times now, the last being one of the shooters in the courthouse. The first time he'd taken a human life he'd brooded over it until Alec had forcefully reminded him of what would have happened if he hadn't done it—that the diplomat he'd been protecting would have been assassinated, and the peace deal the man had been trying to broker would have been destroyed. The second time, Liam had handled on his own. He'd examined his conscience minutely, but had walked away secure in his belief that he'd done the right thing for the innocents involved.

The same went for what he'd done in the courthouse. He regretted the *necessity*, but he didn't regret the killing. He was even more convinced now of the rightness of what he'd done than he'd been at the time, because he knew Cate now. Because he knew what she'd suffered at Vishenko's hands. Because he knew she didn't deserve to die for trying to put Vishenko behind bars where he belonged.

But, just because he could kill and Cate couldn't, didn't make her a coward. He didn't know the circumstances, for one thing. In a life-or-death situation he could pull the trigger. But a preemptive killing? He didn't think so. The rule of law had to be the rule of law for everyone, himself included, or society as a whole would crumble.

He watched as Cate sat at the kitchen table, tugged her sneakers back on and tied the laces. Her slender wrists caught his attention as she did that—wrists that bore the evidence of how brave Cate really was. Somehow he had to make her understand.

They walked in silence for a while, uphill mostly, saving their breath for the climb. Occasionally a leafy branch or two from the tall bushes lining the path blocked their way, and Liam did his best to hold them back so Cate would have clear access. He'd chosen this path because he thought he remembered it led to a waterfall, and the faint sound of rushing water in the distance grew louder the farther they went, confirming his hunch. Eventually the path opened up into a rocky clearing at the base of a pristine waterfall, and they both stopped short.

The water wasn't a rushing torrent, but a steady stream, and as it fell fifty feet and splashed into the basin at the bottom it was even more beautiful than memory had painted it. Cate grasped his arm and said, "Oh, Liam! How lovely!"

"I thought you'd like it." He deliberately didn't look down at her hand holding his arm, not wanting to draw attention to the fact that she was touching him voluntarily. But just the idea sent a thrill coursing through his body.

The face she turned to him was soft and vulnerable, almost the same way she'd looked sleeping in his arms last night, and her silvery-blue eyes were lit from within. "I do like it. Oh I do." She faced the waterfall again. "How close can we get? Can we walk behind the falls?"

"If you don't mind getting wet—and that water is *cold*—we can walk behind it all the way to the other side. I've done it before."

"Oh let's do it." Her excitement was contagious. "I don't mind getting wet."

"Take my hand then. The rocks can be slippery." She hesitated for a second and glanced down, as if she suddenly realized she'd taken hold of his arm as if it came naturally to her. Then she slid her hand in his, and carefully they picked their way across the rocks. Spray from the waterfall hit them occasionally, and Cate squealed like a little girl each time. It made Liam smile, because he'd never seen this youthful side of Cate. Had never known her as anything other than the somewhat somber woman she was now. But at the same time his heart ached that her life for the past nine years had been so restricted, had contained so little *fun*. She was only twenty-five. Far too young to be so serious.

He led her carefully behind the waterfall, then paused so she could gaze through the cascading water. Viewing the world from the back of the falls was a unique experience. They were both damp from the spray and mist, and—as he'd warned—the water was cold. But Cate didn't seem to mind, so neither did he. When she turned back and smiled at him, her face aglow, he couldn't help it—he kissed her. He gently pulled her into his embrace, and when she didn't resist he kissed her until they were both breathless. Then he brushed the mist from her face and kissed her eyes closed.

She stayed like that for a minute, then opened her eyes and stared at him. Dazed. Confused. "Why did you do that?" she asked in a breathless whisper. "Why did you kiss me that way?"

"Because you smiled at me like a woman who wanted to be kissed." He drew a deep breath. "Tell me you wanted me to kiss you, Cate. If it's the truth, please tell me."

"Yes," she said, her face and her voice betraying just how much the truth surprised her. "Yes. I wanted you to kiss me."

Chapter 12

They were almost completely drenched by the time they made their way back to the cabin, but the late summer sun was so warm—even that far up on the mountain—they were still comfortable.

Cate wanted to let Liam shower and change first, but he refused. "I'm okay. You go ahead," he said, pushing her gently in the direction of the bathroom, "and I'll make some lunch for us."

She grabbed clean, dry clothes from her suitcase and hurried into the bathroom, wanting to be quick so Liam wouldn't have to stand around in damp clothes too long. She stripped out of her sodden clothing, then stepped under the warm spray. Only then did she realize she'd been colder than she thought, and the warm shower was welcome. She combed out her damp hair afterward and pinned it back, then stared at herself in the mirror for a minute—at a stranger. This woman was young and almost giddy—with a smile she didn't recognize. A smile that reflected the torch inside her.

Liam had done this to her. Liam had turned her into a stranger to herself. A woman who smiled easily and laughed at the absurdities of life. A woman who could have fun doing simple things. A woman she wanted to be...for him.

Then her smile faded. She wanted to be that woman for Liam...but she couldn't be. Because her past would never let her be that woman. Never.

Liam woke when Cate cried out in her sleep. And he knew the nightmare had come again. This time, though, when he turned on the light, called her name and touched her arm to wake her, she didn't fight him off. But her whole body was trembling uncontrollably, just as it had last night.

And just as he'd done last night, Liam picked her up and carried her to the rocking chair. Cradling her in his arms and rocking until she stopped shaking. He stared sightlessly at the shadowed recesses of the room, his eyes burning with the tears he was crying inside for what she'd suffered...and was still suffering. When she finally lay quiescent against him, he found the strength to overcome his mindless anger at the man who'd instilled this fear in her and said as gently as he could, "Tell me, Cate."

Her little whimper of pain was a dagger in his heart. "I...can't," she breathed in a broken, nearly soundless whisper.

"Yes, you can," he reassured her. "You can tell me anything. Don't you know that by now?" His voice dropped a notch. "Tell me. Whatever it is, it's holding you prisoner now just as much as he held you prisoner then. Tell me and you can let it go. Tell me and the power those memories have over you will fade." He brushed his lips against her forehead in a nonsexual kiss. "Tell me, Cate."

It all came spilling out. Halting, choked sentences. Heartbreaking whispers. She clutched his T-shirt with one desperate hand as words of agony beyond anything he could have imagined poured out of her. And through it all he kept the rocking chair moving. Moving. Letting the repetitive motion soothe and comfort her the way it would a child.

Forever later she came to the end of her story, but still they rocked. His arms were tight bands around her, as if he could shelter her that way from every terrible moment she'd endured. But he knew it was far and away too late for that. All he could do was hold her *now*. Shelter her *now*.

Her breath fluttered in her throat in the silence that followed her confession. Liam wanted to say something—anything—to break that weighty silence, but no words came to him at first. Then he realized what he needed to say. What she needed to hear. "The past is the past, Cate. Let it go. Just let it go." Her grasp on his T-shirt tightened, and she murmured something he couldn't hear. "What did you say?"

"I'm trying," she breathed, loud enough for him to hear this time. "I've *been* trying for seven years. But I—"

He shook his head. "No, you haven't. You haven't

been trying to relinquish the past. You've been trying to outrun it, and that won't work. The past will always catch up with you if you try to outrun it. You've got to just let it go."

Her voice was very small when she said, "I don't know how."

"Give it to me." And as he said the words he knew they were the right ones, even though in one way they made absolutely no sense. But it was what Cate needed to hear. He didn't know *how* he knew, just that the knowledge was branded into his consciousness. "Let me carry that burden for you, sweetheart. You've carried it long enough." The endearment slipped out, but Cate either didn't focus on it, or she accepted it—he wasn't sure which.

"I can't ask you to—"

"You're not asking. I'm volunteering. There's a difference. Let me do this for you."

"Liam." Just his name, but his heart ached at the way she said it. As if he'd given her something wondrous. Something precious and dear to her. Something she'd never forget.

Emotion welled up in Cate's throat as Liam made her that offer, thinking about how wonderful it would be if she *could* surrender her past to him. If he could take the shame and guilt and pain she'd harbored inside her since the day she became Vishenko's prisoner, if he could free her from the weight she'd carried all these years.

Even though she knew—rationally—the only one who could free her was herself, the idea was tempting.

Seductive. Nearly as tempting and seductive as it felt being in Liam's arms. So strong. So protective. In the shelter of his embrace was the only place she wanted to be...now and always.

But that was crazy thinking. No matter what Liam said, her past would always color her future—which meant she could never have a future with a man like him. No matter what he said now, he couldn't erase the knowledge of what she'd been...what she'd done... from his mind any more than she could. No matter how much she wanted to.

And she *did* want to. She wanted that more than anything in the world. More than she could ever put into words. She wanted it with an intensity that swept everything else aside, an intensity she'd only felt once before—the hate she had for Vishenko.

But what she was feeling now wasn't hate—far from it. A new emotion unfurled tiny petals deep within her as she laid with her head pillowed against Liam's shoulder. An emotion she didn't dare name, but which made her wish in a hopeless, helpless way, she could tell him what his offer meant to her. Not just now, but in the future. She would never be completely free of her past. But maybe, just maybe, the guilt and shame could be banished...with Liam's help.

Before she could stop herself, she pressed her lips against the warm, bare column of Liam's neck, so invitingly close.

Liam's entire body was electrified when Cate's lips brushed his skin. He tried not to respond, quickly tried to diagram and parse a complex sentence in his head to get his mind off the fact that he was holding Cate the way he'd dreamed of holding her...and *she'd* kissed *him*. But his body had a mind of its own, and she was having a totally predictable effect on him. An effect he'd be damned if she realized. He tried to surreptitiously pull away, tried to shift in the rocking chair so she wouldn't notice him swelling against her thigh, but it was already too late.

Their gazes met, and Cate's eyes held the knowledge that he wanted her—how had she put it?—*that* way. The knowledge in her eyes was followed by acceptance. And instead of making Liam glad, it made him angry. Not at her, but at himself. At the world. And most especially at Vishenko.

"It's okay," she told him, raising one hand to cradle his cheek.

"No, it's not," he said abruptly, catching her hand with his and forcing it away.

"You want me." She swallowed noticeably. "I don't mind, Liam. I don't."

His anger spilled over. "I don't want you to not *mind*," he grated. "I want you to want it, too. As much as I do."

Her pale blue eyes darkened as shadows filled them. "I can't." Regret colored her words, and Liam knew in her heart she believed it. "Even though I want to, I can't. He...he killed that part of me," she whispered. "I can never...feel those things other women feel."

Liam wasn't given to believe in divine intervention. But he suddenly knew—as if God was whispering in his ear—what he had to do. For Cate. Because it had just become his personal mission—his quest for the Holy Grail—to prove her wrong. He had to prove Vishenko hadn't destroyed the inner woman when he'd tortured and abused her body. He had to prove she *could* feel what other women felt…when the act was done out of love.

The knowledge that he loved her wasn't the revelation he'd thought it would be. It had grown on him steadily, inevitably, like an incoming tide, until he finally accepted it with nothing more than an *Of course!* As if he should have known it all along. Love. All consuming. All encompassing. Flooding his body with an awareness he felt even in his fingertips.

The number of days they'd known each other didn't matter—he'd been with her almost constantly since the moment he'd saved her life. He'd held her as she wept as if her heart were breaking. He'd lain beside her the other night, knowing he couldn't do anything else *but* hold her, but knowing, too, he would have given anything to take away her pain—no matter the cost to him. He'd rocked her to sleep last night, helping her drive off the demons that invaded her dreams. But she'd never given up. She was fighting for her life—her *emotional* life—just as much now as she'd fought to free herself physically years ago. From first to last she'd shown him nothing but unbelievable bravery. He *knew* her. Deep in his soul he knew her…and recognized she was the one.

He raised his hand and lightly brushed his fingertips against her cheek, then tucked her hair behind her ear. She didn't flinch away, as she'd done the first time he'd touched her. And Liam knew this was the moment. It wouldn't be the way he'd dreamed of making love to her. But if he had anything to say about it, it would be the way she'd dreamed of having a man make love to her when she'd been a starry-eyed teenager all those years ago—and still did. Secretly. With every romance novel she read. Totally for her. Nothing for himself, except the knowledge that he was freeing her from a nightmare that had never ended, not even when she escaped seven years ago. Because she was still in chains forged by her mind.

"Cate." Just her name. Nothing more. But the color seeped into her cheeks at the intensity in his voice.

"It's okay," she whispered again, and this time Liam didn't draw back, though he wanted to vehemently deny what she had to be thinking when she made him that offer. She honestly thought he could take her body and use it for his own selfish needs, as if he was no better than men who paid for sex or forced women against their will. But he couldn't *tell* her different. He had to *show* her.

He started slow. And gentle. Stroking his fingers along the contours of her face so delicately she would feel it as the brush of butterfly wings. Whispering her name so she'd know he knew who he was with, who he was making love to. Showing her the wonder, the magic.

Her eyes drifted closed, and Liam took that as a good sign. That, and the soft sighs he knew she wasn't aware of, but which told him he was definitely on the right track. *Oh, sweetheart,* he told her in his mind. *We're just getting started. There's so much more to come. I'm going to make it so good for you, you won't*

remember anything else. Just here. Just now. Just love.
Sweet, sweet love.

He stood, still cradling her in his arms, and carried her back to the bed. Laying her down gently, then following her down and stretching out beside her. Letting her feel him hot and hard everywhere his body touched hers, but not holding her down. Not using his strength against her in any way.

He wanted to blurt out how much he loved her, explain that this experience was as new for him as it was for her, but he knew words were meaningless in this situation. The knight-errant in him assumed control of his body, his mind. Dictating what to do, where to touch her, and for how long. To maximize her pleasure. To leave her shuddering with the intensity love brought to lovemaking. To bring her to completion with just his hands. His lips. His heart.

He didn't try to remove her clothes, sensing she needed that protection, that mental barrier. But his hands roamed her body lightly, caressingly. Letting her know what was coming next, and giving her the chance to object if he did anything she didn't like. She didn't object, and Liam said a little prayer of thanks. He would have stopped instantly if she grew fearful or showed any sign that what he was doing wasn't right, but he didn't want to stop. He had something to prove…to her.

He rubbed his cheek against her nipples—first one, then the other—and felt them bead in response beneath her pajama top. Then he suckled, dampening the material as he pulled both it and her nipple into his mouth.

And knew by her response that she loved what he was doing, which encouraged him to go further.

He slid one hand beneath the waistband of her pajama bottoms and panties, but slowly. Again giving her time to protest what he was doing because he'd be damned before he did anything she didn't want. When his fingers brushed lower her whole body tightened in panic, and he paused. Waiting.

Without removing his hand, he nuzzled her cheek. "It's me, Cate," unerringly discerning she needed the reminder.

She breathed his name, but endless moments passed before she relaxed. He didn't immediately move his hand. Instead he kissed her behind her ear, then teased her earlobe with his tongue and teeth until she shivered with a response she couldn't hide. Then and only then did he proceed.

It didn't take as long as he'd feared it might. He hoped it was a good sign—that Cate had feelings for him, that she might someday love him as he loved her. But that wasn't the most important thing at this moment. His gift to her didn't come with strings attached.

"It's okay, Cate," he whispered when he finally brought her to the brink. When little tremors shook her body and she bit her lip in a last-ditch effort to control the sensations he knew were sweeping through her. "It's okay, sweetheart. Let go. Just let go. I'll catch you. I won't let you fall."

Then she did let go, a tiny cry of completion escaping her throat as her whole body shuddered, as her legs clamped tightly around his hand. Liam crooned wordlessly, his lips pressed against her temple as her climax took her beyond anyplace she had ever thought to go. She didn't have to tell him—he just knew. He didn't remove his hand right away, just continued to hold her, stroke her, extending her pleasure for as long as he could.

Cate was crying. Tears leaked from the corners of her eyes, soundless tears that gladdened his heart and also broke it. Because it killed him to think of her believing the worst of herself. Killed him to think that all these years she'd never known her body could respond the way nature intended.

"I didn't know…" she whispered, almost to herself. She drew a sobbing breath, then turned ever so slightly toward him. "I didn't know," she repeated, placing her hand against his heart. "Oh, Liam…"

A wave of relief swept through him. Relief that he'd done it—he'd somehow found the way to banish her fear long enough for her to experience the beauty, the wonder. He felt like a man who'd climbed Mount Everest and stood triumphant on the summit—because he'd been the man Cate had needed him to be. And at the same time he felt humbled. It hadn't been a conscious effort on his part. He hadn't thought about what he was going to do each step of the way. He'd gone with his instincts, and somehow his instincts had been right. He'd always denied it when his brothers had teased him, but in this case it seemed appropriate—he *was* a knight in shining armor after all. Cate's knight. And it felt damned good.

It hadn't been easy restraining his own desires…and

it still wasn't. His body ached and throbbed, needing the completion he'd just given her and had denied himself. But this wasn't the time. *His* needs weren't important, not at this point.

But he couldn't continue to hold her like this without doing something. So he waited until Cate's eyes fluttered closed and her breathing told him she'd drifted off to sleep before easing himself out of the bed.

He stripped in the bathroom and stepped naked into the shower, letting the hot water pummel him. He was so primed it took him less than a minute to take care of his most pressing need. He toweled off quickly afterward, pulled his boxer shorts and T-shirt back on, then padded silently into the other room.

She was awake again already…and watching him as he came around the folding screen. He climbed into bed next to her as if he had the right, hoping she wouldn't deny it. Then gently drew her into his arms, settling her against his shoulder. Not holding her prisoner, just holding her safe. Secure. Knowing she needed to get used to having him hold her in bed—just like the other night—if she was ever going to accept anything more from him.

After a minute, during which he counted her shallow breaths one after the other, she said, "Why did you do that?"

He didn't pretend to misunderstand her. "Because you're not ready." His voice was a deep rumble in his chest and his arm tightened imperceptibly around her shoulders. "I can wait until you are."

She didn't say anything for a long time, but her

breathing quickened…and not in a good way. Liam knew that as surely as he'd known she wasn't ready in the first place. "But…" she said finally. "What if it's…never?"

"Then it's never," he said simply. She raised her head from his shoulder and stared at him in the light from the bedside lamp Liam had left on, disbelief written plainly on her delicately beautiful face. One corner of his mouth curved up in a deliberately understanding smile that invited her to believe him. Implicitly. "It won't affect how I feel about you, Cate."

"How can you know that?" she asked quickly. Almost sharply. "You're a man, and I know how men—"

"Yes, I'm a man. But I'm not an animal." *Like him,* he thought but didn't say. He didn't want to bring memories of Vishenko into bed with them any more than they already were. "I can control my desires, Cate. I want you so much I'm shaking with it at times—you already know that. But only when you want me too—just as much as I want you—will I ever do anything about it."

"But…" She seemed stunned. "But…never?"

"Why is it so hard to believe? Have I ever lied to you?"

She was silent, gravely considering his question. Then shook her head slowly. "No, you've never lied to me, but…" She still couldn't comprehend it. "Never?"

From somewhere he found the strength to answer with patience, even though part of him was hurt she wouldn't believe him. "I'll never do anything you don't want, Cate, anything you're not ready for."

He could tell he'd confused her. "Then what was that all about…earlier?" she asked. "Why did you…"

"To prove to you—not to me—you were wrong about yourself. That you *could* feel what other women feel. That you could respond when a man makes love to you." He held her gaze, praying she would believe this, if nothing else. "I'm not using those words lightly, Cate. I was making love to you…because I love you."

She caught her breath, and Liam could see she hadn't been expecting that. Not at all. It was another little dagger to his heart, but he was getting used to it where Cate was concerned. He continued, "I waited a long time to find a woman I could love. I finally found her. Okay, so she's not ready to return my love. Not yet. That's my problem, not hers. But I think she will…someday. And I think she'll come to trust me completely. But the only way to win her trust is to be the man she needs me to be. Whatever kind of man that is. For however long it takes."

He ducked his head and kissed her quickly, lightly, on the lips. "It won't be easy—I won't lie to you about that. But a man who can't look and not touch isn't really much of a man…not in my opinion. I can be a very patient man, Cate…when I want something badly enough. When you're ready—and not a moment before—I'll be right here, waiting for you. Waiting to share that part of my love with you."

He tucked her head back down against his shoulder. "Now sleep. Morning will come soon enough, and I'm just going to hold you until you fall asleep. Then I'll go back to my cot over there."

"No," she protested quickly, and at first he thought she meant she didn't want him to hold her. But then she said, "Don't go. Please." Her voice was soft, hesitant, when she asked, "Stay with me?"

Inside he was doing cartwheels, but all he said was, "My pleasure, sweetheart."

Chapter 13

Cate woke before Liam, and at first she panicked at feeling a hard male body next to hers in bed, even though they were both still clothed. Then she realized where she was and who she was with, and she relaxed. But it was too late—she'd already woken Liam.

"Hi," he said, his dark brown eyes fixed on her face.

Liam didn't waken slowly. He was asleep one minute, then wide-awake the next. *Is that a result of his job?* Cate wondered. *Or is he just naturally a light sleeper?* She didn't know. There were so many things she didn't know about him. But she wanted to. She was surprised at how much she wanted to know every little detail about Liam.

And yet, she knew the important things, like his need to protect. He hadn't even known her, but he'd killed to protect her and the others in the courthouse when the machine guns had opened fire. He hadn't hesitated— he'd risked his own life to do what he had to do. Despite that tough side of him, though, he was gentle. So very gentle. Patient, too. And kind. Those things she didn't know about him were superficial. The basic character of the man—she already knew everything she needed to know.

"You okay?" he continued, and Cate knew he wasn't just talking about now, the way she'd started awake, the instant panic. He was also asking about last night. The blood rushed into her cheeks, and a flush of warmth inundated her body as she remembered…and relived everything he'd made her feel.

She hadn't believed it was possible. It was still incomprehensible…but it had happened. Liam had brought her body to life, had proved beyond a shadow of a doubt that Vishenko hadn't killed that part of her. And in a secret recess of her heart, hope quivered to life.

"I'm fine," she answered quickly. Though her first instinct was to turn away as sudden shyness overcame her, there was something about Liam's eyes that refused to let her do that. Something that held her in place with nothing more than his gentle insistence.

"I meant what I said last night." His deep voice resonated through her body, setting off little tremors of awareness. A *good* awareness of him as a man. "I love you, Cate. But I'm not trying to pressure you in any way. And I don't want you to think there's some kind of quid pro quo here—sex in exchange for my protection. My protection is yours for however long you need it, no matter what." He touched her cheek with one finger, the same kind of butterfly caress he'd used last night. Then he threw off the sheet and jumped out of bed so quickly Cate didn't have a chance to protest.

He disappeared into the bathroom, then emerged a minute later. Cate couldn't see what he was doing—the screen shielded him from her view. But the sounds that came to her were the unmistakable sounds of a man dressing, including the rasp of the zipper on his jeans. And Cate's imagination moved into overdrive thinking about the strong male body that had held her through the night.

She slipped out of bed, grabbed her clothes and hurried into the bathroom. She was quick, though not as quick as Liam, and that thought made her smile. As she washed her face and brushed her teeth, she stared at herself in the mirror over the sink. Wondering why she looked so different. Then it came to her. She was still smiling. And not just the perfunctory smiles she used to make the people around her think she was okay. She was really, truly smiling, because she felt good. Energized. Because she was looking forward to the day. Because of Liam.

Then the smile faded when she unbuttoned her pajama top as she started to change into her day clothes. Liam hadn't undressed her last night when he made love to her. *Because of the scars?* she wondered now. Last night she'd been grateful he hadn't attempted to get her naked any more than he'd gotten naked himself. Last night she hadn't been ready to go that far, and somehow Liam had known it. But this morning she couldn't help but wonder if the reason he hadn't was because her scars would turn him off. The way she'd always thought they would turn off any man.

She'd shown him the scars the other night—angrily. Defiantly. Needing in some perverse way for him to know just how damaged she was, physically as well as emotionally. Trying to push him away before he could reject her, so it wouldn't hurt quite so much. He hadn't turned away from her in disgust, though—not the other night. But his actions last night took on a totally different meaning...now. Was that the real reason he hadn't undressed her? Because of her scars?

She turned around and craned her head so she could see the scars in the mirror. It was more than seven years since the last scar had been inflicted, closer to eight. Because when she'd finally realized her only chance for escape would come once Vishenko believed she'd been totally vanquished, she'd surrendered. *Seemed* to surrender. She'd never surrendered in her heart, but she still retained guilt she hadn't fought him to the bitter end. That she hadn't died rather than let him think he'd conquered her.

All these years later the scars had faded. Not completely—nothing would ever erase them. But they weren't the angry red of freshly healed scars the way she always imagined them in her mind. Now they were silvery crisscross traces of where Vishenko had beaten her until her back was bloody and her resistance shredded.

Last night she'd confessed almost everything to Liam. *Almost* everything. The one thing she hadn't told him—the one thing she'd never told anyone except Angelina and Alec, and subsequently the prosecutors—was that she'd eventually surrendered her body to Vishenko. Not willingly. But knowingly.

Which meant that Liam—a man with such strong moral convictions, a man who professed to love her— would never love her if he knew the whole truth. Which also meant she could never tell him.

Dinnertime had come and gone, and so had Callahan. He'd brought news, too. Good news. "One of the marshals wounded in the firefight was discharged this afternoon," he'd said in his dry, acerbic way. "And the other should go home tomorrow." He'd hesitated a second, then added, "The other prosecutor's injuries are more serious, but his condition has been upgraded and he's no longer in intensive care."

"Thank God," Liam had said in such a heartfelt tone Cate had known he meant it literally.

Liam still believes in a just and merciful God, she thought now. *Just like Alec. Just like Angelina.* She wished she could. A tiny voice in the back of her mind reminded her that she *had* escaped. And she'd kept her freedom for more than six years before Alec located her. *But that wasn't God's doing,* she told herself now, ruthlessly squashing that tiny voice. *That was just...happenstance. Luck.* And never settling into a routine. Never staying in one place for very long. Never risking anything, especially her heart. Because what you didn't risk you couldn't lose, and she'd already lost more than she could afford. Her pride. Her dignity. Her self-respect. Survival had depended on risking nothing more.

She dried the last of the dinner dishes—Liam had cooked so she'd washed up—and put them away in the cabinet. Liam had already made a perimeter check, and was now sitting on the back porch, watching the sunset. She squelched the urge to join him, and instead fetched one of her treasured books, settling herself in the rocking chair to read.

But instead of opening the book, she pushed the rocking chair with one foot and stared into the empty fireplace, remembering. Remembering how it felt to lie in the shelter of Liam's arms in this very chair. Remembering how she'd confessed nearly everything to him, and he hadn't judged her. Hadn't condemned her.

Could she tell him the rest? Could she risk it? Could she build a relationship with him if she didn't? And even if she could, he'd know the truth soon enough, and he'd never forgive her for deceiving him.

She rocked slowly until the light left, her thoughts in turmoil. She rocked until shadows crept around the rocking chair, the book still unopened in her lap.

The back door opened and Liam came inside. "You missed the sunset," he told her quietly as he flicked on the overhead light, dispelling the shadows. "Why didn't you come outside?"

"I needed to think." About what, she wasn't ready to tell him. "I needed to be alone."

He nodded as a reflective expression settled over his face. "I'm that way sometimes, too," he told her. "But I missed you." He wasn't saying it in a critical way, Cate knew. Just a statement of fact. He would have liked to share the sunset with her because he enjoyed her company. That was all. Even if no words were exchanged between them, her presence mattered to him.

He went to his duffel bag and pulled something out of it, then sat down at the kitchen table. She watched silently as he pulled his gun from its holster and placed it on the table in front of him. He removed the clip and the bullet in the chamber, then began taking the gun apart. Curious, she left the rocking chair and came to sit across from him.

He glanced up once, then turned his concentration back to what he was doing. He didn't wait for her to ask, volunteering, "Just some regular maintenance on my SIG SAUER. Nothing to worry about."

She propped one elbow on the table and leaned her cheek against her hand as she watched him take a small cloth and carefully wipe each part of his gun. Fascinated by his methodical movements. Then, apropos of nothing, and without looking at her, he said, "I wanted to ask you about what you said yesterday."

She wrinkled her brow in a question, but she knew he couldn't see it, so she asked, "When yesterday?"

"Right before Callahan showed up. When you called yourself a coward because you hadn't killed Vishenko when you had the chance."

She'd forgotten about that…but Liam hadn't. And she could tell it was still bothering him. She hadn't intended to tell him, but it was too late—she couldn't unsay those words.

Liam put down the piece of his gun he was holding and looked at her, his deep brown eyes stern. But there was also something fierce in their depths. "You are not a coward," he said now. "You hear me? You are *not* a coward."

His unshakeable faith in her reverberated in her soul, but she honestly believed his faith was misplaced. "You don't know," she began, but he wouldn't let her finish.

"I *do* know. You think because you couldn't kill him in cold blood that makes you a coward? You're so wrong, Cate. Totally wrong."

"But I—"

"No," he reiterated. "If you could kill him like that, it would make you the monster he is. But you're not. You're not a cold-blooded killer any more than I am, and you never will be. But that doesn't mean you're a coward. It means you have a conscience. It means you know right from wrong. And that's a good thing, Cate. A wonderful thing."

In the silence that followed Liam picked up the piece of his gun he'd put down and continued wiping it. Then he took the little bottle he'd pulled from the case in his duffel bag, applied a minute drop of oil from it and rubbed the oil into the metal.

"How many men have you killed?" Cate asked abruptly, surprising herself as much as him.

His hands stilled for a moment, then continued. "Three," he said finally, not looking up from his task. "Three men who deserved to die." He drew a deep breath and let it out long and slow, then said, "But it wasn't something I planned. Just something I had to do."

"Because you were the only one who could do it."

His gaze met hers, his eyes very dark. Very grave. "Yeah. Something like that."

"That's what Alec said about Angelina. He said she killed a man who was trying to kill him. That she didn't *want* to do it, but she had to…because she was the only one who could save him."

"Alec told me about that."

"I figured he had." She thought for a moment. "How do you *know*, Liam? How do you know when you have to kill someone because it's necessary…and you're the only one who can do it?"

He didn't answer immediately, as if he wanted to consider his response very carefully. "It's not a conscious choice," he said finally. "You don't think, 'I have to kill this man because he's endangering someone.' Or, 'I have to kill this man or he'll kill me.' You don't have time for that. You go on instinct. And you pray your instincts are right."

"Are your instincts always right?"

"For me—so far—yeah. But I don't take that for granted. Every time I hear about a cop shooting an unarmed civilian or a kid with a toy gun that looks real, I think, 'There but for the grace of God goes me.' All I can do is the best I can do at the time, Cate. All I can do is pray I never make the wrong decision."

"But how do you *know* what the right decision is?"

"I train. Constantly. So my reaction time gives me that fraction of a second I need for my brain to assess the situation and respond correctly." One corner of his mouth twitched up into a rueful smile. "Sometimes it's easier than other times. For instance, in the courthouse Alec and I were looking the other way when the gunmen opened fire. But we both knew instantly what was happening—the sound of gunfire is unmistakable—and we both knew what we had to do."

"You saved my life."

"Yeah, we did, both of us. But I don't look at it quite that way. I was going on instinct. I wasn't saving *you* so much as I was reacting to the situation—I just *couldn't* let those machine guns keep firing, endangering everyone. Not a conscious thought, just instinct. And I'm sure that's what Alec was going on, too." He'd finished his task as he was talking, and now he put the reassembled gun back in its shoulder holster. Then his gaze met hers again. "It's a little different when it's personal, though."

Cate caught her breath at the intimate look Liam gave her. "What…what do you mean?"

"My brother-in-law, Cody, told us—my brothers and me, in this very cabin—about the time my sister was shot. About his visceral reaction when he saw it go down, and what he did as a result. I'm not faulting him—in that situation I might have done the same thing. Not that what he *did* was wrong, but his reasons for doing it…maybe. And yet, we're only human, Cate. When someone we love is hurt, we want to hurt back. That's natural. We just have to accept that we're human, and go from there."

"Liam?" She was going to tell him. Everything. She was. She *was*.

"Right here, Cate."

Her courage failed her and she knew she couldn't. *Not yet,* her heart cried. She couldn't bear it if Liam looked at her differently. Even if he said it didn't matter, how could it not? Alec and Angelina hadn't judged her, but the prosecutors had—she knew it. They hadn't said anything, but she'd seen their eyes when she told them…and their tone of voice had changed when they questioned her further. A subtle difference…but a difference all the same.

Would Liam still touch her in that reverent way he'd touched her last night, as if she was something precious? Would he still treat her with respect and that old-fashioned courtesy that reminded her of her youth in Zakhar? Or would his opinion of her be colored by the truth—a truth that damned her in the eyes of most people—the same way the prosecutors' opinions of her had been changed?

She wanted to believe it wouldn't matter to Liam. She wanted so dreadfully to believe…but she couldn't. "Never mind," she said quickly, pasting a fake smile on her face she knew didn't fool him. "It's not important."

Night had fallen hours earlier on the East Coast, and Aleksandrov Vishenko was raging in his Manhattan condo. Raging…and drinking. Slurring his words as he sloshed more Courvoisier into his snifter and cursed the law enforcement bureaucrat—his antecedents, his morals, everything. He tossed back his head and swallowed the contents of his glass in one gulp, then smashed the snifter into the fireplace. A string of Russian obscenities relieved the worst of his frustration, but what made him feel even better was planning his revenge. Once the man revealed Caterina's whereabouts and Vishenko had taken care of her, he would obliterate the bureaucrat. It would be poetic justice. *Bratva* justice. He would recover the ten-million-dollar price he'd paid…and kill Nick D'Arcy.

* * *

Cate had avoided Liam as best she could—which wasn't all that much in a one-room cabin, but she'd tried. She'd brushed her teeth and changed into her pajamas before eight o'clock, pretending she was tired and wanted an early night, and Liam hadn't objected. He'd set up his cot beside the fireplace again, and had turned off the overhead light long since. The rhythmic sound of his breathing—you couldn't really call it snoring—followed soon after, and she knew he was asleep already.

But the book Cate was reading wasn't conducive to making her sleepy, and eventually she turned off the lamp and just laid there wide-awake in bed, listening to Liam sleeping.

"The past is the past, Cate," he'd told her. *"...You haven't been trying to relinquish the past. You've been trying to outrun it, and that won't work. The past will always catch up with you if you try to outrun it. You've got to just let it go."*

She wanted to. She did. She really did. Last night Liam had shown her she could...if she let herself. Last night he'd proved her wrong, too. He'd proved Vishenko hadn't killed that part of her as she'd thought, the part that could respond to a man's loving touch. If she was wrong about that, what else was she wrong about? Was Liam right when he said she wasn't a coward because she'd run instead of killing Vishenko all those years ago?

She wanted to believe it. Just as she wanted to believe in Liam's love. If those things were true...if she could believe them...then maybe her life could be more than just existing day-to-day. Maybe she could have a future…with Liam.

Then she remembered and shuddered uncontrollably, clenching her hands together, digging the nails of one hand into the palm of the other. Liam didn't know *everything*. She hadn't told him because she didn't want him to know. But when she testified, the whole world would know she hadn't fought Vishenko to the bitter end. The whole world would know she'd surrendered… and so would Liam.

Coward, coward, coward, she mocked herself, knowing she should have told him the truth. The whole truth. Keeping that secret from him condemned her just as much as her actions almost eight years ago.

So many things she should have done, but hadn't. Not the least of which was, why hadn't she fought longer? Why had she surrendered? Easy now to say she would never have escaped if Vishenko hadn't believed he'd conquered her. Easy now to say he would never have relaxed his guard around her so she could testify against him if he hadn't believed she was vanquished. Easy now to say she would never have had access to the documents that were so vital to the conspiracy trial if he hadn't believed he'd broken her spirit.

Liam was right that she didn't have it in her to kill Vishenko as he lay sleeping the night she escaped. She'd hated him then with an intense passion that craved vengeance—and she still did. But she hadn't been able to kill him. Even if she'd known what he would do in the future, who would die, could she have killed him? Coldly? Calculatingly?

No. And not because she was a coward. Liam was right about that after all. Was he right about everything?

Suddenly she wanted to see Liam. Talk to him. Thank him for helping her realize the truth about herself—that she wasn't a coward just because she couldn't kill. And more. She wanted what he'd given her last night. She wanted to lie in his arms and believe herself loved. Cherished. She wanted to let the past go and just be… Cate. Cate and Liam. To experience everything he had to offer.

She slipped from the bed and soundlessly made her way to Liam's cot. Moonlight through the front window gave her enough light to see by, and she knelt beside the cot, then hesitated. His face in sleep was just different enough from his waking self so she knew he was asleep, and he seemed so peaceful lying there she didn't have the heart to waken him.

She couldn't help cataloging his face though, as she watched him sleep—feature by feature. Nothing distinctive, except perhaps his eyelashes. Absurdly long for a man, which was even more obvious when seen with his eyes closed. But she was intensely attracted to him. Why? He wasn't traditionally handsome—his features were too stark for that. So what was it about Liam that set him apart from everyone else, even Alec, whom Liam resembled so closely?

It's not his face, she realized eventually. *It's his character. His character is reflected in his face, in his eyes. Morally strong, with a tender heart. So generous, too—a born giver. And kind. A good man, like his brother.* Yes, like Alec, but somehow more. More concerned. More protective. More emotionally involved. All the virtues, in fact, of the best heroes in the romance novels she secretly loved. Her knight in shining armor.

Suddenly she realized he was awake and watching her with those beautiful brown eyes. As if he'd sensed her presence beside his cot. "What's wrong, Cate?" he whispered, reaching immediately for the holstered gun hanging over the edge of the cot.

She put out a hand to stop him. "Nothing's wrong," she said softly. "I just…" She couldn't bring herself to put what she wanted into words.

But he seemed to read her mind, because his hand stopped reaching for his gun and cupped her cheek instead. "Tell me, Cate. Tell me what you need."

At first she couldn't get the words out, then she managed, "You. I need you."

Chapter 14

Cate could never remember exactly how they ended up back in the double bed, but somehow they did. And Liam was touching her as he'd done last night, with lips and hands that made her ache and want something just beyond her grasp. But this time she wanted more. She just didn't know how to ask.

She was also afraid. Afraid that when it came down to it, she'd panic as she'd done this morning when she'd woken in Liam's arms. She didn't want to do that to him, but she didn't know how to prevent it. And the fear made her stiffen against him. Only a tiny movement, but she knew he could feel it.

Again he seemed to read her mind. "Hey," he said as his hands touched hers. "Your hands are cold, sweetheart. Let me warm them up." And he drew them up underneath his T-shirt, pressing them against his chest. Letting the furnace of his body drive the chill from hers. After a moment she daringly slid one hand around beneath his arm and caressed his back, which was even more searingly warm than his chest. Then she hid her face against his shoulder.

"Hey," he said again. "You don't need to be shy with me. It's just me, Cate. You know I won't do anything you don't want me to do."

"That's just it," she said in a small voice. "I want you to…but I… I don't know how to tell you what I… and I'm afraid."

He cuddled her close. "Afraid of me?" The way he said it indicated there was absolutely no reason for her to be afraid of him…and she believed it.

She shook her head. "Afraid of me. Afraid I'll remember…and panic." Her face contracted in fear she wouldn't be able to go through with it. Fear she would hurt him if that happened. And she'd rather do anything except hurt Liam.

Liam marveled that he hadn't thought of it before. He laid back against the pillows and murmured, "Make love to me, Cate."

"What?" She gave him one startled look, then glanced away.

"You want me…*that* way. I know you do. You said it yourself, so you know it, too…in your heart. But the only way to get past what he did to you is to let you be in control of your body. All the way. To let you be in control of *my* body. To take whatever you want, however you want it. However little or however much."

He tore off his T-shirt and stripped away his boxer shorts, letting her see him completely naked for the first time. Letting her see his arousal. "This is what you do to me, Cate," he told her gently. "But this is a good thing…when a man loves a woman the way I love you. I want you to know it in your head. I want you to believe it in your heart. I want you to *feel* it in your bones there's no reason to panic. No need to be afraid. I love you. And I'll never force you in any way. Never take anything you don't willingly give. That's why I want you to make love to me. To prove it to yourself. You can do whatever you want to me, for however long you want. But the minute you stop, we stop."

She hesitated. "How can you know…" Color suffused her face. "What if I can't go through with it? What if I can only go so far, without remembering…"

"Because I love you. That's how I know." His voice was husky with repressed desire. "I want to be inside you, Cate. I want to feel you tight around me, and I want to be so deep it's as if we're one—as if we've never been apart. I want to breathe in unison with you, sharing those little tremors of desire. Then I want to move inside you until we both can't bear it, until the pleasure is so great we both explode." Her shiver of awareness told him his words affected her powerfully, and he knew she *did* want him nearly as much as he wanted her.

"But I swear to you, I'll stop the instant you say stop. Because no matter how much I want you, I want something else more. I want you to trust me in every fiber of

your being. I want you to know you're safe with me…
in every way. Because I love you."

Say it, he begged her in his mind. S*ay the words I
know you want to say. The words I need to hear.*

She touched his face tentatively, then his lips. As
if her fingers were able to distinguish truth from lies
merely by touch. "I love you, Cate," he whispered,
brushing a kiss against her fingers. "Let me prove it to
you. Trust me. Trust me this once, and I swear you'll
never regret it."

"I do trust you." Her voice was barely audible. "And
I… I…" Her breath came in little pants, and Liam could
see in her eyes she wanted to say the words…but was
just as afraid to admit she loved him as she was afraid
she wouldn't be able to go through with making love
with him. He suppressed his regret she couldn't say the
words he longed for, because the words weren't as important as proving to Cate she could do this.

"Touch me," he invited in his deepest voice. "Touch
me. Take me. Whatever you want, I want. Whatever
you need, that's what I want to give you. No force between us, ever." His voice dropped to a seductive whisper. "Touch me, Cate. You want to. So just touch me."

She touched him. Hesitantly at first, her fingertips
just barely touching the proof of his desire. When he
reacted…visibly…she drew her hand back sharply.

Liam laughed softly, reassuringly. "It's okay, sweetheart. That's normal. You touch me and I feel it. And my
body reacts, especially there. That's the way I'm made.
You're made that way, too. When I caress you…your

body reacts. When I stroke your breasts, when I suckle them, you feel it…everywhere. Don't you."

His last words were a statement, not a question, but she answered anyway. "Yes." He knew by the expression on her face she was remembering last night, when he'd proved her wrong. When he'd proved she *could* feel what other women felt during lovemaking.

"And when I touch you *there*, you enjoy that, too."

"Yes." Just a fraction above a whisper. "I do, Liam. I didn't think I could, but I…"

"So when *you* touch *me* there, I enjoy it. Immensely. That's the way it's supposed to work. We touch, we kiss, we caress. We give each other pleasure. One feeds the other, until…" Inside he was begging, *Touch me, Cate. Don't stop touching me. Don't be afraid.*

She touched him again, and this time her fingers curled around his erection. He swelled when her fingers made contact, and he thought he'd explode just from the intimate connection he'd wanted almost since the first moment he'd seen her. What he'd waited so long to have. But he held back by sheer will, wanting her to believe in him.

He tried to speak but found his emotions in the way. He cleared his throat. "Keep going, sweetheart. You're in control. Whatever you want to do, just do. Think about the way I touched you last night, and do the same to me now. You can do it, Cate. You can give me the same pleasure I gave you. But everything stops when you stop, I promise." *Trust me,* his heart pleaded.

He almost arched off the bed when she stroked him, her fingers squeezing just tightly enough for pleasure, not pain. She quickly found a natural rhythm, and Liam's whole body condensed down into a pulsing, pounding need. He tried to hold back, wanting to prolong his pleasure, and wanting, also, to let her see he could control his desire, but it got away from him. Everything got away from him and he cried out as he bucked uncontrollably and thrust himself into her hand. Again. And again.

When it was all over he opened his eyes, afraid he'd shocked Cate, but she surprised him. "I did it," she marveled, almost as if she were talking to herself. "I did it."

Little tremors still transmitted themselves from him to her. "Yeah," he agreed, his voice husky with the remnants of desire. "Hell yeah." He wasn't sure exactly what she was referring to, but whatever it was, it was true—she'd done it.

She reached over to the nightstand and grabbed a tissue, cleaning him inexpertly but with a loving touch. "I was afraid," she explained solemnly, but with a light in her eyes that told him she was thrilled she'd conquered her fear. "I thought I wouldn't be able to…but you… you waited. You let me…all the way. Touch you," she said disjointedly. "My way. I was afraid you would… but you didn't." She smiled a beatific smile. "I did it. And it didn't hurt me."

The sense of euphoria that had enveloped Liam suddenly dissipated as a devastating pain tore through his heart. Cate trusted him…but only so far. No matter what she said, she'd still been afraid he wouldn't let her take him all the way, that at some point he'd force his way into her body the way Vishenko had done. Numerous times. Hurting her. Taking pleasure in hurting her.

Rage at Aleksandrov Vishenko slashed through him. And he knew with startling certainty that if Vishenko was there right now, he'd kill him for what he'd done to Cate. Kill him in that instant like the rabid animal he was. With no more remorse than that it was necessary to protect the innocent.

Vengeance, he realized with a sense of shock. *That's what Cody felt when Keira was shot. That's what I want. Vengeance.*

He reeled mentally. He didn't want to believe it about himself...but it was the truth. He wanted vengeance. Not justice. Vengeance. Exactly what he'd condemned in his brother-in-law, that's what he was feeling.

Then he suppressed that thought ruthlessly. Pushed it out of his mind to consider later, because he had something more important to do at this moment.

He leveraged himself easily into a sitting position, then cradled Cate's face in his hands and kissed her gently on the lips, waiting for her eyes to meet his. "I will never hurt you, Cate," he promised. "Never. I proved it just now, didn't I?" When she didn't answer, he insisted, "Didn't I?"

She smiled again, a tremulous smile that was its own reward. "Yes," she agreed. "You did."

He knew it wasn't enough. But it was a start. He'd shown her last night she was capable of sexual pleasure. Tonight he'd demonstrated a man could find pleasure with a woman without hurting her. But it was a far cry from what he ultimately wanted with Cate. For her. Hell

no, not just for her, for himself, too. He wanted it all…
for both of them.

He sighed mentally, but didn't let it show on his face.
Instead, he drew Cate down to the bed with him and
pulled the sheet over them as he settled her in the crook
of his arm. "Warm enough?" he asked.

"Mmm-hmm." She nodded for emphasis.

"Okay if I hold you like this?" Naked, was what he
meant. Needing to know if she preferred he put his
T-shirt and boxers back on. Needing to know if she was
even the slightest bit uncomfortable with him naked.

She snuggled her cheek against his chest, and slid
her hand down until it was nestled against his bare hip.
"Please."

He smiled in the darkness. *One step at a time,* he reminded himself with a patience that didn't come naturally to him—he had to fight for it. *One baby step at
a time.*

Aleksandrov Vishenko's Learjet landed in the same
private airport in Arlington, Virginia, where it had
landed four days before. Again he was early, which
was par for the course with Vishenko. Meticulous planning had always ensured success…even when it came
to murder.

The sun was setting, and he pulled down the window shade to block the dying sun's rays, waiting with
as much patience as he could muster—hard-won patience given the past four days with no word from Nick
D'Arcy—and reviewing his plan in his mind, looking
for weaknesses.

Item one: pay D'Arcy the bribe and learn Caterina Mateja's whereabouts. Item two: dispatch his chief brigadier to dispose of her. The job wouldn't normally be handled by a man that high in the *Bratva* ranks, but Vishenko was taking no chances. Caterina *had* to die *now*, and he couldn't take the risk she would slip through his fingers again. Item three: recover the bribe. Ten million dollars was a lot of money. He might as well get the money back if he could. Item four: kill Nick D'Arcy in a way that would not only give him the revenge he craved for what D'Arcy had put him through, but would expose the chinks in the agency's armor. How good could they be if they couldn't even keep the head of their agency safe?

The agency had been riding high these past few years. Unknown to the general public, but fast becoming the darling of US law enforcement. D'Arcy's assassination would send shock waves through the entire law enforcement community, not just the agency. And Caterina's death would have the added bonus of sending a chilling message to anyone who was considering betraying him. It wasn't the first time he'd sent such a message—and it wouldn't be the last.

Four days after Cate had made love to him, Liam was still reiterating in his mind what he'd told himself then—*one baby step at a time*.

They'd made progress. He touched Cate constantly now. Natural touches—holding her hand as they hiked the trails around the cabin, touching her arm to draw attention to a doe and her fawn beside the river's edge,

taking the dishes from her as she washed and he dried.
Kissing her on impulse—light kisses, not passionate
ones, but kisses all the same. And she touched him, too.
Maybe not quite as often, but just as naturally. She'd
never again kissed him first, though. But she *had* re-
sponded when he'd kissed her. Shyly to start out with,
but eventually the shyness had given way to something
more. It was the something more that gave him hope.

They'd shared the same bed too, every night. They
hadn't made love, but Cate had slept in his arms. And
at no point had she panicked. At no point had she been
afraid of him. He wanted more, but he fought down his
desire. Cate wasn't ready for more—not yet. When she
was, he would know.

And she looked at him with love shining from her
pale blue eyes, turning them into stars. She never said
the words, but he could live without them. They were
just words. That didn't mean he didn't say the words to
her—he did. Every chance he had. Knowing in some
deep recess of his brain Cate desperately needed to
hear the words she couldn't say. Someday, when he'd
convinced her she was loved—that she was *worthy* of
being loved—she'd trust him enough to say the words
to him. He knew it.

Cate was constantly on his mind, but she wasn't the
only thing on his mind. His conscience was troubling
him, too.

He'd never killed a man with vengeance in his heart.
Although he hadn't felt exactly the same way since, it
bothered him—a lot—that he'd had those thoughts
about Aleksandrov Vishenko the other night. He wanted

to believe he was a better man than that. But he kept hearing Cody's voice in his head as he confessed what he'd done when Keira was shot. And he heard himself telling Cate, *"...we're only human...when someone we love is hurt, we want to hurt back..."*

All he could do was pray he'd never be put to the test. Pray he'd never come face-to-face with the man who'd hurt Cate so grievously. Because he didn't know what he'd do.

Cate sat on the cabin's front porch steps, watching as Liam and Callahan walked the clearing's perimeter. She could have gone with them—neither man would have objected—but she wouldn't have known what she was looking for the way the two men did, and she would probably have slowed them down.

Nick D'Arcy was right, she thought now. *Ryan Callahan's the best at this sort of thing.* Liam had shown her the traps Callahan had rigged, admiration evident in his voice and on his face as he explained what each item was for. *But Liam's the best, too. No one could be more protective. No one could keep me safe the way he can.*

She sighed softly. More than a week was gone. Liam had less than two weeks of his vacation left, and though he'd repeatedly assured her he wasn't leaving, they couldn't stay here forever, even if he didn't have a job to go back to. She'd already heard from D'Arcy via Callahan that the new trial date had been set. In a little less than three weeks she would be in a courtroom in Washington, DC. Face-to-face with Aleksandrov Vishenko and the other conspirators. And the new prosecutors wanted to meet with her ahead of time, so they could prep her testimony. Which meant heading back to DC two weeks from now.

She was terrified of testifying. Not because of Vishenko, but because Liam would know—as the whole world would know—the kind of woman she really was. Angelina had warned her—Alec, too—that the defense attorneys would do everything they could to discredit her. That they would rip her character to shreds if they could. So of course they'd try to make something out of the fact she hadn't literally been a prisoner the entire two years she'd been with Vishenko. They'd do their best to convince the jury she'd been Vishenko's willing mistress. That he'd dumped her. And that she was trying to get revenge on him by lying in court.

She rested her head against her knees. *You have to tell Liam,* her conscience told her sternly. *You can't let him find out when everyone else does.*

Two more weeks, she begged her conscience. *Just two more weeks. Is that too much to ask? Two weeks to be happy for once. Two weeks with the man I—*

Even in her thoughts she couldn't use the word. But it was there. And it hurt. Because even though she'd sworn she wouldn't risk one more thing, she had. She'd risked the only thing she had left to lose. And when she told Liam the truth, when he walked away, he'd take her heart with him. Leaving her with nothing.

Nick D'Arcy leaned back in his leather seat in the cabin of Vishenko's Learjet and shook his head. "No. I don't think so. It's not foolproof."

Vishenko cursed in Russian, then said in English, "It is not your call to make."

D'Arcy smiled coldly. "It is when I haven't told you where she is."

Vishenko clenched his jaw. "You *will* tell me. I will pay you the ten million you want, and you will tell me where she is. My men will take it from there."

"Not a chance. You want Caterina Mateja dead—and I don't blame you. If you don't kill her, if she lives to testify, you're going down. For life. But she's guarded. There's no way your men will get past her protectors—I know these men, and I'm telling you, no way. The only way for this to work is for me to arrange it. For the ten million you offered, I'll take you to her, and I'll get her alone. After that, it's up to you."

Vishenko considered this for a moment, weighing the pros and cons. Then he realized this was the perfect solution to his plan to kill both Caterina *and* Nick D'Arcy. And do it so quickly the chances of recovering his money were improved.

He hid his glee and returned the other man's cold smile. "Fine. I will pay you when you take me to her."

A deep belly laugh rumbled out of D'Arcy. "You must think I'm as stupid as the police and FBI agents you've bribed over the years," he said. "No, no, my friend." Sarcasm dripped from his words. "You will pay me up front, or the deal is off."

Vishenko shook his head. "Pay you ten million dollars for nothing but your word that you will disclose Caterina's location? I think not."

"Of the two of us," D'Arcy said softly, "whose word

can be believed?" He waited a moment, but when Vishenko didn't respond, he stood up. "Ah well," he said as he turned to go. "I guess you will just have to take your chances with the jury."

"Half," Vishenko said quickly, as he realized D'Arcy meant it—he would walk and take his information with him. "I will pay you half up front—a good faith payment. The other half I will pay when she is dead."

D'Arcy smiled again. "Good faith?" He laughed softly. "That's funny, coming from you." Then his smile faded, leaving nothing but cold, hard determination. "Deal," he said. "I won't offer you my hand to shake on it. Neither of us can be trusted that far."

"Deal," Vishenko said. "When will you take me to Caterina?"

"When I have the money safely in my possession, and not a moment before." He held up a cautionary hand. "But don't wait too long. I have arrangements to make if I'm going to get Ms. Mateja's protectors out of the way. It won't be easy doing it in such a way that her death isn't traced back to me. And I don't want to wait until just before the trial. Too many other factors could come into play, like the US Marshals Service and the FBI. So long as the agency has sole custody, I can make it happen. So let's get this done sooner rather than later."

Chapter 15

After lunch Cate asked Liam, "Dessert? There's still one piece of that apple pie left."

He patted his flat stomach and shook his head. "Better not," he said with a rueful smile. "I'm not getting much exercise here at the cabin—not like usual—so I have to be careful how much I eat."

"We've hiked every day," she protested.

"Yeah, but I usually jog five miles or so before breakfast in addition to my other activities. I can't jog up here. You eat it if you want."

She gazed at the covered pan with longing. "It's really good. Sheriff Callahan's wife is a great baker." Liam had told her who'd baked the bread, pie and cookies Callahan had supplied them with.

"I wish I—" She didn't finish her sentence. Cooking and baking were things she hadn't had the chance to do since she'd left Zakhar. Her mother had already been teaching her for several years when she died, so Cate knew much more than the basics. In fact, her father—traditional Zakharian father that he was—had praised Cate's skills in the kitchen, although she hadn't really thought that important at the time. She'd wanted to escape the traditional "home and hearth" role most Zakharians assigned to women and *be* someone. Accomplish something that would set her apart from everyone else.

She didn't feel quite the same way now. Not that she wanted to be a traditional Zakharian housewife, but she would have cherished the opportunity to cook and bake. Renting a furnished room in a boardinghouse though, rarely came with kitchen privileges. Heating things up over a hot plate was about the extent of her cooking nowadays.

"If you like pie, you'll like my mother's," Liam said. "I can't remember a time when she didn't bake every chance she got. There wasn't a holiday or a special occasion—Christmas, Thanksgiving, birthdays, stuff like that—where my mom didn't bake a special treat for the family or the entire neighborhood. Everyone says her pecan pie is to die for—and it is. You'd think she was Southern-born and raised, instead of a native Coloradan."

Cate couldn't keep the wistfulness out of her voice. "She sounds nice. The way you talk about her... I can tell she's special to you."

"Tell you what. After the trial is over, I'll take you

home to meet her. You'll love her, and I know she'll love you. She can teach you to bake, too, if you want. She can teach just about anyone any—" He broke off and started chuckling. "Well, not Keira. My sister refused to learn how to cook, so my mom gave up on her. But if you *want* to learn…"

She wasn't going to tell Liam that with a little practice there probably wasn't a lot his mother could teach her, because her own mother had already taught her well. But she yearned to meet Liam's mother. Not for what she could learn, but for what it meant. Meeting a man's mother in Zakhar was almost a sure sign a proposal was imminent. But even here in the US meeting a man's mother was a serious step—Cate knew that much about her adopted country. And for the first time she realized Liam *was* serious. He really meant it when he said he loved her.

If only she could believe he would still love her…if he knew the truth.

Five million dollars in cash—nothing larger than a hundred—was too much for a briefcase. The money had been delivered via licensed couriers to Vishenko in varying increments from different banks where his money was stashed, so as not to arouse too much suspicion. It now lay neatly stacked in a wheeled suitcase lying near the edge of the massive bed in the master bedroom of his Long Island estate. The same room where he'd first taken his pleasure of Caterina Mateja's body all those years ago—the same bed.

Caterina thought she'd escaped. She thought she

could bring him down. She would know soon just how wrong she was—no one got the better of Aleksandrov Vishenko. And no one testified against him. No one.

Five million. The first—and only—installment. Two hours from now he would be in Virginia again, and the money would exchange hands in the privacy of his plane, which was swept daily for audio and video devices that might have been planted by law enforcement. Which meant complete privacy was assured. No surveillance would record the exchange. And tomorrow… tomorrow his Learjet would take Nick D'Arcy and him to wherever Caterina was. He would teach her a lesson she would never forget. She would beg him one more time—then he would kill her. She would not live long enough to appreciate the lesson, but that could not be helped.

And when she died the sword of Damocles would finally be removed, once and for all, from above Vishenko's head.

Liam and Cate sat on the back porch, watching the sunset. His arm was around her waist, and she was resting her head against his shoulder. "It never gets old," she said as the last dying rays of the sun vanished behind the mountain, the amber sky fading into purple. One by one the stars began to appear, silver dots against the cloudless blue.

"Yeah," Liam said. "It never gets old." But he wasn't looking at the sky, he was looking down at Cate, and his expression was unmistakable.

When she realized where his attention was focused,

she turned her face to hide it against his neck, unable to meet the question in his eyes. "Please don't," she whispered.

"Don't what?"

"Don't look at me that way."

He lifted her chin with one firm but gentle finger, forcing her to face him. "You might as well ask me to stop breathing." He brushed his lips against her forehead. "I love you, Cate. And until you tell me you don't love me...until you tell me you'll *never* love me... I can't look at you and not want you. Fifty years from now I'll still look at you and want you."

"You can't know that."

"Yes, I can." His lips touched hers lightly, then he drew back. "What do you think love is, Cate? It's not just desire. It's not just here and now. It's a choice. A commitment. It's telling yourself 'I want to share everything with this person, now and in the future. Every joy. Every sorrow.'"

He breathed deeply. "But it's more than that. It's sharing the little things, too. Like a sunset. Like a waterfall. Laughing together over nothing—things that wouldn't be funny to anyone else, but are funny to the two of you. Love is going to sleep at night and waking up in the morning next to a woman who is all women to you. It's wanting to shield her from pain—knowing in your heart of hearts you can't—but wanting it all the same. It's giving her children you'll both love and cherish the way you love and cherish each other. It's watching the years take their toll, but still seeing in your mind's eye the beautiful woman she is inside, the woman you first fell in love with. It's wanting to be with her when you draw your last breath…or when she draws hers."

Tears filled her eyes, and she blinked rapidly to hold them back, but two tears escaped and trickled down her cheeks. Liam brushed them away with a gentle hand. "It's knowing she'll cry when you're not there…and that you'll cry when she's gone. But that's okay, Cate, because that's what love is. Needing someone to the exclusion of all others. I haven't just fallen in love with you. I *choose* to love you. That's how I know."

"Oh, Liam…" She was crying in earnest now, her cheeks wet with tears she couldn't suppress. And Liam was kissing her—eyes, cheeks, lips. Soft kisses. Gentle kisses. But when she kissed him back his kisses changed.

"Cate. Oh God, Cate," he breathed in between kisses that stole her breath and made her body ache in secret places. His hands were everywhere. Strong, sure, touching her everyplace that needed his touch.

Soon it wasn't enough. She wanted his hands on her bare skin, wanted to feel his warm body next to hers with nothing between them. She wanted to feel him moving inside her, joining their bodies together so they'd never be apart again. "Please…" she whispered against his lips. "Please love me…oh please…"

They undressed each other in the darkness. Cate wanted to see Liam, but she didn't want him to see her scars again, just in case, so she stopped him from turning on the bedside lamp when he placed something he'd retrieved from his overnight case on the nightstand. But the moonlight was enough for her to see his body—smooth, tanned skin over hard, rippling muscles. And that part of him she was going to take into her body was ready for her. Her breath came a little faster when she touched him and he swelled against her fingers, but she knew in her soul he would never hurt her. She just had to convince her body's reflexes.

He sat her down on the edge of the bed to remove her socks and shoes. Then, "Lift up," he told her, and when she did he slid her jeans down her hips, then off. When they were both completely naked, he knelt at her feet, gazed into her eyes and said, "You trust me, don't you?"

"Yes." She couldn't help that the word came out a little breathless.

"Then before we do anything else, let me do something for you." He placed his hands on her shoulders and exerted just enough pressure so she knew he wanted her to lie back.

"Okay." Again that breathless sound.

His hands moved to the inside of her knees, and again he exerted gentle pressure that told her exactly what he wanted of her. He settled between her parted legs, stroking her thighs with his warm hands, up and down, up and down. Each time coming ever closer to the apex of her thighs, sending tingling chills of excitement all through her. "Trust me, Cate," he said as he lowered his head.

She arched up and caught her breath on a sobbing moan when pleasure unlike anything she'd ever known coursed through her. Liam's tongue touched and teased, his hands held her firm as she writhed beneath him, and his breath was warm, sending shock waves through her as he loved her with his mouth again and again. Cate's hands grasped the sheet beside her, trying to find purchase as every sense concentrated in one location, as every muscle tightened ever tighter. Part of her wanted to beg Liam to stop, but she'd sworn she'd never beg for anything again—and besides, she'd die if he stopped. So she let him lead her higher and higher—up, up, up—until she couldn't take any more and she simply exploded.

She wasn't crying, but the physical and emotional release felt as if she had, and she reveled in it. She floated for a few seconds, just letting the little aftershocks control her, blissful peace permeating her entire being. Then Liam stood.

She heard a tearing sound and was vaguely aware of his movements. Suddenly he was there beside her on the bed, lying on his back and pulling her unresisting body on top of him. His breathing was as ragged as hers when he said, "Spread your legs, sweetheart." When she complied, she felt him nudging at the portal of her womanhood. "Guide me in, Cate," he pleaded. "Show me you want me as much as I want you."

Then and only then did she realize Liam had planned it this way from the beginning. He'd made sure he wouldn't hurt her with his entry, had made her come first so she would be exquisitely ready for him. And he was letting her be on top so she wouldn't feel forced in any way.

Love for him washed through her, an intense emotion she finally acknowledged in her consciousness as love. She grasped his erection—sheathed in the condom he'd donned for her protection—and seated him securely inside her. Then she flexed her muscles and pushed down, throwing her head back and catching her breath in wonder as he filled her completely…without pain. She rocked a little, but it didn't hurt at all. It felt… incredible. It felt…transcendent. It felt…like love.

His big body was trembling, as if his muscles were screaming at him to move…but he wouldn't. And she knew he was waiting for a sign from her that it was okay, that *she* was okay. She rocked again, pushing him even deeper, loving the feel of him so hot and hard and deep within her—the *rightness* of it. "Oh, Liam," she breathed as she braced her hands against his chest and continued rocking. Her nipples tightened until they ached, and she wanted his hands on her. Wanted him to caress her there. Everywhere. But he wouldn't…unless she asked. Because he loved her.

It was all up to her. Her choice. *Choose me,* he was saying. *Choose this. Choose love.* "Please," she whispered. "Please touch me. Please make love to me. Oh please, Liam, please."

She'd released a whirlwind. That was all she could think of as he guided her hips, showing her how to ride him like a wild stallion. Each time he left her body she ached to have him back, moving on him faster and faster, slick and smooth and so hot and tight the friction was sending her toward oblivion again, but it didn't hurt. She moaned his name, not wanting to go anywhere without him, wanting to know she'd pleased him as much as he was pleasing her. Then his hips grew frenzied, thrusting upward as he pulled her down onto him. He cried out her name, his body bucking beneath hers as hers milked his, and they came together.

Cate collapsed onto Liam's chest, boneless. Floating again, but this time was even better because he was inside her. Because she could hear his heart pounding in his chest as if he'd just run ten miles—just as hers was doing. Because his arms were holding her so close it was as if they were one.

When her pulse finally slowed, when she could finally breathe enough to speak, she touched her fingers to his cheek and murmured, "Thank you."

He made a sound as if he was suppressing a laugh, and she could feel him twitching inside her as his body shook. Then said, "You're very welcome." Just like a boy who'd been taught to be polite no matter what, and it made her gurgle with laughter. She sighed dreamily and rubbed her cheek against his chest, loving how it made her feel so warm and contented. Loving *him*.

"You planned it," she said an eternity later, after he'd discarded the condom and they'd settled back into each other's arms.

He seemed uncomfortable with that assessment. "Not exactly."

"Yes, exactly." She let one fingertip circle a flat male nipple. "That's when I knew I loved you," she added quietly.

His hand, which had been slowly stroking her back, stilled. "Say that again."

"That's when I knew I loved you," she dutifully repeated.

He sat up abruptly, bringing her with him. "Cate, are you sure?" He grasped her arms and held her away from him, as if he needed to see her face in the moonlight. "Don't say it because you're grateful and you think you have to."

"I'm not." She didn't care anymore that she was gambling her heart in one reckless move. "When I realized how careful you were to make everything so perfect for me, I knew there could never be another man in the whole world as perfect for me as you. And that's when I finally admitted to myself that I loved you." She smiled tremulously. "I think I loved you almost from the beginning, but I wouldn't let myself." She suddenly realized just how absurd that contradiction sounded, and she laughed softly. "I wouldn't let myself *acknowledge* it," she clarified.

Liam smiled, but then his smile faded. "So where do we go from here, Cate? D'Arcy told me the original plan was for you to disappear after you testify. That the Witness Security Program would provide you with a new identity, a new life somewhere. I want that for you. I want you to be safe. But I…"

After you testify…after you testify…

Those were the only words she could hear. It wasn't the plan for her to disappear that drove a stake in her heart without any warning at all. It was the reminder that once she testified, Liam would know the truth about her. "I don't know," she said, all lightheartedness gone. "I don't even know if I will live to testify."

Liam shook her once, as if to shock her out of the negative mind-set. "Don't say that. Don't even think it. You are *not* going to die."

"You can't know that." Suddenly she remembered saying the same thing to him earlier in the evening, about something completely different.

"Yes, I can." In his eyes was the memory that he'd said those same words to her, too. "I won't *let* anything happen to you, Cate. You hear me? I won't. Even if I die for it."

"Don't." She placed her hand over his mouth. "You think that makes it better for me? Imagining you sacrificing your life for mine?" Her breath was coming fast and ragged. "You really think if you died I would want to go on living?" She threw her arms around him and held him tight, laying her head against his shoulder. "I just found you," she whispered, as if that said it all.

His arms were just as tight around her, and his voice was husky. "I feel the same way. I just found you, Cate. I'm not going to lose you. I won't let it happen."

D'Arcy hefted the suitcase. "I won't bother counting it here," he told Vishenko. "But if it's short by so much as a dollar…"

"That is not a concern," Vishenko assured him. "So where is she? My pilot must file a flight plan."

"Tomorrow," D'Arcy said. "Assuming there is indeed five million dollars in here, I'll tell your pilot what he needs to know." He smiled coldly. "This plane can make the flight without refueling if you start with full tanks. I'll be here at seven. Plenty of time." With that he was gone.

Aleksandrov Vishenko watched D'Arcy walk across the tarmac, carrying the suitcase instead of rolling it. *Five million,* he reminded himself. It wasn't the first time he'd paid a bribe. And he was sure it wouldn't be the last. But he had never paid so much at one time to one man. He had every intention of recovering the down payment after D'Arcy's death tomorrow. His men were already working on a home invasion scheme that would, if necessary, force the location of the money out of D'Arcy's wife if it wasn't found in his house. There was still the slight possibility the money would be unrecoverable—in which case he would have paid five million dollars for his freedom. Expensive, but worth it. And he had the added incentive of making Caterina pay. Not to mention throwing the agency into turmoil once their highest-ranking official was eliminated in a gruesome fashion.

He walked over to a cabinet and removed the semiautomatic pistol it contained. The gun was new to him, but completely untraceable. He checked the action and the clip, even though he'd checked them several times before he left Long Island—he couldn't afford to have the pistol fail when he killed Caterina and the man who had sold her out.

Once they were dead that would leave only the extradition to Zakhar to worry about. And Vishenko wasn't particularly worried about extradition. He had money secreted in bank accounts around the world. If worse came to worst and his high-priced attorneys failed, he would buy himself a safe haven in some country with no extradition treaties. Not with the US, and not with Zakhar.

The cell phone chirped once, then stopped. Liam was out of bed in a flash and picked it up, but it didn't ring again. He tried to see if a missed call had registered, but it hadn't. And when he attempted to check voice mail it wouldn't go through. "Guess I'll have to go outside," he told Cate, who was awake now and watching him from the bed. He tugged yesterday's jeans on, not bothering with his boxers, zipped up but left the button undone and pulled on his T-shirt inside out. When he saw what he'd done he didn't bother changing it. He grabbed his shoulder holster from where he'd left it on the night-stand and shrugged it on, then picked up the cell phone again and went out on the front porch.

The air was early-morning cool, despite being late August. It would warm up later in the day, but right now, with the sun not yet over the horizon, Liam could have done with more than a T-shirt. He didn't worry about it—he didn't plan to be out here very long. Just long enough to check voice mail, and if nothing was recorded there, call Callahan to see if he was trying to contact them for some reason. Voice mail yielded nothing, so Liam punched in the number of Callahan's cell, which was answered almost immediately.

"Callahan."

"It's Liam Jones. Were you trying to reach us?"

"Yeah. I wanted to let you know two things. First, I've got an emergency here—a school bus hit a guardrail. Nobody hurt, but I'm not going to be able to make it out there this morning."

"No problem. Cate and I don't need—"

"Which brings me to the second thing," Callahan said, interrupting him. "D'Arcy called and there's a change of plan."

"Oh yeah? What?"

"The new prosecutors want to interview Cate now, not wait until the week before the trial. D'Arcy's not about to let her go to DC at this point—too dangerous. And he doesn't want the prosecutors to know where this place is—they don't have a need to know, you know?"

"Yeah, I know."

"He never gives away an edge if he can help it." Admiration—not something easily earned where Callahan was concerned, Liam knew—was evident in his voice. "So he doesn't want the prosecutors coming here. He wants Cate to meet them at the agency's safe house in Casper. It's not that far—if you take the other road and don't go through Black Rock it's only a couple of hours away."

"How long will the interview take?"

"He didn't say. Just that he needs her at the safe house this afternoon. He'll meet you there. Knowing him, he wants to make sure security is airtight before the prosecutors arrive."

"Okay," Liam said slowly. "What time?"

"Around two. If you get on the road by noon that should do it. It's not like you have to worry about traffic, even when you get to Casper. I don't have the address or the GPS coordinates of the safe house with me—I'll call you later, once I get back to the office."

"Okay," Liam said again. "Will we be coming back here tonight?"

"D'Arcy wasn't sure, but if I were you, I'd take everything you brought with you. In case there's another change of plan."

"What about the generator? If I turn it off the food in the refrigerator will spoil. But if we're not coming back here it'll go to waste anyway."

"Don't worry about it. Leave the generator on. If you come back tonight there's no problem. If you're gone more than a day, I'll swing by, empty the fridge and turn off the generator."

"Sounds good." He thought for a moment, then voiced his major concern. "You're sure the safe house is secure?"

Callahan chuckled. "Funny you should ask that. I asked Walker the same thing a few years ago when Mandy and my children were brought there for safe-keeping. He told me there are no guarantees in this world, but that he'd stayed there himself on an operation, and he knew the people who ran it. Far as I know, the same people are still running it."

"And?"

Callahan's voice went deadly soft. "And I trusted them to keep my wife and children safe. They did."

And that's the end of that *conversation,* Liam thought to himself with sudden amusement.

Chapter 16

Cate had already taken a quick shower and dressed for the day in jeans and a white cotton top with a blue eyelet ribbon around the neck by the time Liam returned. When he told her they were going to the safe house in Casper to meet with the prosecutors, she didn't object until he added, "Callahan said we should take everything with us, just in case."

"We're not coming back here?"

"It's one possibility. Something we should plan for, just in case. I think we'll come back here after you meet with the prosecutors. No matter how safe that safe house is, this cabin is safer. Especially since only D'Arcy and Callahan know we're here. But Callahan wasn't positive, so..."

"I see." She considered this for a moment. "What about the laundry?"

He stared at her blankly. "Laundry?"

"The sheets, pillowcases, towels, washcloths—all the things we used," she answered patiently. "This isn't a hotel. We can't just leave these dirty things behind for someone else to take care of."

It hadn't even occurred to him. There was no washer or dryer in the cabin, of course, so they'd been hand-washing their few clothes and hanging them to dry on the back porch in order to have clean clothes to wear every day—even their jeans dried in one day in the warm late summer sun. Now he wondered what Keira and Cody did about laundry. Everything had been clean when they arrived, so the Walkers had to do *something*. He just wasn't sure what.

Cate raised her eyebrows at him exactly the way his mom used to do when something should be obvious. "You think maybe there's a Laundromat in town?"

Duh, he thought. "Maybe. Black Rock's kind of small, but we can check. We don't need to be in Casper until two. We have time."

She didn't say anything, just began stripping the bed. Liam went into the bathroom and gathered up all the towels and washcloths, then swung into the kitchen and added the dishrag and kitchen towels to his pile. "Here," he said as he dumped his armful in the middle of the sheets she'd removed from the bed. Cate had already fetched the sheets and pillowcase Liam had used when he was sleeping on the cot, which he'd folded neatly and stacked on top of the collapsed cot he'd stored in the closet so it would be out of the way.

Cate said, "We can wash our dirty clothes at the same time." She quickly added her pajamas and the clothes she'd been wearing yesterday to the pile, then glanced expectantly his way. "Strip."

Liam grinned at her as he shrugged out of his shoulder holster and one-fisted his inside-out T-shirt off. "Why, darlin', I thought you'd never ask."

Her cheeks reddened, and Liam realized Cate was as much a novice at sexual banter as she was at sex. He was naked beneath his jeans, but he had no false modesty, so it took him only a couple of seconds to comply. He hadn't counted on his reaction to her watching him strip, though—which she did…in little sideways glances she thought were covert. Her pretending not to look was more arousing than if she'd openly stared. *Stand down,* he told his body as he tugged on boxers and clean jeans, but it wasn't very obedient, so the jeans were a tight fit.

He dropped his dirty clothes on top of the pile, then slid his arms around her and pulled her flush with his body. "I forgot something."

She looked up at him, questioning. "What?"

"Good morning," he said softly, kissing her forehead. Then his lips found hers and they stood there for several seconds, everything else forgotten. "Oh hell yeah," he said when their lips finally separated. "It's definitely a good morning."

Her cheeks were flushed, but all she said was, "Yes, it is."

When Liam finally let her go, Cate pulled the edges of the bottom sheet together and tied them firmly around the whole bundle. While she was doing that, he pulled on an olive green short-sleeved golf shirt and strapped on his shoulder holster. He grimaced, then added his blazer. "Can't go out strapped without covering up, even if it *is* summer," he explained, though she hadn't asked. "Here, I'll take that." He hefted the bundle over one shoulder.

Liam used the GPS and had no problem finding Black Rock, although it took longer than he expected because of the speed limit in the mountains. As he'd told Cate, Black Rock was small, but they *did* locate a Laundromat two blocks off Main Street. And wonder of wonders, it was already open for business—the sign said it opened at seven and it was just past eight when they arrived. Cate filled two empty washing machines while Liam wandered over to the change machine and tried to insert a twenty. The machine kept spitting the bill back at him, so he tried another without any luck.

"Machine's empty," said a woman sitting in the next row over, reading a magazine and glancing up from time to time to check her laundry in the dryers. "The drugstore next door will give you change…if you buy something. The pharmacy counter doesn't open until nine, but the store itself opened at eight."

"Thanks," Liam told her. To Cate he said quietly, "I don't want you out of my sight, so come with me. I think it's safe to leave the laundry here—we'll be right back."

Startled, she said, "You really think someone will find me here?"

"One in a million chance, but I'm not risking it."

She gave him a somber look, as if he'd reminded her of the constant threat of danger she lived under. "Okay."

Liam made a beeline for the back of the drugstore, Cate in tow. He knew exactly what he was going to buy. He'd used his emergency condom last night, and based on Cate's positive reaction to making love they would need more. No way would he make love to her without protecting her. But no way would he turn Cate down if she wanted to make love again, either, just because he was unprepared. And despite the fact he had a reputation within the DSS for having a way with the ladies—just as his brother had before he'd gotten married—he didn't carry a stash of condoms with him as a general rule. He'd been lucky he had one in the emergency overnight case he kept in his SUV—the case he'd transferred when he'd switched SUVs with the special agent from the agency. But now...

When he found the aisle he wanted he automatically reached for his favorite brand, then hesitated. He hadn't really given it a lot of thought before, but there was quite a variety of condoms to choose from, some of which were designed more to heighten a woman's pleasure rather than a man's. He turned to Cate. Her cheeks were bright pink and she was looking everywhere except at him.

Her shyness over something as prosaic as this charmed him, and he said, "You probably don't have a preference. Right?"

Her gaze flickered toward him, then away again. "Last night…" she managed before her voice trickled away.

Okay, so he wasn't dense. She meant what he normally used was perfectly acceptable to her. He grabbed a box of twenty-four off the shelf.

At the checkout Liam added a couple of packaged honey buns since they'd skipped breakfast, then told the cashier with his most winsome smile, "I need change for the Laundromat, too. Could I get a roll of quarters, please?"

Cate and Liam headed back to the cabin near Granite Peak almost two hours later, with the clean and folded laundry sitting neatly stacked on the backseat. The drugstore bag—with its box of condoms—lay wedged in the space between their seats, and Cate's gaze continually drifted in its direction as she thought about what that meant.

Vishenko had never worn a condom. Why would he? He didn't give a damn about protecting her or any of the women he'd raped and abused in his life. She was profoundly grateful she'd never gotten pregnant, had never ended up with a sexually transmitted disease, either, but neither fact was a virtue in Vishenko—he hadn't cared. If she'd gotten pregnant he would probably have forced her to have an abortion, a dilemma that had torn her apart at the time. Not that she wanted his child—the idea made her sick—but that in aborting his child she would also be aborting her own, something she couldn't fathom.

But she hadn't gotten pregnant. Maybe she couldn't get pregnant at all—how could she know? Early on Liam had said his mother wanted more grandchildren, and the way he'd talked last night told her children were something he envisioned for himself, too...eventually. Which meant that even if he didn't walk away when he found out the truth, would he still want her if she was barren?

Then other words Liam had said last night came back to her. *"What do you think love is, Cate?... It's a choice. A commitment... I haven't just fallen in love with you. I choose to love you..."*

She wanted to believe him. She wanted to believe he'd chosen to love her and always would, no matter what, just as she would always love him. But that last little doubt clung to her, refusing to go away. Because if he could *choose* to love her, he could also choose differently—he could choose not to love her.

"Let's pack up," Liam told Cate once they'd put away the clean sheets and towels.

"Okay." Cate pulled her small suitcase from beneath the bed where she'd stored it. She didn't have much to pack. A few changes of clothing—including what they'd just washed that morning. Her toothbrush and toothpaste. The comb and brush the Morgans had provided her with at the first safe house.

When everything had been packed she stared at the pitiful contents of her suitcase for a minute, the sum total of her possessions at this point. It wasn't all she owned, of course. She had a few belongings back in

Zakhar, in her suite in the palace. And she had some clothes and things in her hotel room in DC—which reminded her she needed to ask someone about that.

As she stood there she realized she'd spent her entire adult life expecting to move on at a moment's notice. She'd always told herself she couldn't afford to become attached to *things* she might have to abandon. And not just things. People, too. She'd made no friends in the six years she'd been on the run—for their safety as well as for her own. She'd reconnected with Angelina after Alec rescued her, and Queen Juliana had been exceptionally kind and friendly toward her once she'd moved into the palace, but Cate had made no attempt to get in touch with any of her former friends in Zakhar— she couldn't have lied about where she'd been all these years, but she couldn't have borne to tell anyone the truth, either, and have them look at her with disdain... or even worse, with pity.

But she wasn't the same woman she'd been a year ago. Not the same woman she'd been a month ago, or even two weeks ago. Liam had changed her. Despite telling herself not to hope...not to dream about the fairy-tale ending, she *was* hoping. She *was* dreaming. Despite her fear that Liam would no longer love her if he knew the truth, hope refused to die.

She absentmindedly picked up her book from the nightstand and tucked it beneath her pajamas, then closed the suitcase lid and zipped it up. "I'm packed," she told Liam in a voice that didn't betray any of what she'd been thinking.

"Me too," he said as he swung his duffel bag over one

shoulder. "How about a late lunch on the road? I don't know about you, but I'm a little tired of eating stuff out of a can. If we leave now we can stop in Kaycee and have a nice lunch, and still be in Casper by two."

"Sounds good."

Cate realized she was going to miss the cabin as she followed Liam out the door. And not just the cabin—she would miss her life here. She would miss hiking the trails with Liam, which reminded her of hiking the mountains around Drago when she was a girl. She would miss the quiet serenity. She would miss the isolation. Most of all, she would miss the sense of peace and security that had flowed around her this past week. *You were happy here,* she told herself now. And not just because of Liam, although nothing would have been the same without him.

"I hope we come back," she told him as she pulled the door shut behind her.

Aleksandrov Vishenko's Learjet landed at the airport in Buffalo, Wyoming, and taxied toward the terminal. The two passengers—Vishenko and D'Arcy—had barely spoken to each other for the entire duration of the flight. Now D'Arcy unbuckled his seat belt and said, "I've arranged an agency car for myself. I knew you'd want to rent your own."

Vishenko turned his cold gaze on the other man. "You are not taking me to Caterina? What did I pay you for?"

"You paid me for her location. And you paid me to make sure her protectors were out of the way, which

I've done. So I'll take you to her, but I won't stay. I'm sure you don't want a witness to murder."

Vishenko's mind was working furiously. He'd planned on killing D'Arcy first, then taking his time with Caterina. But if D'Arcy had his own transportation, if he merely pointed him in the right direction instead of taking him all the way there, that could throw a kink in the works. He would have to somehow lure D'Arcy into accompanying him to wherever Caterina was located. He would also have to assume D'Arcy would be armed, and take that into account. He wasn't armed now—his men would never have let the other man board the plane otherwise—but D'Arcy wasn't a fool. Just because he'd never been able to legally pin anything on Vishenko didn't mean he was foolish.

Perhaps D'Arcy suspected a double cross, and that's why he'd arranged his own transportation. Perhaps he suspected what Vishenko had in mind for him—he *did* have the reputation for being uncannily omniscient. If that was the case, Vishenko would have to postpone killing him.

The other five million was sitting in a suitcase by Vishenko's seat. He'd brought it along just in case D'Arcy had insisted on seeing it before their departure—and he had. But Vishenko had no intention of giving it to him now...or ever.

Liam and Cate were almost all the way to Kaycee when she suddenly gasped and turned to him, dismayed. "My books! I left my books in the cabin."

Liam eased his foot off the accelerator. "Are you sure?"

"Yes, I'm sure." She pounded the heels of her hands against her forehead as if to knock some sense into her head. "I put them in the closet so they'd be out of the way. I only packed the one I was reading." She grasped his arm. "We have to go back. We have to!"

"If we do we'll be late getting to Casper. And we won't have time to stop for lunch."

"Please, Liam. I don't care about lunch."

"It's likely we'll be going back there tomorrow or the next day anyway, so—"

"But you said yourself we might not. I can't leave my books, I just can't." Her voice took on a note of desperation. "*You* gave them to me."

How well he remembered that moment. Cate had been as giddily happy over those few books he'd bought her as if he'd given her diamonds. If anything prevented them from going back to the cabin...

He saw an exit coming up and flicked on his turn indicator. His stomach was already growling—one honey bun while doing laundry didn't really cut it for him—and now they would miss lunch, too. But Cate expected so little and asked for even less—he was damned if he wouldn't do this one little thing for her.

They pulled into the dead end near the cabin just before one. Liam hadn't even shifted into Park before Cate had her seat belt off and her door open. He snagged her arm just in time, and pulled her back. "Hang on a sec," he told her, turning off the engine and pocketing the keys. "Don't go anywhere without me, okay?"

"Sorry. I was just—"

"I know," he said, cutting her off. "But just because we were safe here when we left doesn't mean we shouldn't exercise caution now." He undid his own seat belt and said, "Come on, let's get those books and get back on the road."

They made their careful way down the path to the cabin, Liam in the lead. They were halfway there when Liam stopped abruptly, his eyes on the ground, and Cate almost ran into him.

"What's wrong?"

His face was grim. "Something's not right."

"What do you mean?"

"Look." He pointed at the dirt path. At first she didn't know what he was talking about because all she saw were several sets of footprints crisscrossing each other, leading to and from the cabin. But then she got it— the top set of footprints headed *toward* the cabin, not away from it.

"Sheriff Callahan?" she suggested.

"Maybe. But if it's him, where's his SUV? Besides, he knows we're not there. And he told me he wouldn't come out here unless we were gone more than a day."

An icy chill ran down her spine, and despite the warm summer day she shivered. And when Liam drew his SIG SAUER from its shoulder holster, she knew it was scarier than he was letting on—which was bad enough. She touched his forearm. "Let's go back."

He shook his head. "We need to know if someone

found this place. If he tried to take this path without knowing what to watch out for and avoid, Callahan's trap—the one right before the clearing—would stop him. If it's Callahan, the trap will be unsprung. Come on." Quietly, so quietly Cate couldn't believe it, Liam moved toward the clearing. He'd gone several yards before he turned around and saw her standing frozen exactly where he'd left her. He held a finger to his lips, then waggled his fingers for her to move toward him. She wasn't quite as stealthy as he'd been, but she was proud of the way she managed to make very little sound.

Even though Cate knew it was there, she couldn't actually see Callahan's trap until Liam pointed at it silently, and when she saw it was intact she let out the breath she'd been holding. She started to speak, but again he put his finger to his lips, indicating silence. His left hand pulled her close and he pressed his lips to her ear.

"Even though there's no one in the trap, something still feels off." It was uttered in an undertone, not a whisper. "It's probably nothing, but stay here just in case. I'm going to reconnoiter a bit. If everything's okay, I'll come back and get you."

He tugged the keys to the agency's SUV from his pocket and started to press them into her hand, but then he must have remembered she couldn't drive and a look of frustration crossed his face as he shoved the keys back into his pocket. Then he said in that same undertone, with his lips next to her ear, "If you hear gunfire, run back toward the SUV but keep going until you hit the main road. Don't stop for anything."

She started to protest that she wasn't going to leave him if he was in trouble, but he put his hand over her mouth before she could utter a word. "Please, Cate. Just do it, okay? It's the only way you can help me."

She struggled with her heart, but knew she had to do this for him. "Okay." She mouthed the word against his hand.

He slid his watch from his wrist and handed it to her. "If I'm not back in ten minutes, gunfire or no gunfire, run like hell. Promise?"

She nodded, then glanced down at the watch to see what time it was now. When she looked up Liam was gone. Her heart had already been pounding, but the minute he disappeared from sight it kicked into overdrive. She tried to calm her heartbeat by taking several deep breaths and watching the second hand on Liam's analog watch tick around one full circuit, then two. But watching the second hand only made her more anxious, so after another minute she stopped and looked up instead.

A sound from the path behind her made her whirl around. Her heart skipped a beat, then accelerated into the rat-a-tat-tat of machine gun fire.

Evil incarnate confronted her. "Hello, Caterina," Aleksandrov Vishenko said. Then he raised his pistol.

Chapter 17

Liam crept around the cabin's perimeter, easily avoiding Callahan's traps. Thanking God silently he knew the location of every single one. The only sounds he heard were natural to the forest, and there was no movement from the direction of the cabin. But he wasn't convinced. His sixth sense still had him on high alert. A burst of speed brought him to the steps at the bottom of the back porch, his SIG SAUER raised, his finger on the trigger.

When there was still no sound or movement from the cabin, Liam mounted the steps slowly, cautiously, placing his feet where the nails bound the cross boards to the supporting beams, so they wouldn't creak. Then he was at the back door. He peered through the window and spied a blonde woman sitting at the kitchen table drinking a cup of something, with her back to the door.

Suddenly the barrel of a gun was pressed against his temple, and a rough voice said, "Federal agent. Move and you're dead."

Adrenaline jolted through Liam's system—the body's natural fight-or-flight response. But then he realized with shock he recognized the voice. Incredulous, he said, "Cody?"

"Liam?" A large hand grabbed his shoulder and pulled him around. Then his brother-in-law cursed, long and low. "What the hell are you *doing* here?" Cody demanded.

"I could ask you the same thing."

"You're supposed to be halfway to Casper by now."

"How the hell do you know that?" Then Liam got it. "Callahan. Callahan told you. What the hell is going on?"

Cody reached around Liam and shoved open the kitchen door, then pushed him inside. When he did, the blonde turned around, and Liam's startled eyes met his sister's beneath the blond wig that was remarkable in its resemblance to Cate's hairstyle. "Keira?"

"Damn it, Liam, what are you doing here?" she threw at him. "You're not supposed to be here. Where's Cate?"

Like the wheels on a slot machine spinning round and round, then falling into place one by one, everything suddenly clicked for Liam. "It's a trap," he said slowly, knowing the truth of his words even before it was confirmed by the expression on Keira's face. "You set a trap for Vishenko with Cate as the bait. And you're Cate."

He whirled on Cody. "Why didn't you tell me?"

Cody shook his head. "Need to know," he said softly. "This is an agency op…and you're DSS, not one of ours. You weren't supposed to be here, so you didn't need to know."

"Damn it, you should have told me anyway." Then his eyes widened and his voice dropped to a whisper. "Cate. Oh my God. Cate." He spun around to his sister. "Vishenko's on his way, isn't he?" He grabbed her arms and shook her hard. *"Isn't he!"*

She didn't answer his question, just posed one of her own. "Where is Cate?"

Cate's throat was so dry she couldn't have spoken even if she'd wanted to. Horrifying dreams of this moment had haunted her for years, nightmare visions of Vishenko finding her. Touching her. *Owning* her. She would rather die than submit to him again.

Then she saw the expression in his eyes, and she knew she *was* going to die. The only thing she didn't know was whether she would die in time to prevent him from raping her again.

"No," she whispered to herself, shaking her head slightly. "No." Her fingers tightened until they formed fists. *"No."*

"I left her on the path…told her to run if she heard gunfire." Liam made a rush for the back door but Cody blocked him with his body and pushed him backward.

"Where on the path?" Cody demanded. "Just, *wait!*" he ordered when Liam tried to fight him off.

"Right before the clearing. Right beside Callahan's

trap. Let me go, Cody," he panted, desperate to get to Cate. "She's out there alone."

"No, she's not. Callahan's out there. McKinnon, too. She's not alone."

"You really thought you could get away with it?" Vishenko asked softly, dropping the hand with the pistol to his side as he took a step closer. As if his ego wanted to control her even without the gun, the way he'd controlled her years ago. "You really thought I would let you testify against me? *You?*" He laughed sardonically, and she took a step backward as he took another forward. "Ah, Caterina," he mocked. "I always enjoyed that little game."

She found her voice. "What game?"

"That little game you played, pretending to fight me."

Her breath rasped in her throat. "It wasn't a game."

His smile widened. "Not at first, true. You fought me like a woman possessed. Your screams that first time…ahh, I can still hear them in my mind." The sick, twisted pleasure in his voice, the avid expression on his face appalled and repulsed her, just as they had all those years ago.

"You should never have run, Caterina. You forced me to find substitutes for you." She closed her eyes momentarily, sick to her soul, imaging the terror and agony countless other women must have suffered, just as she'd suffered.

"But none of them were as beautiful as you," he continued. "And none of them were as satisfying because none of them fought me as you did…until you surrendered."

Her eyes shot open and she shook her head. "Never," she said fiercely. "I never surrendered."

He laughed, an ugly, gloating sound. "Oh but you did, Caterina. You can't have forgotten."

"*That* was the game," she insisted.

"Was it? You think a jury would believe it?" When her eyes widened, he said, "I have associates who will testify—truthfully—to what they saw." He laughed again. "They don't even need to lie under oath."

"*Never* willingly. Yes, I submitted." And had despised herself for years because she'd done so. But now—facing Vishenko—she faced the truth. The *real* truth. And she knew she'd been wrong to blame herself for surviving the only way she could. *I did what I had to do,* she told herself now. *No one else was going to save me back then. I had to save myself.* "I would never have escaped if I hadn't submitted. But I was *never* willing."

"We will never know who the jury will believe, will we?" He took a step closer. "Beg me, Caterina," he said now. "I promised myself you would beg me again to let you go, just as you did the first time."

"No."

He gestured with the gun. "To save your life, you will not beg?"

"You'll kill me anyway."

He smiled and said softly, "You were always too smart for your own good." When she didn't respond, he admitted, "Yes, I will kill you anyway. I need to make an example of you. No one has dared testify against me for years—I can't allow you to testify either. Even with the witnesses I have lined up to discredit your testimony, I can't risk it." He smiled his ice-cold smile. "But first I will make you beg…and scream." His head inclined toward the dense woods surrounding them. "Go ahead, Caterina. Scream. No one will hear you… except me."

He was wrong. If she screamed, Liam would come running, would try to save her. If she screamed, Vishenko would shoot him, too. *"You really think if you died I would want to go on living?"* she'd told Liam and she knew it for the truth. She couldn't risk his life.

Memories of him flooded her consciousness, and as plain as if he was standing next to her, she could hear him saying, *"What do you think love is, Cate?… It's wanting to be with her when you draw your last breath…or when she draws hers."*

An eerie calm settled over her, almost as if Liam's arms were enfolding her, holding her safe, and she drew courage from it. She knew she was going to die, but Liam was with her in her mind and that was all that mattered. "No," she said, shaking her head, determination tightening her muscles. "I won't scream. I won't beg. And you won't rape me, ever again."

He cocked his head to one side, considering. "No? Perhaps you are right." He sighed with real regret. "It is too bad, Caterina. I would have enjoyed having you one last time."

"Federal agents! Freeze!"

The harsh voices came out of nowhere, slicing through the air, just as Vishenko raised his gun once more. But even before that, a hard, male body crashed into Cate's, knocking her out of Vishenko's line of fire as he squeezed the trigger.

Gunshots rang out from several directions almost simultaneously, slamming into Vishenko's body. He tottered a few steps, a look of utter surprise on his face. He dropped the gun and fell to his knees, his hands clutching his chest, while the small blossoms of red that had first appeared there grew larger and larger. Then he pitched forward.

Pinned to the ground by the heavy weight on top of her, dazed and confused by everything that had just happened, Cate tried to take it all in as four people swarmed onto the narrow path. The smallest person—a woman she realized, with blond hair similar to her own—kicked the gun away from Vishenko's outstretched hand while still keeping her own gun steadfastly pointed at him. Another person—a man she'd met when Alec and Angelina found her—knelt beside the body and felt for a pulse.

"Dead," Cody Walker said, and by his tone Cate knew he wasn't sorry.

A third person, another man she recognized—Trace McKinnon—lowered his weapon, then glanced in Cate's direction and cursed fluently.

From behind her, strong hands lifted the weight from her body. Only then did she realize something warm and sticky was seeping through her clothing. When she rolled over she saw Sheriff Callahan propping Liam upright against his shoulder. She watched in horror as

Liam coughed up blood once…twice…then sagged unconscious against the man holding him.

"Walker!" Callahan barked, reaching over and ripping Liam's jacket open, then raising up his shirt to expose the two bloody gunshot wounds caused by the bullet that had entered Liam's body just above his waist and exited out the other side.

"Oh no!" The words didn't come from her own mouth, Cate realized. They were coming from the blonde as she and Walker hurriedly converged on Liam, blocking Cate's view.

Gentle hands helped her rise to a sitting position. "You okay?" McKinnon asked her as one hand moved impersonally over the damp patches of blood on her back. "Were you shot?"

"No, I… Liam," she said disjointedly. "His blood, not mine." She clutched McKinnon's arms. "He's going to be okay, isn't he?"

He didn't answer her, just tapped an earpiece in his ear. "We've got a situation here. We need a medical team, stat. No, sir," he continued. "It's Jones—explanations can wait." Cate couldn't hear the other side of the conversation, but even hearing only one side was enough to get the gist. McKinnon glanced around and made a face of frustration. "You can't land a medevac chopper here at the cabin—there's no way. The main road's our only chance. You get a chopper there, we'll meet you." He listened for a couple of seconds. "Yes, sir, will do."

Desperate to know Liam was going to make it, Cate turned back to stare at the knot of people frantically working on him, but she couldn't see much.

McKinnon's voice was sharp and staccato when he told the people surrounding Liam, "D'Arcy's calling for a medevac chopper. I told him we'd meet him at the main road."

Walker stood up, and suddenly Cate could see Liam's ashen face, bloody lips and the pressure bandage they'd strapped around his body. "The cot," Walker said, his voice harder than she'd ever heard it. And she knew it was bad. Really bad. "I'll get the cot from the cabin and we can carry him that way."

"SUV," Cate choked out, unable to tear her gaze away from Liam's face, willing his eyes to open. Willing him to speak. "The keys are in his pocket. If you get him as far as the SUV, you can save time by driving to the main road."

Cate sat in the waiting room, apart from the others. Liam had been airlifted to this hospital in Sheridan and was still in surgery, even though it had taken them more than an hour to drive here after the helicopter had thundered away. *Still in surgery is a good thing,* she reminded herself. It meant he was still alive. She clung to that hope, but in her head she was hearing Liam's voice telling her, *"I won't let anything happen to you, Cate... even if I die for it."*

"Don't die," she whispered now, wishing Liam could hear her. "Don't die." She stared at the scars on her wrists, remembering how Liam had kissed them and called them badges of honor. She would give anything to have him kiss her again. Hold her tight. Hold her safe. But not sacrifice his life for her. Not that. She'd never wanted that.

Cate was vaguely aware when Sheriff Callahan walked into the room, joining the other three. She knew he'd stayed behind to officially see to the disposition of Vishenko's body, and to confer with Nick D'Arcy. She didn't know why D'Arcy had been close by and not in Casper where he was supposed to meet her—and she hadn't asked. She'd been too concerned about Liam to worry about inconsequential things.

Since the sheriff was wearing a shirt again—he'd used his for the pressure bandage on Liam—Cate assumed he'd stopped off at his home. But everything seemed so distant, as if she was seeing the world through a camera lens, and nothing around her really reached her. All she could think of was Liam as she'd last seen him, strapped to a gurney, being loaded into the helicopter that just might make it to the hospital in time to save his life.

Liam. *Maybe he's okay,* she thought, desperately wanting it to be the truth. *Maybe it's not that bad.* Or maybe he needed a miracle.

She clasped her hands together and bent her head as a sudden, urgent need rose in her, a need she tried to quash...but couldn't. She hadn't prayed for more than eight years. Had thought what she'd suffered at Vishenko's hands had killed her faith...in God and in the goodness of mankind. But Liam had proved her wrong—there *was* goodness in the world, and he was a shining example. Her knight in shining armor. If she was wrong about mankind, then...

At this moment she fervently wanted to believe in a just and merciful God, the way Liam believed. "Don't let him die," she prayed. "Oh God, if You can hear me, please don't let him die."

Someone came over and sat down beside her, placing her hand on Cate's folded hands. She glanced up and saw it was Liam's sister. Keira had removed the blond wig on the way to the hospital and ruffled her red-gold curls. Now she looked just as Cate remembered her from when they'd met last year.

"What were you and Liam doing at the cabin?" Keira asked quietly. "You were supposed to be long gone."

Cate bit her lip. "My fault," she said, guilt swamping her. "I left my books behind." She squeezed her eyes shut as the memory came into sharp focus—Liam turning the SUV around and driving back miles for nothing more than books that were precious to her because… "Liam gave them to me," she whispered. "I just wanted…just wanted…" She pressed the heels of her palms against her closed eyes to hold back the tears.

Keira didn't say anything, just waited patiently for Cate to regain her composure. Cate breathed slowly, deeply, until she had herself under control, then dropped her hands in her lap and looked at the woman Liam called his baby sister. Remembering everything he'd told Cate about her. Remembering Keira had been shot a few years back, had deliberately stepped in front of someone to take a bullet meant for him, to save his life. The same way Liam had done for Cate.

In her head she could hear Liam saying, *"What do you think bravery is, Cate? It's conquering your fear*

*and doing what you have to do in the instant you have
to do it..."*

"Were you afraid?" she blurted out, needing to know
what Liam had felt when he'd thrown his body over hers,
shielding her from harm. When Keira's brows drew together in a question, she rushed to clarify. "When you
were shot. When you put yourself between a bullet and
someone else, were you afraid?"

Keira considered the question for a moment. "If I'd
thought about it, probably. I'd probably have been terrified. But I didn't have time to think about it—I just
did it. It was something I had to do...because I was the
only one who could do it."

"That's what Alec said last year about my cousin,
Angelina," Cate whispered. "She saved his life, you
know."

Keira nodded. "I know."

"Liam said—" She swallowed hard to keep her emotions at bay. "Liam said you have to go on instinct. You
don't have time to consciously think about what you're
doing. You just have to pray your instincts are right."

"He's right." Keira was silent for a moment, watching Cate with those soft brown eyes so like Liam's,
then shattered the last remnants of Cate's self-control.
"You love him."

Cate caught her breath on a sob as tears welled, but
she fought them back. "How could I not?" she asked,
choking a little. "You...he's your brother, so maybe you
don't see him as I do, but..."

"He's my brother, but I know he's pretty special. All
my brothers are."

"Alec is a wonderful man, and I admire him, too. But Liam…" Fresh tears threatened. "I didn't want to love him. I didn't want to love anyone because I don't des—" She broke off as she realized what she was saying. Who she was saying it to.

"Because you don't deserve to be loved?" Keira asked, her voice steady. "Is that what you were going to say?" When Cate didn't respond, just turned her head away, Keira said softly, "You're so wrong about yourself, Cate. If Liam loves you—and he *does* love you, doesn't he?"

"He thinks he does."

"I know my brother. If he says he loves you, he does. And if he loves you, then you deserve to be loved."

"He doesn't know…" Cate's voice trailed off miserably.

"Doesn't know what?"

"That I… I wasn't Vishenko's prisoner for the entire time I was with him." The confession poured out of her. "Yes, he raped me." She shuddered at the memories she would never be able to completely suppress. "And yes, he kept me a prisoner for…it seemed like forever. And I *did* fight him…at first. But eventually I realized the only way to escape was to…to pretend. To let him think he'd won. To let him think I was…willing."

Keira's next words dropped like a bombshell. "I know. We heard."

"What?" Suddenly light-headed, Cate stared at Liam's sister in incomprehension.

"When Vishenko confronted you on the path, we heard everything he said. Everything you said."

The constriction in her throat only allowed her to utter one rasping word. "Liam?"

Keira nodded. "All of us. But, Cate," she said, placing a comforting hand over both of Cate's hands again. "He already knew."

She shook her head in denial. "He couldn't. I never told him."

"He had to know, because he wasn't shocked. I saw his face, Cate. He… I've never seen him so angry. But he wasn't shocked."

She couldn't take it in. Liam had known? Had he known all along? *Did Alec tell him?* she wondered feverishly. Then she remembered Liam denying Alec had told him anything except who she was running from when she went underground. That Alec had said anything else should come from Cate herself.

She breathed a quick sigh of relief that Alec hadn't betrayed her trust. But the pain returned sharp and deep when she realized somehow Liam had known the truth anyway, even though she'd never told him. Had he known when he said, *"You can tell me anything. Don't you know that by now?"* Had he known when he said, *"What do you think love is, Cate?... It's a choice. A commitment..."* Had he known when he said, *"I haven't just fallen in love with you. I choose to love you..."*

And when he'd made love to her so tenderly, so carefully. Wanting to make it right for her however he could, because he knew what she'd endured at Vishenko's hands and wanted to break through her mental barriers. Had he already known the truth, the truth she so desperately wanted to keep from him…because she so desperately wanted him to love her?

Then she thought about what Keira had said, that Liam—that all of them—had overheard what had passed between Vishenko and her, and a hot tide of shame and humiliation swept through her. She'd walked into that courthouse days ago, prepared to enter the courtroom and be vilified in the eyes of the jury…and in the eyes of the world. "'I am one,'" she'd told herself that morning—a lifetime ago—believing she could do it. But she hadn't been prepared for this. To be confronted with her sordid past after Liam had told her to relinquish it, to let him shoulder the burden for her because she'd carried it long enough…

A sudden churning in her stomach warned her and she lurched to her feet, making a mad dash for the ladies' room. She made it just in time. When the violent reaction was over, she realized Keira had followed her and was silently offering her a warm, damp wad of paper towels to wipe her mouth.

Still shaking, Cate used the paper towels, then rinsed out her mouth several times. Keira watched her, then asked quietly, "You want to talk about it?" When Cate shook her head, Keira leaned against the sink, crossed one leg over the other and said conversationally, "You know, when Nick D'Arcy asked me to participate in this op, Cody didn't want me to do it. He thought it was too dangerous."

"Op?" Cate's brain hadn't focused on it before, but all at once she wondered what Keira had been doing there at the cabin. Not to mention her husband and Trace

McKinnon. Wondered how Vishenko had known where to find her. "You asked me what I was doing at the cabin," she said slowly, "but you didn't say why you were there. No one was supposed to know where Liam and I were except Nick D'Arcy and Sheriff Callahan."

Keira drew a deep breath and exhaled slowly through pursed lips, whistling under her breath, obviously trying to decide how much to tell Cate. "Baker Street—Nick D'Arcy," she amended, then explained, "We call him Baker Street in the agency. Anyway, D'Arcy knew the attempt on you in the courthouse had to be an inside job. Nothing else made sense. And even though you were still willing to testify, without corroborating testimony from the other witness—the one he was fairly sure Vishenko had killed—he knew there was a chance Vishenko would get off. With you in safekeeping, he decided to go for a long shot."

"I don't under—"

"Bait a trap…with you."

Chapter 18

"Only not you, if you see what I mean," Keira was quick to add. "I was supposed to be the bait, made up to look like you from a distance. D'Arcy couldn't risk you because he still needed you to testify in the conspiracy trial. And besides, he has a thing about keeping witnesses safe. Long story."

"I know," Cate said. "He used to be a US marshal. He told me about it when he...when he convinced me to come here."

Keira continued as if Cate hadn't interrupted. "So he set it all up to make Vishenko believe he was willing to sell you out. Since your location was a closely guarded secret—*no* one knew where you were except the four of you, and he put out the word through channels that only the agency knew where you were—he knew Vishenko couldn't get that information from any other source. It *had* to come from D'Arcy. Which meant Vishenko had to try to bribe him.

"His plan worked beautifully. D'Arcy had Vishenko dead to rights on bribery and conspiracy to commit murder. In addition to the money—the serial numbers of which, by the way, were recorded by the banks where Vishenko withdrew the cash from his various accounts for the bribe, proving the money came from him—he also had Vishenko on audiotape offering the bribe and soliciting your murder."

Cate was puzzled. "How did he manage that? When I knew him, Vishenko was extremely cautious about wiretaps, listening devices and…oh, everything of that nature. I can't see him letting himself be recorded by Mr. D'Arcy."

Keira's lips twitched in sudden amusement. "Two years ago D'Arcy had knee replacement surgery on his left knee. He had the brilliant idea of using that as cover for the wire. Do you know that when you go through airport security screening after you've had a knee replaced, the replacement knee sets off the metal detector? And when they run a hand scanner over you, it'll ping on your knee?"

Cate shook her head.

"Well it does, so whenever you get a new knee, the manufacturer sends you an ID card stating you've had the surgery, and showing what the knee looks like under X-rays. It's supposed to help you get through the airport screening. Doesn't really work that way," she added as an aside. "D'Arcy found that out the hard way. But that's the theory.

"Anyway, D'Arcy knew Vishenko's men would physically search him, use a metal detector to check for weapons and an electronic scanner to detect a wire. Sure enough, the metal detector pinged on his left knee. But he showed them his surgical scar and the ID card, and they bought that explanation. So when they ran the electronic scanner over him, they skipped his left knee—*exactly* what he was counting on. The wire was hidden in a prosthesis that looked like real skin and muscle, attached to his knee."

Keira's expression grew serious. "But that evidence wasn't enough for Baker Street. He wanted more. That's where I came in."

A sudden knock on the ladies' room door startled them both, and they turned sharply as the door opened just far enough to allow Cody Walker to stick his head in. "Liam's out of surgery."

Cate caught her breath. She hadn't forgotten Liam was fighting for his life—it had been constantly in the back of her mind. But she'd allowed Keira to distract her for a few minutes. A warm, sisterly feeling permeated her when she glanced at the other woman and realized that's what Keira had been trying to do—distract her from worrying about something over which she had no control. But now...

She looked at Cody. "Is he...?" She couldn't get the question out.

He shook his head. "Don't know. The surgeon just

came out to talk to the family. But she's smiling, for what that's worth."

Cate closed her eyes briefly. *He's alive. Liam's alive. Thank You, God. If You're there...thank You.*

In no time at all they'd joined the others in the waiting room, where a woman wearing surgical scrubs quietly watched their approach. Her gaze moved from Cate to Keira as she asked, "Are you...?"

"I'm his sister," Keira said quickly.

Cate couldn't say anything. What was she? She had no official role in Liam's life. She wasn't his wife. She wasn't his fiancée. She wasn't even his girlfriend. *But you* are *the woman he loves,* she reminded herself. *You're the woman he risked his life to save...not once, but twice.*

The surgeon was talking, and Cate forced herself to listen.

"He's a very lucky man. It must have been a coated or jacketed bullet, because it didn't deform on impact and cause massive damage. The bullet entered below his right rib cage and nicked his left lung, but it went right on through, out his left side. The paramedics inserted an endotracheal tube into his lungs to help him breathe, and they started an IV right away—our first responders are the best in the business—and that helped. He's on a ventilator, but we'll try to get him off that as soon as possible—hopefully tomorrow."

Cate wanted to ask why that seemed to be so important to the surgeon, but wasn't about to interrupt.

"We reinflated his left lung—no problem. And we didn't have to remove the lower lobe since it was just nicked—we repaired it and I'm fairly confident that will hold. He's also got a thoracostomy tube in place—more commonly known as a chest tube."

"What's that?" Keira asked, and Cate threw her a grateful glance because she wanted to know, too.

"It's a flexible plastic tube inserted through the chest wall into the cavity between the lung and the chest wall. It's hooked up to a suction device that will evacuate air and any remaining blood from the chest cavity, which will help keep the lung inflated. That tube will stay in place longer, maybe as long as a week. We'll have to wait and see. I just wanted you to be prepared when you see him. The endotracheal and thoracostomy tubes will make it will look worse than it actually is."

"So we can see him?" Keira asked in a hopeful voice, and again Cate was grateful.

"He's still in recovery, but yes, we'll let you see him as soon as we can. Not for too long, please, and not all of you at once—you don't want to exhaust him. We've got him on antibiotics, of course, and pain meds. He won't be able to talk to you, not even after he regains consciousness—not until he comes off the ventilator—but you'll be able to talk to him." She smiled. "You might not know it, but the presence of family and friends is great medicine and can actually aid in the healing process. So we encourage visitors…in limited doses." She smiled again, this time at her little joke, then glanced at the clock on the waiting room wall. "Is there anything else you wanted to know?"

Cate finally found her voice before anyone else had

a chance to ask a question. "You said you want to get him off the ventilator as soon as possible. Why?"

The surgeon hesitated. "He's young. He seems to be in splendid physical shape. And his wounds in and of themselves aren't that serious. But there *can* be...complications," she said reluctantly.

"Complications?" Cate's heart skipped a beat.

"Pneumonia is the most common. But when the patient is immobilized with a ventilator, we also have to worry about deep venous thrombosis and possibly a pulmonary embolus." Before Cate could ask, the surgeon explained, "DVT, that's blood clots in the leg veins. And if that occurs, the blood clot could break free and travel to the lungs, causing the pulmonary embolus—PE." She held up a cautionary hand. "Don't be alarmed, I'm not saying any of these things are going to happen. Just that they might. We're taking steps to prevent them, but the most important thing is to get him off the ventilator as soon as possible." She gave them an encouraging smile, and glanced again at the clock. "If that's all... I really do need to get back. One of the recovery nurses will let you know when you can see him."

When the nurse came out to tell them they could visit Liam one at a time, Cate had no intention of stepping forward. And when Keira turned to her and said, "You first, Cate," she demurred.

"You're his sister. I'm just—"

"You're just the woman he loves," Keira said swiftly. Her smile was woman to woman, and full of understanding. "He'll want to see you first." And when Cate still hesitated, she added, "Go on. I know him. He'll want to know you're okay. And since he can't ask..."

Another burst of sisterly affection for Keira filled Cate—similar to what she felt for Angelina—and she blinked back sudden tears. Liam's sister was just like Liam, and Cate could so easily see herself fitting into their family, if...

She didn't hug Keira, but the urge was there. "Thank you."

The nurse led Cate through the double doors and down a long hallway, to a dimly lit hospital room filled with so many monitors, pumps and other pieces of life-saving equipment there was scarcely room to maneuver except right next to the bed. "Ten minutes," the nurse said.

Cate hesitated in the doorway until Liam turned his head toward her, and his eyes—those beautiful dark brown eyes—lit up at the sight of her, despite how weak he obviously felt. Then she was at his side in a flash, leaning over and kissing his cheek as emotion welled up in her throat. She wasn't going to cry, she told herself with a kind of desperation. She *wasn't*.

Only...she was. Tears coated her cheeks as she whispered, "Please don't ever scare me like that again." Then kissed his shoulder, his arm, his hand—the one without the IV drip. Hot, frantic kisses, because she was so overcome with emotion that he was alive and she had to let it out somehow.

She shushed him when he tried to speak even though the ventilator tube made it impossible. "Don't, Liam.

Just listen." She brushed a hand over his forehead, then cupped his cheek. "I'm sure there are lots of questions you want to ask…but you'll have to wait until that tube comes out. All you need to know right now is I'm okay…and Vishenko is dead." She kissed his cheek again for good measure. "And you are a lucky man, according to your surgeon."

He gripped her hand and squeezed, his eyes telling her he knew he was a lucky man…and *not* because his injuries weren't life-threatening. His eyes said plain as words he was a lucky man because she loved him. "I do," she whispered. "I do love you, Liam. More than you know. More than I can ever tell you."

He tugged on her hand until she let him guide it to his chest and splay her fingers over his heart. Then he moved her hand to her own chest and pressed it against her heart, and she knew he was trying to tell her the only way he could that he loved her, too.

She swallowed the lump in her throat. "When I saw him on the path," she said in a voice that trembled, "I was afraid at first. Then… I can't explain it…but I felt your arms around me. Holding me safe. Loving me. And I knew no matter what happened, he couldn't touch me. Not the *real* me. Only you can do that. Only you."

The ventilator had been removed and Liam had been moved to a regular hospital room when Cate returned the next day. The IV was still inserted in a vein on the back of his right hand, and the chest tube was still in place, too. Despite that, he was sitting in a chair beside his bed, trying to interest himself in a not-so-recent swimsuit issue of *Sports Illustrated* one of the nurses had provided him with from the waiting room...but thinking about Cate. Thinking that none of the swimsuit models could hold a candle to her. Remembering, too, that she'd once dreamed of being a model herself... before the *Bratva* and Vishenko entered her life.

He looked up when the door opened, and there she stood in a simple cotton T-shirt tucked into snug jeans, her shoulder-length blond hair shining. But all he really saw was the radiance in her face, her eyes, and his heart turned over at the sight of her. *It probably always will,* he realized. *Fifty years from now she'll still make my heart skip a beat.* And he wasn't the least bit sorry.

"Hey, sweetheart." He tossed the magazine onto the bed and held his left arm out to her. She moved into his embrace and kissed him lightly, careful not to touch his chest tube. "I was just thinking about you."

Still in the circle of his arm, she reached over and picked up the magazine from the bed. Her gaze moved from the nearly naked cover model on the front of *Sports Illustrated* to him. "Oh really? Thinking of *me*?"

Her attempt at the sexual banter most women engaged in without a second thought was endearing, and he gave her his most flirtatious grin. "Yeah, darlin'. I was thinking you might pose like that for me...a private showing." His grin deepened when her cheeks turned crimson. But his grin was erased when a stricken expression entered her eyes and she turned her face away from him.

"Hey," he said, attempting to use his right hand to turn her face back to his, but the IV wouldn't let him reach that far. Frustrated, he said, "Cate. Sweetheart. What is it?" When she still refused to look at him, he suddenly realized what the problem was and mentally cursed. He shifted his left arm so his hand was at her waist, then he was tugging her T-shirt out of her jeans.

"What are you doing?" Her voice was breathless.

He slid his hand beneath her shirt and ran his fingers up her back. Slowly. Gently. Feeling the scars he knew were there. The scars she'd shown him once, but never again.

"Don't," she choked out, but she didn't try to escape so he refused to obey. Instead, he continued to caress her with his fingertips until she shivered with sexual awareness. Until her nipples betrayed her body's reaction to his touch.

"Look at me, Cate." When she did, he knew from her expression that her arousal warred with shame that her body was no longer model-perfect…and why. Fury again slashed through him at the man who'd done this to her, the same fury that had possessed him when he'd heard Vishenko yesterday. *I didn't kill him,* he reminded himself as he fought his fury down, just as he'd done the day before. *I wanted to kill him. And I could have. But I didn't.*

But he wasn't sorry Vishenko was dead.

"I know the scars are there," he said, his voice as gentle as he could make it. "But they don't have a damn thing to do with you, sweetheart. They don't affect my love. And they damn sure don't affect my desire for you—couldn't you tell the other night?"

"How can you say that?"

"Because it's true." He drew a deep breath—as deep a breath as he could with his damaged lung—as he searched his heart for the words. "The shame is his, Cate. Not yours. Don't be ashamed. Not of the scars. Not of what you did to survive, to escape. You did what you had to do…because you were the only one who could do it."

After several moments she said, "You're right." Her voice was low, but firm. "For the longest time I blamed myself…*despised* myself for giving in. But yesterday… when I saw him…when I thought I was going to die, I realized I was wrong. It's like you said. You can only do the best you can do at the time." Her voice dropped to a whisper. "I did the best I could—the only way I knew how."

"I know you did."

Her eyes met his, and his heart was gladdened by the new expression he saw there. "It's not easy, though," she said. "Letting go of the past. It's not easy changing how you think of yourself."

"I know that, too."

She shifted in his embrace so she was facing him fully, looking down at him, her hands resting on his shoulders. "Yesterday, when you were in surgery, Keira said that if you loved me, then I deserved to be loved." He waited, unsure how to respond, but she wasn't done. "And I realized Keira was right. Not because of me— but because of the man you are. You couldn't love the woman I thought I was. You could only love the woman I really am."

She touched his face with reverent fingers, her eyes

misty. "You saw things in me I never saw in myself. And you made me see them, too. That's what makes you unique, Liam. That's what makes me love you."

"Does that mean you'll marry me?"

"What?" Her fingers stilled, and her stunned expression told him he'd taken her completely by surprise.

"I know," he said quickly. "We haven't even known each other two weeks—I know that. But I also know you're the one. I *know* it, Cate. If you're not sure…if you need time… I can wait. But I'm committed—that's not going to change. Believe it."

"I do," she whispered. "I do believe it. And I *am* sure I love you, but…"

"I want to be your husband," he said stubbornly. "I want the rights that come with it—the right to be at your side, keeping you safe. The right to love and cherish you, now and forever. The right to expect the same from you."

But there was something else he wanted, too. He finally understood why Cate no longer wanted to be called Caterina—even though she hadn't been on the run for nearly a year and no longer needed to hide her identity. He'd heard the way Vishenko had called her by that name—and it had sickened him. How much worse was it for her? "I want to change your name to Jones… legally. Cate Jones." His voice dropped a notch. "Say yes, Cate. If you want to wait, I'm good with that. Just say you'll marry me."

She opened her mouth—to say what, he wasn't sure—when a rap on the door frame of his hospital room interrupted them. Liam glanced over and saw

Nick D'Arcy standing there, grinning. Right beside him was Alec. And crowded behind them were Keira, Cody, Shane and...

"Mom?" he asked in a disbelieving voice.

Cate abruptly attempted to move out of his embrace when she heard him, but he tightened his left arm around her and kept her anchored at his side. "Don't think you can escape because my right arm's out of commission with the IV," he murmured for her ears alone. "I'm ambidextrous. I thought you already knew."

He knew she'd heard him—and had made the connection—because her cheeks turned pink. But she stayed right where she was as his mother squeezed through the people blocking the doorway and headed straight for him.

"My baby," she said, cupping his cheeks in her hands and raining kisses over his face. "My baby's okay."

"I'm not your baby, Mom," he protested, embarrassed but laughing. "That's Keira."

"You're my baby boy," she insisted, taking a step back to look him over. "And don't you forget it, Liam Thermopolis Jones," she added with a militant gleam in her eyes.

Cate glanced down at him, her eyes brimming over with sudden amusement. She raised her eyebrows. "Thermopolis?"

Liam flushed. "Yeah," he growled. "But don't even think about calling me by that name." He wasn't about to explain how his mother—a romantic at heart—had named him that because he'd been conceived at the mineral hot springs located in Thermopolis, Wyoming. He'd had a hard enough time living down the name when he was a kid. Liam was unusual enough, but Thermopolis...

All at once the room was crowded with the other members of his family who'd been able to make it to his sickbed. Only Niall was missing, and Liam understood—black ops warriors were rarely free on short notice.

All Alec said was, "Looking good, bro," but the warm respect in his eyes spoke volumes.

Keira pressed her cheek against his and whispered in his ear, "I'm so proud of you."

Shane came around the other side, clapped him on the right shoulder and teased, "Trust Mr. Knight-Errant to find a way to save the damsel in distress and make himself look like a hero...without getting himself killed."

"Like you should talk, Senator," Liam said, lifting his chin in the direction of the barely visible scar on the left side of his oldest brother's head beneath his close-cropped hair—Shane's own badge of honor.

Shane just laughed and made way for Cody, who tapped Liam's jaw with his fist, saying, "Thought you told me there was no bullet out there with your name on it."

Liam had forgotten he'd said that to Cody not too long ago. Now he said, "There wasn't. It wasn't meant for me."

The hushed silence that greeted his words was broken by Nick D'Arcy. "If you don't mind, everyone," he said, moving away from the doorway. "I need to speak to these two…in private. It won't take long, I promise."

It was amazing how quickly the room emptied, as if D'Arcy had waved a magic wand. He pulled a chair away from the wall and put it next to Liam's, then indicated Cate sit in it. When she did, he said, "I can't even begin to apologize for putting you in danger, Ms. Mateja—"

"Cate," she interjected.

He nodded. "Cate." His gaze moved to Liam and he smiled slightly. "I told you I wasn't really omniscient, much as I'd like to be. This proves it."

"No one is." Liam sucked in air, feeling a twinge in his chest. "But you had the right idea." When Cate turned startled eyes his way, he explained to her, "Keira told me about the op yesterday, after you left and she came in to see me." He turned back to D'Arcy. "So I know the whole setup, what all went down, everything. But what Keira couldn't—or *wouldn't*—tell me, was what progress the agency or the FBI has made in finding out who set Cate up to be assassinated in the first place. And I couldn't talk to ask. Who smuggled the Uzis into the courthouse?"

"The FBI got lucky there," D'Arcy said. "They raised the serial numbers and tracked down the shipment they were stolen from. You were right—no one is better than the FBI at following a paper trail. One thing led to another…and so on. Turns out, it was someone in the US Attorney's Office—the prosecutor who was shot but wasn't killed."

When Liam's eyes widened, D'Arcy said, "Yeah.

Go figure. I'm sure he had no idea he'd signed his own death warrant by arranging to get the guns into the courthouse. But he was a target, same as Cate. When the FBI's investigation led straight to him and they questioned him, he caved. Guess he was terrified the *Bratva* would come after him again once he was out of the hospital, once the protection on him was lifted. He spilled everything he knew...but not until he'd negotiated a plea deal with his former colleagues in the US Attorney's Office."

He smiled, but his eyes didn't. "*And* he knew a lot more than just the attempt on Cate. A hell of a lot more, including how they got to the other witness. The *Bratva* needed to silence him, too, and not just to make sure the hit on Cate was never traced back to Vishenko. I can't tell you the details, but he'll be the key witness at some new trials, both here and in Zakhar. After which, he'll spend a couple of years in prison, in protective custody. Then he'll go into the Witness Security Program."

He grimaced. "We don't always get to choose who rots in prison and who gets a second chance at a new life under a new name—sometimes we have to choose between the lesser of two evils. I don't like it any more now than I did when I was in the US Marshals Service—I just have to live with it. The good news, Cate, is that with Vishenko dead, I don't think you'll need to go into the Witness Security Program after all. But we'll see."

"What about the trial I was supposed to testify at?" Cate asked abruptly. "If one of the prosecutors was working for Vishenko...how does that affect the case?"

"No impact," D'Arcy explained. "The original trial never started. A jury was never seated. Vishenko's dead, but the trial for the rest of the conspirators will go ahead with the new prosecutors the US Attorney's Office has already assigned to the case."

Cate didn't respond, and Liam glanced at her to see how she was taking the news the human trafficking conspiracy trial was still on. Which meant she still needed to testify. Which meant the defense teams would still do everything they could to discredit her testimony. Which meant the whole world would know…everything.

"I understand," she said finally. Determination pulled her face into resolute lines. "'I am one,'" she whispered under her breath. She glanced down at the scars on her wrists for a moment, and an ache speared through Liam as he realized he couldn't shield her from the mental and emotional trauma of the upcoming trial—much as he wanted to—any more than he could shield her from the abuse she'd suffered in the past.

Then she looked him full in the face, dauntless courage shining from her silvery-blue eyes. The courage that had ensnared his heart almost from the beginning. "I can do this," she said softly. "I can." She turned to D'Arcy. "I will."

Epilogue

Cate walked into the Washington, DC, federal court-house, Liam at her side, her right hand clasped firmly in his left one. Four US Marshals surrounded them. Even though Vishenko was dead, even though two of the conspirators in the human trafficking case had accepted plea bargains three days before the trial, the prosecution of the other men was going forward as scheduled. Cate's eyewitness testimony was still key to the prosecution, and the various federal agencies involved—the FBI, the US Marshals Service, the US Attorney's Office and the agency—were taking no chances with her safety.

Nor was Liam. He was still on medical leave from his job with the DSS, but he'd scarcely left her side since he'd been discharged from the hospital. Just as he'd scarcely left her side from the moment he'd met her—keeping her safe as only he could do.

Cate glanced down at the diamond on her left hand. She'd told Liam she didn't need an engagement ring. That she didn't need *things* to know he loved her. And besides, they weren't *engaged*, they were *married*. But he'd insisted. And now that it was on her finger, she loved it. Not just because it was beautiful—the most gorgeous ring she'd ever seen—but as its symbol. Along with her wedding ring, it was a reminder that Liam had *chosen* to love her, as he put it...and always would. A reminder, too, that she was worthy of being loved. Whenever she slipped back into her old mind-set, all she had to do was look at the ring to know the truth. It was her talisman.

They paused at the doorway to the witness room and she turned to Liam. She had to leave him here. He would be in the courtroom for the entire trial, but she wouldn't. As was often the case with witnesses, only when she was on the witness stand would she be allowed inside the courtroom. On the witness stand... and when the verdicts were read. She took a deep breath and forced a smile.

"You okay?" he asked her. When she nodded, he said softly, "Remember, 'I am only one, but I am one. I cannot do everything, but I can do something. And I will not let what I cannot do interfere with what I can do...'"

"'...And by the grace of God, I will,'" she finished. "I know. I just wish it was over."

"It will be...soon enough. Just think about how much this means to every woman who was ever trafficked—

and those who will never be trafficked because of your willingness to stand up and testify against these men."

"'This stops here,'" she quoted softly, nodding to herself as she remembered Alec saying this to her almost a year ago when he'd first convinced her to testify. Drawing courage from the memory. "'This stops *now*!'"

"A verdict was reached in a federal courtroom in Washington, DC, today," announced the CNN news anchor, "in a complicated and hard-fought human trafficking conspiracy case. Correspondent Carly Edwards is standing by at the courthouse with the verdict. Carly, can you hear me?"

"Yes, Tom," Carly Edwards said into the microphone from the top of the courthouse steps. "Guilty on all counts for all the conspirators. Let me repeat, guilty on all counts. The verdict was announced an hour ago, in a trial that was postponed when two gunmen opened fire in this same federal courthouse, killing the lead prosecutor and wounding—"

Liam clicked the remote to turn off the TV in their DC hotel room. He'd been in the courtroom with Cate this afternoon when the verdict was announced, but it still gave him a surge of satisfaction hearing "guilty on all counts." Later tonight he and Cate were meeting Alec and Angelina for a victory dinner to celebrate.

They also had something else to celebrate, something Alec had confided in him just as Angelina had confided in Cate—Alec and Angelina were expecting a baby. Sometime in the new year he was going to be an uncle for the second time.

Cate had been ecstatic for them. And her reaction to their pregnancy news had laid to rest Liam's last, lingering doubt about her feelings for Alec. He hadn't known that doubt still existed—until it was dispelled. Until she'd slipped her hand in his, her eyes like stars, and whispered, "If there *is* a God, that will be us, Liam. Someday."

Cate had refused to marry him until she'd confided her fear to him that she might be sterile and why she suspected it, and it had nearly broken his heart. Not so much for himself—although the idea of never having children of his own had been a body blow—but for her. Because it was just one more thing to add to her insecurities. One more potential heartbreak for a woman who'd already suffered enough heartbreak in her relatively short life.

Cate had wanted a fertility test performed on herself before their wedding, but Liam had adamantly refused. *"Hell no!"* he'd told Cate, the only time he'd lost his temper with her. *"If we can't get pregnant we'll adopt."* And though she'd argued with him that *her* problem didn't have to be *his*, he'd stood resolute, and eventually she'd conceded.

So they were trying. Maybe some people would say it was too early in their marriage, but Liam was thirty-six and ready to be a father. Not that he'd actively been seeking a mother for his children when he'd met Cate—he hadn't. But now that he'd found the woman he would love and cherish for the rest of his life, he was ready to give her all the children she wanted—he hadn't worn a condom since the day they were married in a quiet ceremony ten weeks ago, shortly before the trial began. He'd been out of the hospital only a week at that point and still recovering, so their honeymoon had been somewhat…limited.

Liam smiled suddenly. Despite his limitations, Cate had managed to make their honeymoon memorable. Creatively memorable. In fact, she'd reveled in taking charge. His shy bride had been transformed into every man's bedroom fantasy, and he hadn't complained. It was proof she trusted him completely—with her body as well as her heart.

Now that the trial was over, now that all the conspirators had been found guilty and faced long prison sentences, he still wasn't sure where they went from here. D'Arcy was confident Cate didn't need to assume a new identity…and Liam was almost convinced Baker Street was right. But he'd already resolved in his mind to resign from the DSS, if necessary, and go with Cate wherever she needed to go. He hadn't told her that—she had enough to worry about with the trial. The king of Zakhar had made him a respectable offer, too—more than respectable, actually. That was another thing Cate wasn't aware of. But he didn't really want to leave the DSS unless he was forced to. He'd only consider the king's offer if he couldn't stay in his current job, if he and Cate couldn't make the US their home base.

So they had options…which he'd worry about later. The only absolute in Liam's mind was Cate. Keeping that glow of love in her eyes for the next fifty years. Being with her when he drew his last breath…or when she drew hers.

He turned when the bathroom door opened and Cate

walked out. She was still wearing the slacks and sweater she'd worn earlier in the day—not the dress she'd been going to change into for their upcoming dinner with Alec and Angelina. His smile faded at the sight of her pale, shocked face. "What is it?" he asked sharply. His anxious gaze swept over her, searching for injuries. "Are you hurt?"

She shook her head. "Blue," she whispered, dazed. "Plus blue."

He stared blankly. "Plus blue?"

A smile started in her eyes and spread over her face, then she threw herself at him, wound her arms around his neck and held on tight. "Plus blue," she repeated. "I took a home pregnancy test and it turned blue. Plus blue. We're pregnant, Liam! Can you believe it? We're pregnant!"

"Pregnant?" His arms closed around her automatically, but he was stunned. Cate hadn't let on at all, so he couldn't take it in for a moment.

"Pregnant!" She was laughing and crying at the same time. "A baby, Liam. We're going to have a baby. Oh, there *is* a God. There *is*!"

His eyes were suddenly burning with the tears his father had told him more than once men never cried. But he didn't care. Because some things deserved tears, and Cate's renewed faith was one of them.

He cradled her face in his hands and kissed her tenderly. "Yes," he said, unashamed to let her see his damp eyes. "There *is* a God. I know, because He brought me you."

* * * * *

LIAM'S WITNESS PROTECTION
by Amelia Autin

*Don't miss the next thrilling installment
in the* MAN ON A MISSION *miniseries,
coming soon!*
And don't forget the previous titles in the miniseries:

ALEC'S ROYAL ASSIGNMENT
KING'S RANSOM
MCKINNON'S ROYAL MISSION
CODY WALKER'S WOMAN

Available now from Harlequin Romantic Suspense!

*When horse trainer Greta Colton is wrongfully
imprisoned, oilman Tyler Stanton gives her an alibi—and
provides protection. But Tyler aims to safeguard more
than Greta's body. He'll also have to lasso her heart…*

*Read on for a sneak preview of
THE COLTON BODYGUARD,
the thrilling conclusion to the 2015
COLTONS OF OKLAHOMA continuity.*

"If all this hadn't happened, then you wouldn't have known
that you were about to marry the wrong man," Tyler coun-
tered. "Not that I'm suggesting I'm the right man."

She tilted her head slightly and looked at him
curiously. "Why haven't you married? You're handsome
and successful and I'm sure plenty of women would be
happy to become Mrs. Tyler Stanton."

"The women who want to be my wife aren't the kind
of woman I'd want for a wife. They want it for all the
wrong reasons," he replied. "I got close to marrying once,
but it didn't work out and since then I haven't found the
right woman. Besides, I work long hours and don't have
a lot of time to do the whole dating thing."

"So you just invite emotionally vulnerable women to
share your bed for the night and then move on to the next
woman." She stared at him boldly.

A small laugh escaped him. "You don't appear to me
to be an emotionally vulnerable woman and no, I don't

make a habit of inviting women into my bed. In fact, you're the first who has gotten an official invitation."

She eyed him dubiously.

He leaned closer to her, so close that if he wanted to, he could wrap her in his arms and take full possession of her lush lips with his. It was tempting. It was oh so tempting.

"It's true, Greta," he said and watched her eyes spark with gold and green hues. "I don't invite women into my bed. I wait for them to invite me into theirs. But you're different and the desire, the passion, I have for you is stronger than anything I've ever felt for any other woman."

Her mouth trembled slightly and he continued, "In all of my life I've never been jealous of Mark, but when he hooked up with you, I was jealous of him for the first time. He had what I wanted…what I still want."

Don't miss
THE COLTON BODYGUARD
by New York Times *bestselling author Carla Cassidy,*
available November 2015 wherever
Harlequin® Romantic Suspense
books and ebooks are sold.

www.Harlequin.com

HRSEXP1015

THE WORLD IS BETTER WITH

Romance

Harlequin has everything from contemporary, passionate and heartwarming to suspenseful and inspirational stories.

Whatever your mood, we have a romance just for you!

Connect with us to find your next great read, special offers and more.

f /HarlequinBooks

🐦 @HarlequinBooks

www.HarlequinBlog.com

www.Harlequin.com/Newsletters

⬧ HARLEQUIN®

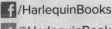

A *Romance* FOR EVERY MOOD™

www.Harlequin.com